Marlie

Marlie

Anneli Purchase

ACQUILINE

Manufactured in the United States of America

Published in 2017 by Acquiline

Library and Archives Canada Cataloguing in Publicaton
Marlie / Anneli Purchase

Issued also in electronic format.

ISBN 978-0-9947557-6-6

This is a work of fiction. All characters in this novel are the products of imagination. Although places named in the novel are real, liberty has been taken in the use of buildings, businesses, and organizations in these locations to suit the story. In no way do they refer to the actual places or enterprises. Any resemblance to real persons or places of business are purely coincidental. The two rape scenes in this novel may be offensive to some, but the focus of the novel is on love and justice for women.

To Myrtle Purchase, who never tires of listening to my stories.

Other Books by Anneli Purchase

Julia's Violinist

The Wind Weeps

Reckoning Tide

Orion's Gift

Acknowledgements

I have the most patient friends. When the muse left me and I despaired of finishing this novel, they gently but constantly nudged and prodded me to pick up the pen again. Maggie Dunn, Dawn Hill, and Ursula Kurz, thank you for not giving up on me.

My writing and editing partner, Darlene Jones, thank you for continuing to encourage me to reach for a higher standard, and for proofreading the manuscript many times.

Kathleen Price, thank you for helping to publish my work, setting up the layout of the paperback version, and for being so supportive, with sound and practical advice.

Jan Brown, your painting nearly leaped off the wall at me, calling, "I'm Marlie! Put me on your book cover." Thank you, Jan, for trusting me and giving your generous permission to use this painting.

And of course, I have the ongoing encouragement and support of "The Captain," who keeps me informed of the correct fishing and boating terms and still puts up with having lost me to the computer.

CHAPTER 1
Marlie

The bow of the car ferry cut through the smooth silvery water. It almost looked as if the gods had spilled mercury over the ocean. Marlie bounced on her toes, then self-consciously whirled around to check if anyone was watching her childish excitement as the ferry approached the dock at the village of Skidegate. She was about to set foot on these remote islands for the first time. All she had wanted was to get away from her messed up life in the city. Any distant place would do, but she hadn't expected such beauty. The scenery took her breath away. Rocky islets with stands of tall cedars dotted the bay. Yellow-green seaweed clung to black rocks that stepped down into the sea. The Northern Expedition was about to dock on Graham Island, the larger, northernmost of the Queen Charlotte Islands, recently renamed Haida Gwaii. A gray gravel beach without one speck of litter stretched northward from the ferry terminal. Not a soul in sight. The islands promised to be the escape she hoped for.

She hurried down the metal stairs to the car deck. It would be a while before the ferry finished docking and passengers could drive off, but the intercom had called drivers to return to their vehicles several minutes ago. She shook her head. No, it was not a dream. She was really here. Alone, yes, but she could handle that. She hoped.

Marlie drove off the ferry ramp following a line of traffic, with many more vehicles behind hers. Much to her relief, the highway to Masset was paved. In this quiet, remote place, she had expected it to be gravel. In the gaps between the stands of cedars along the right side of the road, she caught glimpses of the beach as she drove north. She even had a quick peek at Balance Rock. She had seen it advertised in tourist brochures. This huge boulder on the beach appeared as if it were in danger of toppling over, but had apparently been balancing there for thousands of years. Once she was settled in her new place in Masset she would make a point of driving back down here to have a closer look.

No gas stations, no houses, no sign of human encroachment into nature. Tall evergreens, small meadows, seemingly untouched beauty pushed in on both sides of her. Marlie chuckled to herself as she thought of a silly saying that seemed to fit the scene. "It was like a virgin forest; a place where the hand of man has never set foot." She wanted to preserve it all with her camera.

Marlie cursed herself for packing her Nikon somewhere on the floor in the back. Hadn't she learned yet, that she should always have it handy? She reached behind the seat, groping for it under bags and boxes as she drove. When the car swerved she thought it was because she had taken her right hand off the wheel so she corrected with the left. At least, she thought she could correct it! The pull to the right was incredible. She yanked her arm back to grasp the steering wheel more tightly with both hands. A stab of panic attacked her stomach. She had to keep the car out of the ditch. She gripped the wheel with all the strength she could muster, white knuckles bulging. Her whole body clenched with fright as a meeting with the edge of the pavement seemed inevitable. She pumped the brakes and the car slowed down, but it behaved strangely, as if the wheels were turned completely to the right. At last she forced it to a crawl. Her knees shook as adrenaline coursed through her. Noticing she was still halfway in the lane, she took her foot off the brake and let the car roll onto the shoulder in case any traffic should come along. Not bloody likely, she snorted, as she looked up and down the desolate highway. Not a soul in sight.

After leaving the ferry, the other northbound vehicles had sped by her. In one passing car, she saw Don, the tall gangly man she'd chatted with briefly on the ferry earlier. He hadn't seemed to be aware of his strange attire. He was on his way back from a doctor appointment in Prince Rupert, he'd told her. Marlie guessed that he had dug out his only suit to wear to the city. The baggy dress pants and brown checkered jacket were dated and ill fitting. She'd almost laughed when she saw that he wore knee-high gum boots instead of leather shoes to go with the suit, but she would never be that cruel. Don told her he lived in a log cabin on one of the tiny islands accessible only by boat. Leather shoes would be useless for getting in and out of the skiff. It was obvious he felt quite comfortable in his gum boots and why not? He had to wear them. Why bother to change to shoes just for show? A pretty young blonde woman in a granny dress had picked him up at the terminal. Don had given Marlie a nod and a wave as they passed her Corolla on their way north. *If only they were still behind me,* she thought, *they might have helped me out.*

At least she was dressed in clean, comfortable clothes. Her jeans and jersey top and a light quilted vest had been perfect for the ferry ride in this cool northern sea air. Standing out on the highway now, she was glad she didn't look like a freak. Not that she was a snob, but she liked to take care of herself.

It was about 5:30 but she had plenty of time yet before dark. July in these northern latitudes meant the sun rose early and set late. She stepped out to see what was going on with the car. The passenger side seemed to be lower than the driver's side, but she reasoned that could be the slope of the shoulder of the road. She walked around the front past the hood and gasped at the sight. Not only was the tire flat, but it was mashed so badly that the car was resting on the rim.

Marlie kicked the flaccid tire. "Shit-shit-shit!" She looked up and down the empty highway. Nobody. Surely someone would come along to help her? Minutes ticked by. At last her shoulders slumped and she blew out a long breath.

"Okay, I know how to change a tire," she said. But where was the spare? She groaned as she remembered. It was in the trunk, under the floor. Easy to access. Unless you had everything you owned piled on top of that floor.

A wave of misery and disappointment washed over her. The whole idea of moving to the Charlottes was to outrun her string of bad luck. Tears welled. She could easily sit down and cry, or she could get to work and move all her earthly belongings onto the side of the road. She glanced up at the sky, thankful it wasn't raining, but the air was chilly and those dark clouds moving in from the southeast looked ominous. She would have to get a move on and save her crying for later.

CHAPTER 2
Brent

What the hell? Brent pulled over and stopped behind a little blue car. Heaps of boxes, bags, and clothing lay haphazardly tossed onto the shoulder of the highway. The car trunk gaped open with a shapely pair of buttocks displayed at center stage.

As he got out and closed his truck door, the woman whirled around to face him. Her mane of curly gold-red hair bounced as she turned, giving her that sexy popstar look. She stepped around to the side of her car, looking over her shoulder and then back at Brent.

He half raised his palms in a hands off gesture. "Don't worry!" he said. "I'm not here to mug you."

She gave a nervous laugh. "Oh, that's good. I don't think I could handle one more problem."

"What's the problem?"

"Tire blew out. I was about to change it."

Brent gestured at all the things on the ground. "Thought you were setting up for a garage sale."

"I guess it does look that way." Her face flushed slightly pink. "I was looking for the spare tire, and wouldn't you know they put it under the floorboards of the trunk. Stupidest place." She swept her arm around indicating her belongings on the roadside. "That's why...."

Brent nodded. "It is kind of a dumb place to put the spare. Let's have a look at that flat. Maybe I can help." He checked the front passenger side and gave a little whistle. He stuck out his hand. "My name's Brent."

"Marlie," she said, reaching out.

Firm grip. Confident. "Nice to meet you, Marlie."

Brent didn't really want to spend the extra time changing a tire. He had plenty of things to take care of that night, but he couldn't leave a pretty lady in a lurch. For that matter, he wouldn't leave anyone that needed help. He hadn't been raised to be that selfish. "I should have that tire changed in no time. If you really do have a spare in the trunk, that is." He pointed at the flooring in the trunk. "Do you mind?" He lifted the trunk floorboard and took out the jack, tire iron, and spare tire.

Dark clouds and a cold wind were moving in. Brent glanced at the sky and worked more quickly.

He got the old tire off, new one on, and about the time he tightened the last nut on the spare, the first drops of rain dotted the pavement.

"Oh no! All my stuff will get soaked." Marlie grabbed the tire iron and jack and jammed them into the trunk. Then she took them out again. "The tire. I need to put the tire in the trunk first." She picked up the dirty flat tire.

He couldn't let her lug that dirty old tire. Looked like she had on her best traveling clothes. Gently he took it from her. "Here. I'll do that." He fit it back into the trunk and put the tire iron and jack back in their place. The moment the floorboard dropped she was already heaving her boxes and bags into the trunk.

"Dammit! My bedding is all wet." She pushed the bundles on top of the boxes and tried to cram them down to make room for more of her belongings. "There's way too much left over." She grabbed two big bunches of curly hair on the sides of her head and stared wide-eyed at the car. "How did I ever get it in there in the first place?" Her eyebrows furrowed as she squinted her eyes, trying not to cry. Her chin quivered as the rain pelted down harder now, soaking them. Her vest was not much protection against the rain and without a toque her hair hung in her face in long wet ringlets. She had to be new to the islands.

"Look," he said. "I'm heading to Masset, so I can take some of your stuff in the back of my truck if you want. You just moving here?"

"Yup. First day on the Queen Charlotte Islands—I mean Haida Gwaii."

"Where are you going?"

"Masset," she said. "But—"

"Okay, you go sit in the car and I'll take care of the rest." When she nodded, Brent grabbed a few things from the roadside and walked to the back of his truck. She was right behind him with an armful of odds and ends.

Brent opened the canopy door and as she shrieked, he whirled around. "Oh my God! You killer!" Her face was contorted into a mask of horror.

"What's wrong?" he asked.

"You murderer! How could you kill that sweet little thing? Give me my stuff." She tried to grab the bags from his hand but dropped what she was carrying. They both bent to pick the things up and bumped heads.

"What the hell's the matter with you?" Brent stared at her in disbelief. The popstar image was fading fast and she was looking more like one of those angry protestors he'd seen on TV.

Her hazel eyes were huge as she glared at him. "You killed that helpless animal."

"Yeah, I shot a deer. So what? I eat venison."

"Is that even legal?"

"Lady, what planet did you beam down from? Of course it's legal. Everybody eats venison here."

"Not everyone! Not me!" She picked up her things and stomped back to her car but there was no place to put anything. She threw him a disgusted look, frowned, shook her head. She opened the back door and punched and pushed and shoved her belongings, desperate to cram her things into the Corolla's back seat. No room. She squeezed out a growl of frustration, and looked back at Brent again. Her shoulders sagged and that's when the tears came.

He blew out a long breath. "Look. Nothing is going to happen to your stuff in the back of my truck. The deer won't do anything to it. You don't even have to think about it being there. We'll load up and you can follow me to Masset." He waited and she appeared to mull that over. It was taking too long. "Oh, piss on it. This was a mistake. I'm leaving. You can wait for another car to pull over to pack your stuff to Masset for you. I don't need this shit."

She wiped her eyes with the back of her wrist and sniffed. "No wait! Yes, okay. Would you please bring my stuff for me? I guess I have to trust that you won't take off with my belongings."

"Have to trust me?! Jeezus you've got some bloody nerve. What the hell would I want your stuff for?" Brent turned to get into the truck.

"Please." She closed her eyes and pulled herself up straight. "I'm sorry. I do need your help. If you could take some of my things in your truck.... I do trust you."

"This is the only road that goes up or down the island, so you won't lose sight of your boxes." *What does she think I'd do with a bunch of ladies' clothes? Christ! What a loonie! How did I get myself mixed up with this nutcase?*

"Of course. You're right."

"Where in Masset are you headed?"

"The teachers' trailer court," she said.

He straightened up and inhaled a long slow breath through his nose. *Oh man. One of those!* "That explains a lot."

CHAPTER 3

Marlie

Marlie drove faster than she was used to, trying to keep up with the green Ford truck in front of her. Sure he'd helped her out, but what a jerk. "That explains a lot," he'd said. What the hell was that supposed to mean?

What was wrong with being a teacher? Teachers were caring people. They taught kids how to read and do math, taught them social skills, how to get along with others. Teachers cared about the kids in their classes. They really cared.

And how caring was he when he killed that beautiful deer?

If she hadn't had to dig for her spare and the tools, she would have had her tire changed and been miles up the road before that deer murderer came along. Or maybe not. She hadn't expected not to be able to fit everything back in the car. She supposed she could have said no to his help in the first place. But then she would have been all by herself at the side of that lonely road. She'd seen pictures of some of the huge black bears on the islands.

But that poor deer lying there in the back of his truck with its tongue hanging out, so undignified. It deserved better. She shuddered as she remembered its green eyes staring at her when she loaded her things into the truck. Poor thing!

She wiped the tears away so she could see the road. Still, she had to turn the wipers to a higher speed. That rain was coming down pretty hard. She was thankful to be on her way again, and not broken down on the roadside, which is where she would be if Brent hadn't helped her. She sighed.

Maybe she had been rude. All he was doing was trying to help. *I bet he's wishing he hadn't stopped. I don't think I even said thank you.*

She drove as fast as she dared making sure to keep Brent's truck in sight. The thought hit her that she had no idea who he was. All she knew was that his name was Brent. She had made a rather rash decision to enlist his help. Whatever had possessed her to put her belongings in his truck—along with his oily power saw, dirty coils of rope, an axe, a jerry can of fuel, and the deer, of course. What if he took off someplace where she didn't want to go? But another reason she needed to keep him in sight was because she didn't know where she was going herself.

At Port Clements, Brent pulled into the gas station to fuel up. She glanced at her gas gauge and did the same.

The rain had eased and they chatted as they filled their tanks. "So you're going to the teachers' trailer court in Masset?" he asked.

"Yes, but first I have to find out where Mr.Wilkinson, the vice-principal, lives. He has the trailer key."

"Why don't you call him and get him to meet us at the trailer and we can get the stuff unloaded? Otherwise, I'll have to leave your bags in the rain or wait around and I've got things to do ... like dealing with the deer."

Obviously she had thrown a wrench in the clockwork of his finely tuned schedule. "Yeah, sure. I can do that."

She pulled over to the side of the gas station after she gassed up, and made the call. At the pumps Brent was leaning his shoulder into the side of his truck, staring off into space as he held the nozzle in the gas tank. The profile of his face was perfect—manly, but fine. His blue checkered work shirt had a tear in the elbow. Jeans were dirty and smeared with dried blood—from the deer, she presumed. She sure hoped that was what the blood was from. How was she to know? She'd only just met him. His canvas vest had lots of pockets, more practical than fashionable. Seemed like islanders tended to be that way. Kodiak boots half unlaced told her he must have walked a lot today and maybe his feet were sore. Fancy, he was not.

"Mr. Wilkinson agreed to meet us at the trailer park," she called over.

Brent nodded, replaced the nozzle, and got on the road again. Marlie rushed to get back in the car and keep up with him.

She would never forget her first sight of Masset. She hadn't realized that the road had climbed some distance above sea level. Not really high, but high enough that it gave a memorable view of the town in the distance. The road dropped down to sea level then and the anticipation of the pretty community that shimmered with white buildings in the sunlight was dashed as she drove past the shacks on the outskirts of Masset.

Grass a foot high seemed to be the normal landscaping. Car parts and shells of broken down cars and trucks littered many of the front yards. Remnants of kitchen chairs—even an old sofa—sat out in the drizzly rain surrounded by beer cans and whisky bottles.

Closer to town, partway down a poorly maintained side road, they turned into a trailer park. Perhaps "park" was giving it too much credit. She bounced into a long driveway full of potholes and pulled up to the middle trailer of three that faced three more on the other side of the lot. It was the only empty one, so she figured that had to be it. The pale yellow vinyl walls were green with mildew on the shadier side. Worn and wobbly looking wooden steps led into a shabby porch with a bare plywood floor and ill-fitting walls thrown together in a hurry. Marlie turned to look at her front yard. Between the trailer and the driveway, a few clumps of grass dotted a muddy field like mini islands of green. No mowing needed.

She peered through the windows of the trailer. It was empty all right. Downright bleak. Brent was already opening the back of his canopy.

"Where is he?" She raised her arms, dropped them, and blew out a sigh. Dammit! She fumbled for her cell phone and waited for a signal. At Spring Break in Vancouver, Bob Wilkinson had hired her to teach at the elementary school in Masset. Well, here she was, but where was he? Marlie was stuck outside this trailer until he brought her the key. Finally the rings went through. No answer. Not even voice mail to leave a message.

Brent had come up behind her with the first load of her bags from the back of his truck.

"I'll stash them by the steps for now," he said. "Sorry, but I'm in a hurry."

Tears prickled behind her eyes. She swallowed, blinking them back quickly. Just then an old 1980s Chevy two-door sedan bounced into the driveway. "Marlie!" A short, stocky man in jeans and a coffee-stained T-shirt stepped out from behind the steering wheel. "Sorry," he wheezed. "Couldn't get the car started."

"Bob?" She stuck out her hand. It had been a while, and the last time she saw him he'd been wearing a suit.

He shook her cold hand with his warm, clammy one. "Right, yes, Bob Wilkinson." He eyed the Corolla. "Brought a few things with you, eh?"

"Well, I wasn't sure what I'd need, so I brought lots. Too much, probably." She pointed at Brent who was getting the last load of her belongings out of his truck.

"Brent here helped me out when I had a flat tire after I got off the ferry at Skidegate." The men shook hands.

The wind whipped her hair into her face. She put her hood up and tucked her hair inside. "Brr. That's a cold wind for July."

"Always like that around here. Might as well get used to it. Anyway, I need to show you a few things about the trailer and turn on the propane for you. That'll warm you up."

"Propane?" What did she need propane for?

"The furnace. The range is propane, too." She thought she must have looked stunned because he added, "You know.... Gas?"

A tremor of insecurity ran through her. Would she know how to work the range if it was propane? All she'd ever used was an electric stove. "So you'll show me how it works, right?"

"Let's leave your belongings here in the joey shack until we check out the inside." Bob fumbled through his keychain, finally deciding on a plain brass one.

"Joey shack? This porch here? That's called a joey shack?"

Bob nodded and his brow furrowed slightly. "You really are a city girl, aren't you?"

She shrugged.

"Well, that will soon change if you're going to last at this job. Most don't."

"Don't what? Change or last?"

"Last. Or change, for that matter. The ones that don't change, don't last. We have 23 teachers on our staff and this year 19 of them are new to the school."

Her eyebrows went up. "Why?"

Bob let out a long, tired sigh. "You'll see soon enough."

Brent had brought the last of the bags from the back of his truck and stashed them in the joey shack.

"I'll be going now," he said. "See you around."

She barely had time to call out a thank you, before he slammed his truck door and bounced away through the potholes.

CHAPTER 4
Marlie

Since she had nearly two months before school started, Marlie reasoned that once she had the basics set up—phone, bank, mailing address—she could spend some of that free time touring up and down the island, getting to know the geography better. She started with Masset. The highway ended here. Beyond that was the north coast of Graham Island.

A spur of the highway that continued to the west, ended at the village of Haida. This First Nation community was in the perfect location for monitoring traffic arriving by sea. It occupied the point of land overlooking an inlet that entered from the north. All fishing boats leaving or entering the town of Masset had to pass by Haida Village, or Old Massett, as it was once called. It was a perfect lookout point, and on a clear day one could see the mountains of Alaska in the distance.

Marlie started her day looking for a place to have breakfast. At the Coffee House, she ordered an Americano and a Danish, and laughed to herself about how worldly it sounded. She sat in a booth and raised a hand to wave at a thin, fortyish woman she had seen shopping with the vice-principal a few days earlier.

"I'm Pat Wilkinson, Bob's wife," she said. "Are you expecting company, or can I join you?"

"Happy to have some company. I'm Marlie Mitchell."

"Bob told me you were new to the islands, and would be teaching at Tahayghen this fall. How are you managing? All moved in okay?"

"Getting there, thanks. I thought I'd get familiar with Masset and the rest of the island while I had the time and the weather to do it."

"And what do you think, so far? Different, isn't it?" Pat said.

Marlie smiled and shrugged her shoulders. "Definitely different from the city, but that's what I like about it. The pace is a lot slower, and I like that. Shopping is a bit ... ah ... minimal."

Pat laughed. "No kidding! Bob and I fly out to Vancouver at least once a year, sometimes twice, to catch up on our shopping."

"Well, I won't be doing that. At least not for a while. Anyway, I just got here. But I'll manage."

"One thing that may help," Pat offered, "is the Sears mail order outlet. I use it for all the home décor kinds of things or bulky things I don't want to load in my baggage on our out-of-town shopping trips."

"That's a good idea. Where can I find that?"

"Oh, just along the main street, up from the Co-op," Pat said. "And I just remembered another thing you might be interested in. If you want to get in on a bulk food order once or twice a year, I can give you the number of the lady who puts in the order."

"Now that sounds like something I could be interested in. What kinds of food?"

"Just about anything you might find in a health food store—nuts, seeds, tea, flour, cheeses...."

"I'm sure I'd be interested," Marlie said.

Pat dug around in her purse. "Here's Betty Gibson's number." She wrote the name and number on a page she tore out of a tiny notebook. "She'll be happy to have another person on her order list. The more people who get together on an order, the easier it is for everyone. Like they'll order a whole round of cheese and cut it into portions when it gets here. If four people ordered a cheese, you'd get a quarter of a round. The more you order, the cheaper it is, not only from the wholesale store, but also for the price of the freight. It's really worth it."

"Wow! Well, thanks for telling me about that, Pat." Marlie laughed quietly. "I have to admit, I haven't been impressed by the groceries in the Co-op so far."

"Oh, you probably went there on the day before freight day," Pat said. "You need to shop on Wednesdays. That's when they have the fresh stuff out."

"Thanks so much for all the tips, Pat. I'm so glad I met you here today."

"Me too," she said. She picked up her leather bag and slid out of the booth. "Enjoy the rest of the summer then. It's going to be a long winter."

"So I keep hearing," Marlie said.

"If you ever need a cup of tea or some company, give me a call and we can do this again sometime. It's been nice to meet you, Marlie. Good luck with your class."

After Pat left, Marlie thought about how well dressed the principal's wife was, and how "together" she seemed to be. She remembered Bob's stained T-shirt the day he let her into the trailer. She doubted that Pat would ever leave the house in a blouse with a big stain on the front. But maybe women were not responsible for their husbands every minute of every day. It was enough to be responsible for oneself, she thought.

After her coffee shop breakfast, Marlie went to the Credit Union, the only bank in town. It wasn't her first choice, but she needed someplace local to keep her money so it would have to be the Credit Union. Some things about this small place annoyed her and the lack of a proper bank was one of them, but it was another one of those situations she had no choice about if she was going to live here.

From the Credit Union, she went next door to the post office and rented a mailbox. Now she only had to get her telephone line connected and she would be in business.

Once the necessities were taken care of Marlie spent her days with her camera. She visited the government wharf, taking pictures of the boats and the wharf facilities. She explored the retail shops in town. That took all of ten minutes. Nothing much for sale in any of them. Then she widened her circle of exploration. She had an extensive beach photo collection from any of the places where beach access was available. Driftwood, shells, and items that had fallen off boats always made good subjects for her photography. She had finished the tour of the small town in a few days. It became clear to Marlie that the beauty of Haida Gwaii was in places outside of town.

With her camera along for the ride, she headed south. She first came to the old logging town of Port Clements, and beyond that the small community of Tlell, basically a few houses and hobby farms on the Tlell River— gorgeous farming area for cool-weather crops. It was so scenic that she used up one of her camera batteries taking pictures. She thought Tlell might be a wonderful place to live ... for a while ... but she knew she'd be too lonely there for a long-term stay.

After Tlell she drove through miles of natural landscape until she came to Queen Charlotte City. She had to laugh at it being called a city. It was barely big enough to call a village. But it was important because it was near the First Nations community of Skidegate which was where the ferry docked, and because it was the place where a smaller ferry connected Graham and Moresby, the two main islands of Haida Gwaii.

She concluded that Graham Island was beautiful as far as the scenery was concerned, but there wasn't much in the way of shopping. Not that she had any money to spare anyway. It would be perfect for someone who had a dream of living off the land and doing most things the hard way. Beautiful lifestyle, and possibly satisfying for the soul, but a lot of work. She considered herself a realist and had to admit she wasn't sure how she would manage when the novelty of Haida Gwaii wore off.

As the middle of August rolled around, with the summer holiday coming to an end, she knew she should already have made the trailer more livable. If she was going to live there for the winter, she had to make it cozier, more like a home. The empty trailer was ugly and unwelcoming, and she hadn't wanted to spend much time in it. The touring and sightseeing helped fill her days, but she was good at procrastinating about things she didn't want to tackle. It was time to get herself organized. She didn't need another bout of depression when summer was over, and staring at the plastic walls of that shell on the gray days of winter could bring it on. She would use the time she had left and do what she could to perk it up. Maybe she could get some house plants from the little shop next to the Co-op. A spider plant with those skinny leaves dangling down might distract the eye from the synthetic walls. The mustard yellow upholstery of the worn and stained sofa and chair made her want to vomit every time she looked at the furniture. She had covered the couch and chair with blankets for the time being. A cushion would help. Some extra towels and facecloths would make life easier, so she wouldn't feel the need to do laundry every second day.

She found the Sears mail order outlet that Pat Wilkinson had mentioned to her. She'd make a point of getting a catalogue and placing an order right away. Meanwhile she would make a wish list. She had to brighten the place up. Everyone had warned her about the long, dreary winter. "Wind and rain," she'd heard one person say, "and after that you get rain and wind."

Although bedding was provided, she was glad she had her own sleeping bag and pillow. She wasn't sure how clean the previous tenants were. Sometimes at night as she lay in bed, she thought she got whiffs of engine oil. *Can't be,* she thought. *This is the bedroom.* More than once she got out of bed and tried to track down the smell. If anyone could have heard her, they'd wonder if some wild animal was loose, sniffing in the corners of the room. The floor looked clean enough and there was nothing under the bed or in the closet. The mattress smelled a bit musty and used, but not too bad. As soon as she could afford it, she would order a new one. But that oil smell…. She couldn't figure it out. She made a mental note to scour the bedroom floor with a powerful cleaner again the next day.

As she lay in bed, she wondered if next year she would be one of the nineteen teachers who would leave the island for someplace else, or if she would be one of the four who remained. Failure was not an option. Starting tomorrow, she would make this place livable. She was not a quitter.

CHAPTER 5
Marlie

Marlie had been to the school a few times to get her room ready for September's opening day of classes. Built in the '70s the school was still modern enough, even forty-something years later, but she was surprised that her classroom doors opened to the central library and had no windows to the outside. She had to keep the constantly humming fluorescent lights turned on. The inner classroom wall had window panes on the upper half and the only natural light coming in through them was from the library ceiling skylights. Would it be enough? She doubted it. If it was like this in the late August sunshine, those short winter days ahead could only make the problem worse.

For more than a week before classes started Marlie immersed herself in her work. Bulletin boards covered with coloured paper looked a lot less institutional than a sheet of white chipboard with a thousand pinpricks. Using some of her collection of mounted and laminated magazine pictures, she pinned images with fall colours around a seasonal poem on a chart. Later she would get the students to colour and cut out paper leaves to add to the display.

On the wall near the 9 foot by 12 foot carpet where she would have the class gather for story time, news, and discussions, she put up a calendar she had made a couple of years ago in her school at Maple Ridge, in the Lower Mainland. Slots with paper clips to hold a new number tag each day and a picture that looked Septemberish on the top, a folder to hold cards for the days of the week, the date numbers, and a card with the weather symbol for the day (sun, cloud, rain, snow, wind)—all these she pinned to the wall in a way that made the corner look inviting. Each morning they would start with the updating of the calendar, weather charts, and news. After that they would begin their lessons.

On top of the waist-high shelf that ran along one wall of the room, she placed a decorated coffee can with extra pencils, a stack of foolscap, and some spare erasers and rulers she had bought, providing the basics for those students who came to school without their supplies. If this district was like her last one, there would be parents who didn't send the school supplies on time, or, in some cases, ever.

Working in her classroom that last week of August filled her days and gave her a deep sense of satisfaction. It was the time when she was not in her classroom that gave her pause. She had hoped to find a kindred spirit among those twenty-three staff members, but most were a disappointment to her.

On the first morning of prep week, two old women, Jean and Tilly, sat on the sofa in the staff room talking quietly over a cup of coffee. Marlie came into the room, and in a gap in their conversation said, "Good morning." They glanced up at her, wrinkled their noses ever so slightly, and then went back to their conversation. Did she imagine their rudeness?

She tried again. "How is your week going?"

Tilly threw out one word, "Fine," and stuck her head close to Jean's to whisper something that made them both giggle.

Marlie gasped inaudibly. She hadn't imagined the rudeness. How could they treat anyone like this? And these women taught young impressionable children? She made a mental note to have as little as possible to do with them. If they didn't want to speak to her, that was the way it would be, but she wouldn't initiate any more conversations with them either. It would only invite more ridicule from them.

Another teacher, a young woman named Skylar, breezed into the staff room. Marlie did a double take. The thin material of the pale blue muslin blouse was very revealing. Skylar certainly had a strong sense of body image. "Uh-er-uh … hello, Skylar."

"Hey, Marlie! What's happenin'?" she said. "That's really cool what you've done in your room. I like the 'All About Me' bulletin board. Kids need to choose their own destiny. Adults mess with their heads way too much." Skylar stopped to adjust the red bandanna she was using as a head covering. "It's nifty that your classroom's right next to mine. You can keep an eye on the kids if I have to pop out of the room any time."

She leaves the kids alone! "How's your room coming along, Skylar?" she asked. "It's grade four you have, isn't it?"

"Yeah, there's really not much to do until after the first day."

"What do you mean? Aren't you putting up any bulletin board coverings or calendars? We always did that kind of thing at my old school."

"Naw! I figure by the time they're in grade four, they're old enough to do it themselves. Besides, we're going to spend the first day or two having class meetings to talk about what they want to learn. Fuck if I'm going to do all the work. Child-centered learning means less for me to do. I throw it right back in their lap."

Oh my Gawd! She's smoked a few too many. "But, Skylar, they're only nine years old."

"Yeah? So?" Skylar blew a bubble with her chewing gum and popped it between her teeth. "You've got to please the parents. They want to hear that you're doing the modern stuff. Letting the kids decide what they want to do."

Marlie frowned. "I don't know.... I think I'll stick with 'tried and true.' I want to make sure the kids learn to read."

Skylar shrugged. "Suit yourself." As she left, she looked over her shoulder. "Lot more work for you."

Well, for heaven's sake, that's what they pay me for.

$$***$$

First thing Saturday morning on the Labour Day long weekend, Marlie once again scrubbed her bedroom floor and walls with a bucket of hot soapy water, a brush, and a rag. A dash of bleach wouldn't hurt either. Somehow she had to get rid of that smell of engine oil. The water had turned darker than she expected by the time she finished scrubbing what she had thought was a clean floor. Her hands stunk of bleach but without rubber gloves it couldn't be helped. She lugged the bucket to the trailer door and tossed the washing water out onto the weedy ground.

With that taken care of, she thought she'd take a drive to the wharf to see if there was any fish for sale. The sky was overcast so she dug out a pullover and grabbed her windbreaker. A plastic potato chip bag blew across the trailer court. Her first instinct was to go pick it up, but that one was soon followed by a candy wrapper and a plastic grocery bag. The litter situation was hopeless. She tried to shut her mind to it. A brisk gust of wind reminded her to put on her windbreaker and her toque. You'd think it was October, not the beginning of September, it was so cold. The weather gods had obviously forgotten to include the Charlottes when they doled out warm summer weather. At least she could still get away with wearing runners and not boots. The roads in town were paved. It was only back alleys and driveways like those in the trailer court that were a mess.

As she walked over to the car, she raised her hand to wave to Roger, a high school math teacher who lived in the trailer across the yard.

"How ya doin', Marlie?" he called over. "I see you've been busy already this morning."

"Oh—the water—I hope it was okay to toss it out here. It's not like they have a clippy-clippy lawn here." She felt herself blushing at the thought that he'd seen her toss out the bucket of water.

Roger smiled. "Very third world."

"I was trying to get rid of the smell of engine oil in the bedroom. I can't figure it out. Smells like a car repair shop in there."

Roger's head went back slowly and he closed his eyes. "Oh. My. God. No wonder it smells. The teacher who lived in that trailer quit at Christmas time. Couldn't hack it. The place sat empty for a month and, not to lose money, the School Board rented it to three guys who were up here on a construction job. They used to take their motorcycles right into the trailer and work on them. I'm guessing that's where the oil smell came from."

Marlie thought her jaw would hit the ground. "You mean they used it like a repair shop? No wonder it stinks." She shook her head. "Men!"

Roger grimaced. "I hope you get the smell out. Don't worry about tossing the wash water out here." He waved his arm around, indicating the potholes and patches of weeds. "I don't think you're going to hurt anything. Good luck!"

She drove towards town, still shaking her head. Men had no appreciation for keeping their living quarters clean. At least now she knew the whiffs of motor oil weren't her imagination. She had more scrubbing to do, but she would think about that later. For now, she was going to plan a great weekend for herself.

A special dinner would be a treat. Surely with all the fishermen working out of Masset, she could buy a fish at the wharf. She had looked in the Co-op but found nothing she would consider buying there. The wharf should be a better bet. A fancy dinner, a glass of wine, and then she'd relax and enjoy her last days of freedom. Maybe she'd go for a walk on the beach on Monday to get her head sorted before the big first day.

It wasn't that far to the dock, but she took the Corolla in case she could get a fish. No need to walk home with a bag of fishy slime bumping on her leg at every step. She didn't mind the smell of fish, but she'd rather not have it on her pantleg. A few cars went by but traffic was light. Foot traffic was light too, as most of the streets were residential. Only the two main streets, with the Co-op and the liquor store had a few pedestrians. A couple of blocks from the causeway, she turned down the slope to the top of the wharf and parked the car. It was busier here—a lot busier.

A guy wearing a gray wool Stanfield's undershirt heaved a large box into the back of his truck. He gave her a nod and a smile when she walked by. Another, in filthy coveralls, was bent forward as he walked up the ramp from the floats with a big black garbage bag over his shoulders, probably off to do laundry somewhere. He should have put the coveralls in too. A pot-bellied fellow with several days' growth on his face squeezed past him on his way down the ramp. He hopped onto a boat a little way along the float. Everyone was working and no one seemed to care about how they looked. She guessed they had different priorities from city people. They were dressed for practicality, not for looks; something she was only beginning to appreciate.

When Marlie was still living at home, she used to like going down to the docks in Victoria, watching the boats come and go, but it was mostly sailboats there. The boating crowd dressed in the latest fashion; shiny yellow Helly Hansen boots rather than the cheap black rubber gumboots, and bright yellow sailing jackets instead of the black or green slicker sets the fishermen used. It was one thing to go out in a sailboat for a leisurely cruise and dress the part, but quite another to brave harsh sea conditions to scratch out a living. Even in Victoria, fishermen had no time for the fancy raingear.

Masset was a far smaller place than Victoria, but it was bustling just the same. She wandered down the float to the end looking for any sign of fish being handled. She was fascinated by the names of all the boats and wondered how the owners came up with them. Some, like Lillian B. and My Rhonda had to be the names of wives or girlfriends. Others were names of places. Yet others had aggressive sounding names like Ocean Warrior, or Sea Raider. One was named Serenity. She liked that name. Sounded so peaceful.

A pretty young woman came out of the Serenity's wheelhouse, laughing. Over her shoulder, she said to someone inside the boat, "You'd like that, wouldn't you?"

She stepped onto the float in front of Marlie, still smiling, and said, "Hi. Haven't seen you here before. Are you on one of the boats?"

"Oh, no. Just down for a walk. I'm a teacher, new in town. Actually I was looking for someone who might have fish for sale."

"We've sold our load, so we can't help you out, but a friend of ours might have some. He just came in and won't be unloading until this afternoon. I can show you where he's tied up if you like."

"That would be great." She reached out her hand. "My name's Marlie."

"Andrea." She smiled and shook Marlie's hand. "It's so nice to meet you. It's mostly a man's world down here. Come on, I'll take you over to my friend's boat."

They walked back up the float. Halfway along, Andrea stopped and stepped onto a boat. She motioned for Marlie to follow. Choosing their steps carefully, they crossed over it. They twisted and turned to avoid all the clutter on the boat and the rigging hanging down from the poles. It stank of fish guts. The boat that was tied outside of it was quite different. Clean, tidy, and without bad smells. Marlie looked up into the face of the skipper as he came out of the wheelhouse. For a moment she forgot how to speak.

"Er ... ah ... hi, Brent," she managed to stammer.

CHAPTER 6
Brent

"Careful there. Don't lean on that anchor winch. You'll get grease on your pants." He looked from one to the other. What the hell was Andrea doing with Marlie in tow?

Andrea's brow wrinkled and she shook her head slightly. "You two know each other?"

"Er...," they answered together, and then laughed.

"Brent fixed my flat tire a couple of months ago," Marlie said. "I haven't even thanked you properly...." She hesitated. "So thank you."

He nodded. God, she was a knockout. Those curls. "Are you settling in at the trailer court? Need anything?" Then he remembered how her car was crammed full, and snorted as he tried in vain to stifle a laugh. "Of course not. You brought everything you could possibly need. How could I forget?"

She blushed then. *Stupid! Why did I say that?* "Sorry. I mean ... you did have a lot of stuff."

"I was wondering if you had any fish for sale." She was quick to change the subject. "I had hoped to make a nice dinner tonight. School starts Tuesday and I wanted to give myself a treat before it's back to work."

"I have a small fish I could give you." Brent opened the hatch cover and hopped down into the hold. In the top layer of ice he had a few fish that were too small to sell—his food fish. He liked to have some in his freezer at home. No need to sell every single fish. He held up a coho. "Would this do?"

Marlie's eyes widened. Her smile was dazzling. "Wow! Yes, that'll do fine." She started digging in her purse. "How much is it?"

He couldn't take her money, but knew she'd insist. He hated that kind of polite bickering. Andrea hadn't said a word. She leaned against the rigging, arms folded across her chest, big grin on her face as she watched them.

"I have an idea," she said. "Why don't we go up to Foissy's Chipmobile and Marlie can buy you lunch?"

"Great idea," they said. He rolled his eyes. This really had to stop. Saying the same things together.

Andrea said she'd go back and see if Jim wanted to come along and they'd meet on the float in a couple of minutes. Brent put the fish in a bag and stuck it back in the hold on ice for pick up later, grabbed a jacket, and followed Marlie across the stinking boat he was tied next to. He hoped she didn't think this was how all fish boats were kept. If he wasn't going to be moving his boat in an hour anyway to go unload his catch, he would have found a better place to tie up.

Jim smiled as Andrea introduced Marlie. He shook her hand enthusiastically. "Hey, Marlie. Nice to meet you." Couldn't seem to take his eyes off her. Brent was surprised at himself to think that it kind of pissed him off. Not that Jim had designs on Marlie, but he wished his friend wouldn't be quite so eagerly friendly. He already had a gorgeous girl.

"So ... let's get going then. I can taste that burger already. Come on, Marlie," Jim said. "We want to get over to Foissy's before the lunchtime lineup starts."

Jim and Andrea led the way, and Marlie fell into step beside Brent, following behind them.

Brent thought it looked like a double date, the four of them walking up the floats together. He had a surprising feeling of well-being and pride as he walked beside Marlie. She might have walked out of an L.L. Bean catalogue, sporty and healthy. She was gorgeous. A sigh escaped him. If only she wasn't such a left-winger—teachers always were—with her anti-hunting sentiments. *She's probably totally naive about real life. The fish will be a big change from her steady diet of granola. Wonder if she knows how to cook it?*

CHAPTER 7
Marlie

Marlie was pleasantly surprised that Brent seemed like a different person in the wharf setting. He was agile as he moved around the boat. When he went to get the fish for her, he'd put a hand on each side of the hatch cover and easily hopped down into the hold, completely disappearing below the deck. As they walked up the ramp towards the main road, she glanced over at his muscular arms. It was hard work to turn her eyes away and not stare.

She thought of James and his flaccid muscles. James was a city boy. His only exercise was on machines in the gym once in a while, and he wasn't dedicated enough that it made a difference. For that matter, his brain was slack too. He was bookish, but not a deep thinker. So why had she moved in with him? She had wondered about that many times. How did she get tangled up with such a useless person? Thinking back now, the answer was easy. He was her ticket to get out of the house—her mother's house, that is.

In her fourth year of university, she was paying her own way at school as well as handing over a substantial amount of rent to her mom—her student loan and the money her dad sent her allowed for that. After a while, she wondered why she should have to spend her evenings and weekends doing housekeeping chores and avoiding her mom's boyfriend, Dean, when she needed to be studying. Sure she helped out with dishes, kept her own room clean, and took care of her own laundry. That was expected, but her mother practically used her as a full time maid. While Dean spent his time nursing the bottle and secretly chasing Marlie around the house, her mom sat around smoking cigarettes and complaining to her friends on the phone about what a burden her daughter was.

Marlie sat on her bed with legs propped up to hold her psychology textbook. She was trying to tune out her mother's voice as she talked to her friend Madge on the phone downstairs. The door to her room inched open and Dean slipped in, beer in hand and fingers to his lips.

"Shh…," he'd warned with a leer as he came over to sit on her bed.

"Dean, I'm trying to study," she told him.

He reached over to touch her knee and let his hand slide down the inside of her calf. Marlie put the book down and swung her legs off the bed. Dean hooked his hand under her arm as she tried to get off the bed. "Come on, Marlie. You know you want it."

Marlie gave him a shove and jumped up. Dean was right after her, pulling her away from the door just as she reached for the handle. As he yanked her towards him, Marlie used the momentum to swing at him, slapping Dean's face hard. His Coor's can flew across the room, the beer fizzing onto her psych book. Marlie grabbed the ruined book and thundered down the stairs. Her mother lowered the phone to her lap.

"I caught her drinking beer," Dean said. "She's supposed to be studying. If I'm paying her keep, she can damn well earn it," he said, "not lie around swilling beer."

"Gotta go, Madge. I got trouble with that girl again. I'll call you later," Marlie's mother said. "Now what the hell is this? You're drinking now? Thought you said you had to study?"

"I was! Until Dean came barging into my room."

"Bullshit, Marlie! I can smell the beer on you," her mother said.

"'Cuz I had to wipe it off my psych book when Dean spilled it."

"If Dean was in your room because you were drinking, then he's perfectly within his rights to stop you."

"Mother! You're not hearing me. Dean had the beer. Dean came into my room. DEAN put his hands on me!"

Her mother's face turned red and her hand flung out instantly to slap Marlie's face. When Marlie caught the look on Dean's face, her own anger boiled over. "That's it! I'm out of here. If you take the word of this sleazy gold digger over your own daughter's, that's the last straw. You're so pathetic, both of you." She took the stairs two at a time and locked the door to her room while she packed. One suitcase and a backpack was all she needed to take with her.

She phoned James, who was happy to have her stay over in his small suite. That night they decided to find a place together. James was her escape. She had known him only slightly from around campus. He looked presentable, seemed to care about her, and made her laugh—at first anyway.

"Two can live cheaper than one," he had said. If anyone could disprove that old cliché, he sure could. She didn't have much money for university. Her dad was sending what he could from Saskatchewan where he was teaching at a college. They had only lived together a few months when Marlie realized that James made short work of his own money and then waited for her dad's monthly cheques more eagerly than she did.

When her dad had phoned one day, he asked how she was doing.

"Scraping by," she'd told him. "My part time library job doesn't pay much."

"I'd send you more if I could, honey, but they only pay me so much. Are you managing the rent?"

"It's going to be tough this month. James used most of my savings for some investment that he says will give us a good return, but not for a few months yet."

"But the money I've been sending should more than cover your rent," he'd said.

"It used to, but I thought you were having a hard time and couldn't send anymore. I really appreciated it, Dad, but I understand."

"What do you mean 'couldn't send anymore'?"

"You haven't sent me anything for three months now. I didn't want to say anything. Thought you were having some problems...."

"Marlie, I've never missed a payment. If you're not getting the cheques, we'd better find out where they're going."

That night she confronted James about the cheques. He must have thought he could lie his way out of it. Denial was his defense. They fought about it until three in the morning, and finally James admitted that he was cashing the cheques and not letting on that they'd arrived. That was the beginning of the end for them. The trust was gone. So much for James being her ticket. It was more like she was his ticket. What a mistake she'd made. She'd jumped out of the proverbial frying pan and into the fire.

James had been fun at a party or with a group of friends. He'd be the first to say let's all go to the lounge. They'd have a few fancy drinks, laugh with his buddies, and he'd insist he was fine to drive home. Somehow they always made it home safely. A miracle, in hindsight. She would never do that now—drive, or ride with a driver under the influence of alcohol. All they remembered in the morning was that they'd had a good time.

When her Visa bill came, she was reminded that in spite of James's love for a party, real life was not one big party. There were bills to be paid, not least of which was her Visa with expensive drinks adding up to more than she could afford. She tried to speak to James about reining in the fun times, but his response was always the same. "You only live once!" If she nagged, and insisted, he'd say with a sneer, "Yes, Mother," and then go out to a party on his own. Still, she was not a quitter. She hung in there for another two years, while she taught in Maple Ridge. She kept hoping James would change. It didn't happen. Not for the better anyway.

That was a chapter she had closed nearly a year ago. She was moving on, and coming up here to the Charlottes was an escape from James' leg-breaking associates, and also a way to prove to herself that she could cope. Just because her relationship with James had been a total failure, didn't mean that she was hopeless.

"What was that all about?" Brent asked.

"What?"

"That big sigh." Brent looked at the ground as they walked, but his glance slid in her direction. "Or maybe I shouldn't ask."

"Oh, just remembering something I don't want to remember."

The aroma of French fries and frying onions wafted towards them as they walked the two blocks from the dock. Her mouth watered in anticipation of a burger and fries. So what if it didn't fit with the Mediterranean diet she'd been trying to follow. She could eat healthy tomorrow.

The converted delivery truck was parked in a roadside gravel parking area. Bright red lettering on the top of the truck wall advertised "Foissy's Chipmobile." Below the name was a long window with a sliding pane. Ketchup, salt, pepper, and napkins stood ready to use on the counter below the window sill.

Inside, a petite thirty-something woman flipped burgers and pushed onions around on the grill next to the deep fryer. The apron wrapped around her gleamed white except for the many fresh grease splatters. A green ball cap struggled to contain the dark curls that kept popping out until she repositioned the cap. Her face was flushed and covered in a light film of steam from the grill. As she served two young native people who stood beside her chipmobile, she wiped the counter and laughed with them about some private joke they shared. She asked after their family and friends. Apparently these fellows were regulars. Marlie's suspicions were confirmed when one said, "I'll have the usual," and the other asked, "Can you put it on my tab please?"

Foissy gave Jim and Andrea a wave. "How are you guys doing? Haven't seen you in ages." She turned to build the burgers and in a short time handed the orders to the two fellows.

Foissy took their orders and Marlie paid for Brent's burger and fries. He kept reaching for his wallet, and

Andrea kept pushing his hand back down and giving him a little shake of her head. "Let Marlie pay," she said. "She's happy to have the fish." She turned back to Foissy. "So where have you been? We came up here looking for you a few times this summer but you weren't around."

Foissy waved a flipper. "Oh, this darned old van. I had to get a valve job and some other stuff done on it. Took forever to get parts. Well, you know how it is up here. Having parts shipped up takes twice as long as anywhere else and costs three times the price. But finally the old Masset Garage came through for me."

"We've missed you," Jim said. "And we'll never forget how you stood up to Robert and tried to help us last year."

"It's so good to see you and Andrea together," Foissy said. "How's the season going this year? No troubles, I guess?"

"It's been great," Andrea said. "So much easier with Robert gone."

"That guy got exactly what he deserved." Foissy shrugged. "I know he was your husband, but he should have known better than to treat you like that. I'm glad he's gone."

"Yup," Jim said. "His own damn fault."

"Did they find him after he fell off the boat?" Foissy asked.

Jim nodded. "Eventually. He washed up on the point. Lucky thing too. If he'd been out in the middle more, he would have been swept into Grenville Channel and sunk so deep they would never have found him."

"What did they ever do with his boat—the Hawkeye, was it?"

"The Coast Guard had it run back to Lund, and when the estate's all settled, the boat will belong to Andrea." Jim pulled Andrea close and rubbed her arm. "But we'll probably put it up for sale. Bad reminders."

"Great to be able to visit you without looking over my shoulder." Andrea turned to Marlie then and said, "Robert was my ex-husband. Very abusive. Long story. Anyway, he fell overboard and drowned. You'll probably hear all about it around the dock. Not like it's a big secret." She put her arm around Jim's waist and pulled him close as he kissed the top of her head. "Everything's good now."

"So Brent, who's your new friend?" Foissy asked, as she placed their orders on the counter.

"Oh, sorry. Scuse my manners. This is Marlie. I fixed her flat tire when she got off the ferry. She had to take some things out of the trunk to get at the spare and then she couldn't fit all her stuff back in the car."

"That was embarrassing, and frustrating," Marlie said.

"I offered to bring it along in my truck and she freaked out because I had a deer in the back."

Marlie gasped at his detailed telling of the story, but no one even noticed.

"What? That deer we had a roast of a few weeks ago?" Jim asked.

"Yup!" Brent kept his head down as he bit into his burger. "She thinks it was too pretty to shoot."

"Oh, I do not!" She couldn't take any more of this. "I don't see why you have to kill animals."

"Well ... to eat them, of course."

"But I don't eat deer—"

"Venison."

"What?"

"Venison. It's called venison once Bambi is dead." Brent was trying to hide a smirk and she knew he was making fun of her. She felt a prickle of annoyance.

"So, okay," Brent continued, "you don't eat deer—venison. So what will you eat while you live here?"

"Chicken, pork, beef, like most people do."

"Not most people up here. We eat a lot of venison. Once you've had a taste of the meat they bring us up here—pretty on the top of the package and going green underneath—you'll soon wish you had some venison."

Foissy leaned her forearms on the counter and said to her quietly, "Marlie, if I were allowed, I'd be making my burgers from venison too. The meat is clean and healthy and not full of steroids and antibiotics. You'll soon get used to it."

She opened her mouth to speak and then thought better of it. From what she could tell, Foissy was a sensible, gentle soul and she seemed to be in the know. Maybe she needed some time to ponder these new developments. Anyway, it seemed she was outnumbered on this issue. Still, she was pissed off with Brent for embarrassing her like that.

***

They finished their burgers and fries, said goodbye to Foissy, and wandered back down to the floats. "She's sure nice, isn't she?" Marlie said.

"A very good friend," Andrea said. "If you ever need help or a friendly ear, she won't let you down."

She sensed there was a lot more to the relationship between Andrea and Foissy, but judging by the way Andrea's eyes were misting over, that story was for another day.

She said goodbye to Jim and Andrea. "Hope to see you again."

"We're doing one more trip and then we'll be heading home to Vancouver Island."

"Maybe I'll see you before you leave. Nice meeting you anyway." She turned to follow Brent onto his boat, the Huckleberry.

He dug the coho out of the ice in the hold and was about to hand it over to her, but pulled it back at the last second. "I don't suppose you know what to do with it?"

"I ... ah...."

He hardly gave her time to consider. "Didn't think so."

She heard the disappointment and dismissal in his voice. "Would you like me to cut the head off? Maybe fillet the fish?" He was already going into the wheelhouse. Seconds later he came out with a long knife.

She wanted to stick her nose in the air and reclaim some of her hurt pride, but she pictured the mess she would make in the trailer dealing with a slimy fish. She swallowed and said, "Sure, that would be great."

Brent reached into the wheelhouse and grabbed a cutting board to put on the hatch cover. He laid the salmon on it and cut off the fish's head at an angle, not wasting a bit of meat. He was amazing to watch. He made a cut beside and all along the length of the backbone. Once the skin was cut, he slid the knife through, pressing it along the fish's bones, and separated the side of the fish from its ribs. He flipped the fish over and did the same on the other side. In a little over a minute he had two smooth salmon fillets.

"There," he said, smiling. "Now all you need to do is give them a rinse and pat them dry with a paper towel. Don't overcook them. Enjoy."

"That's really good of you, Brent. Thanks a lot."

Brent stood there, holding the bag of fillets. He hesitated. "Um ... ah...."

"Yes?"

"Well, it's just that ... I have to apologize for embarrassing you in front of my friends—about the flat tire thing."

Marlie waved at the air.

"No, I'm really sorry. I shouldn't have done that."

"Don't worry about it. We're good," Marlie said with a smile, as Brent handed her the fish.

She stood there holding the bag of fish with her fingertips, trying not to get too much slime on herself. "Will you be going out fishing again now?"

"I have to unload this afternoon, then shovel out the ice. I'll grab a few groceries tomorrow morning and then head out. Jim and I fish near each other. He and Andrea will be pulling out tomorrow too."

"How much longer will you be fishing this year?"

"Maybe another trip or two, and then the weather will start to get ugly."

She looked up at the sky. "It's already not very nice."

Brent laughed. "No, I mean really ugly. Windy.... Well, you'll see for yourself."

She shrugged. "I guess.... So then are you heading back to Vancouver Island with Jim and Andrea?"

He laughed. "Nope. I'm staying right here."

"You live on the boat?"

"No. I have a house outside town, on the way to Tow Hill."

"Oh! You live here." She felt a buzz of joy go through her and coughed to hide her emotions and the grin that tried to give her away. "Okay, well, maybe I'll be seeing you around town sometime then." Her face was heating up. She turned away and called, "Thanks again for the fish." She held up the bag, and then worked her way over the inside boat. "And be careful out there."

"Will do." He held up a hand in goodbye. "Say, Marlie?" He leaned forward, holding onto the rigging. "When I come back in, do you maybe want to go for a cup of coffee with me?"

"Okay, sure." She hopped onto the float and turned to give him a last wave, but he had already disappeared into the wheelhouse.

CHAPTER 8
Marlie

Marlie's class of twenty-six eight-year-olds was a split of about one-third Haida and two-thirds children of non-native people who worked around town or had alternate lifestyles.

The children whose parents were local business people or worked for one of the essential services were the kind who went unnoticed. They did what was expected of them and seemed normal in every way. One or two had attitude but she treated everyone fairly and made it her goal to become friends with them all.

One little Haida girl sat with her head bowed, looking down at her lap, and wouldn't start writing. Marlie bent over and quietly said, "Come on, Heather. Let's start." The girl kept her head down and above her lap she held a pencil from the coffee can, one end in each hand. She twirled the pencil round and round, and whispered half to Marlie and half to herself, "Look how s'arp this is." And it was very sharp. She was so fascinated with the sharp pencil that she forgot all about using it.

Heather quickly became one of her favourite students. She was pretty but shy. Marlie always had the feeling that Heather would love to have been a part of everything going on around her, but she seemed afraid to do anything. Maybe afraid of being reprimanded?

Skylar had filled her in on Heather's background. "Her parents died in a house fire. Lives with her grandparents and an uncle. All alcoholics. Breaks your heart."

Heather came to school in the coolest weather in a white sleeveless blouse, and rarely a sweater or jacket. No school supplies. No lunch. Ever.

One day she was late coming back from lunch break. "Heather! Where have you been?" Marlie asked. "The bell went half an hour ago."

Heather stood still, seemingly unsure of what to do.

"And what's happened to you?" Marlie couldn't figure out why Heather's face was smudged purple.

Heather clutched her arms around herself in an effort to get warm. She stared at the floor, unwilling to meet Marlie's gaze, and whispered, "I bin eatin' salal berries."

"Oh. My...." It was then that Marlie put the clues together. Heather's face was stained from the berries. The poor girl had nothing to eat. Salal grew everywhere in the Charlottes and luckily for Heather, the salal berries were ripe.

Marlie picked up her water bottle, and took several tissues from the box on her desk and walked to the door. "Heather could you come over here please?"

Heather looked scared to death. "It's okay. I just want to talk to you. You're not in trouble." She waved her hand for her to come.

Outside the classroom door, she said to Heather, "I'm just going to get the salal berry stains off your face if that's okay." She poured some water on the tissues and gently rubbed the stains from Heather's face. "Didn't you have any lunch?" she asked.

Heather shook her head ever so slightly and whispered. "Noni is always sleepin' when I go to school."

"Could you make yourself a sandwich at night and put it in the fridge for the morning?"

"We don't got no food. Noni don't got no money for shoppin'."

"Oh, I see. And that's why you were eating salal berries?"

Heather nodded.

"Okay." She finished cleaning up Heather's face. "You go on back and get a book out."

After school, Marlie left a note for the liaison aide to contact her. She made arrangements to have her visit Heather's home and deal with the situation in what she hoped would be a discreet manner. In the meantime, Marlie made up her mind from then on always to bring along something extra in her lunch and slip it to Heather.

Some of the other native kids also had very little, but Heather was the poorest. The rest of the class seemed to be taken care of well enough.

It was a chore that first week to keep the kids busy and interested in every lesson. Every job she prepared for them to do was dashed off in a fraction of the time allowed. It was more like a race to be finished first, regardless of the quality of the work. After a while Marlie began to say, at the beginning of each job she assigned, "Many times, 'first is worst,'" and eventually the message got through. "Take your time and do a good job, and you'll get praise for doing your best job, not your fastest."

Before the kids arrived in the morning, Marlie, like most teachers, had already been on her feet for an hour, and again doing her prep work for the next day after the students left. By the end of that first week, after standing on a cement floor for eight hours a day, even with comfortable shoes on, her feet and legs felt swollen and on fire. It made her so angry when she heard people say that all teachers did was sit at a desk all day. If she could only trade feet with them for one school day....

It was still a half hour before home time on Friday and she sank into her chair to rest her aching legs. Of all times for the principal to walk in. He surveyed the room. A small man with a sharp nose and greasy hair, he fell short of the image one usually associated with his job. "Having a break, I see, Ms. Mitchell." She leaped up onto aching feet and continued wandering around the desks as she had been doing for most of the afternoon. "What's on your lesson plan for this afternoon?"

"We've been learning about fish," she said, "and now the kids are drawing salmon on an underwater scene." She hoped that would meet with his approval. She needed a good report this first year on Haida Gwaii or she'd be looking for work in places even more remote than this one. Beginning teachers always had a hard time getting jobs in the most desirable districts. Marlie was in her third year of teaching, so still very much a beginner.

Marlie was used to having shops and supplies of all sorts handy when she taught in Maple Ridge, outside of Vancouver, but she was willing to forego those conveniences and work in a place where she could learn to be more self-reliant. Someplace remote like Haida Gwaii was perfect. It was far from urban living but still had a major airport for getting out if she wanted to. She knew there were places in northern BC where you could literally be stuck in the bush. No transportation in or out for days at a time. She didn't need that much of an adventure. Masset was quite remote enough. But there was no way she wanted to go back to any place where James—or his creditors—might come looking for her.

Mr. Dupuis spun her daybook around on her desk so he could see the daily plans. He glanced at her over the black plastic frames of his thick spectacles and raised his bushy salt-and-pepper eyebrows. He flipped through the daybook, on each page putting his finger on the time slot after recess when the class always had math. His face clouded over.

Oh, shit! What now? Did I screw up? "Something wrong?" she asked.

"On the contrary. Everything's fine," he said.

Apparently that disappointed him. He must be bored. Jean and Tilly had probably sicced him onto her, suggesting he check on her because she had little experience. They seemed to have special standing with Mr. Dupuis. She'd seen Tilly talking to him with her head awfully close to his. Something was going on. For all their charmed status, they were anything but charming. She didn't know how long she could tolerate their rudeness. She knew she would have a run-in with them. It was just a matter of time.

Mr. Dupuis' visit went well though. For now she was in the clear. Jean and Tilly would be disappointed. *Better luck next time, you old bats.*

Soon after he had satisfied himself that all was well in her classroom, Mr. Dupuis drifted out, and Marlie breathed a sigh of relief. She hated herself for caring what he thought. She remembered her mother's words from long ago when she was still a caring parent. "We were all born naked, Marlie. You're just as good as they are." Her mother was right. She shouldn't feel intimidated, but she wanted a good report and Mr. Dupuis held the power to make or break her career.

Now with only ten minutes before dismissal time, they had to hurry to get things put away. Marlie was disappointed that they didn't get the project finished by the end of the day. They would have to work on it again on Monday, but for now, she was glad this week was over.

A little later, when the classroom was empty, Skylar stuck her head in through the doorway. "Hey, Marlie! Coming out to play volleyball tonight?" She had a big grin on her face, unabashedly showing off the braces on her teeth. Marlie wished she had Skylar's bold self-confidence.

"Volleyball? Where?" She loved playing volleyball.

"Right here at the school. Seven o'clock." Skylar nodded expectantly.

"Yeah, I guess." She didn't know why she hesitated. She would meet a lot of new people at volleyball, and although she wanted to make friends, she was shy. "Yes … YES! I'd love to! I'll be there."

The tiredness of the day fell away once she had made the commitment to play volleyball. She'd been looking for something fun to do. Skylar told her they played every Friday and anyone from the community was welcome.

It was a beautiful afternoon so she decided to walk back to the school after supper. The fresh air would do her good. She put her gym runners in a small drawstring bag and, for a Friday afternoon, found a surprising amount of spring in her step.

She had come to the Charlottes to get away from all her old acquaintances and baggage, but her idea in coming to this remote place was not to be isolated from everyone. New friends were out there. She just had to find them. Volleyball nights were a good place to start.

Marlie arrived at the school gym with fifteen minutes to spare. The varnished hardwood floor glistened, having been buffed by the wide mop of the custodian. She loved how the hardwood shone like new in September, before so many children's runners scuffed the floor. Several of the teachers from her school were there, along with some from the high school and a handful of people she'd seen around town.

They made up two teams of six and the extra two on each side would substitute in at each rotation. Skylar, Wendy, and John from her school ended up on the opposing team with Mike, Josie, and Ryan from the high school. She didn't know anyone else on her team, except to see them. One woman was a cashier at the Co-op and another was a physiotherapist at the Human Resources building. A lean, handsome fellow stood in the front row to her right. He had wild blond hair that kept falling into his face at the most inconvenient times. She didn't know how he managed to hit the ball so well when he could barely see. He sent some great smashes over the net and won lots of points for their team. She learned quickly that if she set him up for a spike, he would most likely score for them. After the second amazing spike, he grinned at her and came over for a high-five.

"Name's Clancy," he said. She introduced herself, and they shook hands. He had a warm, firm grip and held her hand a split second longer than she expected. From then on they were like magnets and the other four players hardly existed. His lightweight beige cargo pants and pale green T-shirt hung on him loosely, but he was obviously fit enough to play volleyball like a pro. No fat on him. Her eyes wandered over in his direction often, and many times she caught him sneaking glances at her. Sparks were flying.

At the end of the evening, most people pitched in to take the net down and put the equipment away. Clancy reached up to unhook the net from the pole and she stood ready to pull out the post to put it back in the equipment room.

"How are you getting home?" he asked.

"I walked over tonight," she said. "It's a nice night for walking."

"Might be starting to get dark soon. Mind if I walk you home?"

"Oh, I'm fine," she said. "You don't need to do that." *Now why did I say that? I'm so stupid.*

"It's Friday night. It may have been a good walk earlier in the evening, but trust me, you'd be safer with an escort once it starts to get dark. Lots of drinking on Friday nights. Some guys get a bit wound up."

A flurry of nerves gave her stomach a twinge. How could she not have thought of that? "I didn't know," she said. "All right then. Next time I'll bring my car."

She was surprised how quickly it was starting to get dark. It had been bright daylight when she arrived at the school gym after supper at 6:45 but by a little after 9:00 the sun was gone from the sky.

"Our shadows look like we're walking on stilts," she said. "I didn't think it would be this dark so soon."

"It changes quickly from those long daylight hours we had in the summer," Clancy said.

"I didn't think to bring a light either," she said. "Let's walk fast so it's not pitch dark before—oh, what about you? Where do you live? You'll have to walk in the dark by yourself."

"No worries there. I'm a couple of streets over from you," he said. "It's not that big a town, you know. But the thing is, a pretty young woman walking in the dark alone on a rowdy Friday night ... not a good idea."

What a gentleman, she thought.

They crossed the causeway over the slough that separated the two parts of town. The shoulder was narrow so she walked partly on the road. When a vehicle approached from behind, she turned to look back. Blinded by the headlights, she threw her arm up against the glare, but did nothing to get out of the way. Clancy grabbed her shoulder and pulled her to the side. She stumbled into him and he clamped his arm around her. The truck slowed down and the driver stared at them as he crept past. By the light of the streetlight, she saw a man shaking his head. A few yards past them, the truck stopped. Then it lurched ahead again and sped over the causeway.

"Oh, no," she wailed.

"You're okay," Clancy said. "You just got a scare."

"Yeah, I'll be fine. Thanks," she whispered. But her insides fluttered and her stomach did flip-flops while her happy evening dissolved into disappointment and regret. She knew that face. Brent.

CHAPTER 9

Marlie

W"ould you like to come in for a cup of tea? Glass of wine?" Marlie asked more out of politeness than anything else. After all, Clancy had been good enough to escort her home in the dark.

"Got any beer?" Clancy asked. "I could go a beer."

"I think I might have one." She hoped she'd remembered to make the bed. An unmade bed was a sign of slovenliness, her mother always said. But what was she thinking? Clancy wasn't interested in her bed any more than she was hoping to get him into it. But the trailer was so small and it seemed like everything was on display. She rushed down the hall to close the bedroom door. "Have a seat." She indicated the couch. "I'll get you that beer."

"How are you settling in?" Clancy asked. "Anything you need?"

"It's coming along okay. I ordered a bunch of things from Sears—sheets, towels, that kind of thing." She hesitated. "I even ordered a pair of shoes."

"Let's see them."

"Had to send them back." She giggled. "Not only were they two different sizes, but they were different styles. They were like those old-fashioned penny loafers, but the part where you would put the penny was a different shape on each shoe."

Clancy grinned and shrugged. "That's how it is up here. When you order something, like from Sears, the stores in Vancouver must think we're so desperate up here, we'll keep any kind of crap they send us. Same thing happened to me when I ordered paint supplies. They sent the cheapest brushes—not at all what I ordered—so I sent them back." He took big thirsty gulps of his beer and belched softly.

Marlie settled into the sofa chair and tucked her feet under her. "Some things are okay though. I got good towels and a new set of dishes. Only one cup broken."

He looked different sitting there on the couch. Smaller, somehow, and his hair fell into his face and looked messy rather than sexy like it had in the gym.

"Well, I guess I'd better get going," he said. "See you next Friday?"

"Huh? What are we doing on Friday?" She followed him to the door.

"Volleyball, of course."

"Oh, of course." How stupid she must have sounded. "I'll bring my car next time," she added, "so it won't be a problem walking home."

"No problem. But maybe you can give me a ride back next time? I think Mike's having the volleyball people over for a party after the games. Thought you might like to go."

"Okay, sounds good." What else did she have to do? It wasn't as if it was like a date. They would just go there together.

He leaned over to give her a kiss. She pulled away and saw his brow crinkle.

"Sorry," he said. "I didn't mean anything by it. Small places like this ... everybody is pretty informal. Do you not do that with friends—a little kiss?"

She wasn't crazy about getting involved right away, but since he put it that way, like it was no big deal, she thought, why not? He was kind of cute and they'd been like a team on fire at the volleyball game. A kiss wouldn't hurt. She didn't want to seem like a prude. His lips looked soft and welcoming, but they were cold and he tasted of beer. She tried not to show her disappointment. He pulled back and smiled at her as if he had given her the greatest thrill on Earth. "See you next Friday."

She switched on the porch light as he hopped down the stairs of the joey shack and turned to give her a last wave.

Marlie moaned. *If only you were Brent.*

CHAPTER 10
Marlie

Late that Friday night a weather system moved in. Marlie was surprised at how violently the wind buffeted the trailer as raindrops rattled a tattoo on the roof. She lay in bed, eyes wide open, listening to the screaming of the wind. Every creak and groan of the trailer had her wondering if this was the gust that would make it lift off and blow away. The power went off sometime after three in the morning which was the last time she looked at the digital alarm clock on her night table.

The next day, the storm had already cleared when Skylar dropped in to see her. "Hey, Marlie. I was wondering if you'd like to come with me tomorrow. The Baileys and I are going beachcombing. You could come along with us."

"Sounds like fun. Where and what time?"

"North Beach. I'll pick you up here at 10? Tide will be going out so we'll have a few hours to poke around. Never know what you might find. With the wind we had last night there might even be some scallops washed up on the beach."

"Okay, why not? See you tomorrow."

Sunday morning, Skylar pulled up in her orange and white VW van. Like Marlie, she had on her gum boots, windbreaker, and a toque. The van had been partly camperized, the bench seats in the back taken out and replaced by a bed. Behind the front seats, just in front of the bed, was a large storage space where Marlie stashed her backpack next to Skylar's. She sniffed the air. Skylar was tuned up for an enjoyable day, if the sweet smell of dope in the van was any indication.

They headed for the closest beach access past the Masset cemetery. At the graveyard, Skylar pulled the van off to the roadside. "Look at the moss on those markers." Skylar shrugged her shoulders. "Guess nobody cares."

Marlie had never seen a cemetery like this one, so uncared for, yet quiet, calm, and mystical. "But it's kind of pretty in a natural sort of way, don't you think?" The whole place reminded her of an Emily Carr painting. "I can think of worse places to spend eternity."

"I was thinking some flowers would be nice, but they'd have to be plastic. Too ugly. And they'd probably blow away. Anyway, it does look peaceful with that moss over the graves ...over the gravestones ... over the trees...." She laughed. "Hardly any place that isn't covered by moss."

"I like it though."

Skylar gave her a puzzled look.

"Don't worry. I'm not ready for the grave yet. So, how far to the beach?"

Skylar pulled back onto the road. "We'll park down here a little way. There's a turn-around and beach access."

The sea air begged to be inhaled deeply, so fresh and cool, soothing on the lungs. Marlie could think of no better way to clear her head of any worries. "This is beautiful, Skylar. I'm so glad you asked me to come."

Marlie saw the Baileys way down the beach with about a half hour's head start. It looked like they would do their own thing, but it was good to know other people were about. These islands were so sparsely settled, it was easy to spend time alone if you wanted it. The downside of that was that if you needed help, tripped and broke a leg on the driftwood or something like that, it might not be easy to find—as she had learned when she had the blowout on that empty highway—and you always had to be able to look after yourself.

She liked the idea of being independent and capable. Her goal was to be a survivor under any circumstances that might arise. She had started carrying a knife in her backpack. A practical tool, it could be used to cut kindling to make a fire or cut rope. It was a last measure of self-defense, not that she anticipated any problems here at the beach. The sand stretched on for miles. Gorgeous! Here and there, Marlie and Skylar detoured around tidal pools, many with small crabs in them probably desperately hoping that the tide would come in before they were picked off by seagulls and eagles. They found some unusual shells and uniquely shaped driftwood and in no time had quite a collection in their backpacks. No scallops this time but there was so much else of interest that they didn't miss them. Her white and amber agate collection was growing quickly and adding weight to the pack.

She and Skylar hadn't had much opportunity to get to know each other and their walk on the beach was a good chance to talk. Like her, Skylar had come to Haida Gwaii to get away. She thought half the islands' population was there to "get away."

"Do you have a big family?" Marlie asked her.

"No, there's just my brother and me."

"No parents?"

"Dad died ten years ago. Mom and I didn't get along. After we had a big fight, I decided it was a good time for me to go traveling." She laughed in a bitter tone. "I took off to India. Thought I'd find myself and become enlightened. I still have to laugh at that, how people think they'll become enlightened and they don't even know what that means."

"What does it mean?"

"Hell if I know!" she snorted. They giggled. "I did get enlightened, but not spiritually. I got a bug or ate something bad and was looking for a toilet constantly. Lost a lot of weight."

"I guess that's one way to do it."

"But the worst thing was that I was on a bus trip in northern India crossing miles and miles of bleak landscape when it struck. I managed to get the bus driver to stop, but there was absolutely no place to find privacy. Not a shrub or a rock bigger than a pebble. And all the people on the bus gawking. It was awful."

"Oh no! You poor thing. What did you do?"

"I did what I had to do." Skylar stopped walking and turned to her. "You get to a point where it doesn't matter anymore. Your bodily needs take over and you remind yourself that we were all born naked."

Marlie stood with her mouth half open. "Hah! That's what my mom always said. Isn't that too funny? Well, when it comes right down to it, it's true, isn't it? Nothing like being sick to take us all back to the basics."

Skylar nodded as she stood, lost in thought, probably remembering that terrible trip.

"It must have been awful for you," Marlie said. Skylar was a lot tougher than she had given her credit for.

"But that wasn't the worst of it," Skylar continued.

Marlie's hands went to her cheeks. "Oh my God! What could be worse than that?"

"Turns out that along with the bug I picked up, I had Hep A."

She stopped in her tracks and Skylar reached for her. "Don't worry, you aren't going to catch anything. I think I ate something prepared by someone who hadn't washed their hands. But oh God, I was sick. And getting sicker by the day."

"What did you do? Did you have a friend to look after you?"

"No, I was traveling alone." She stopped talking for a while, then shook her head and said, "Anyway, it was time for me to get back to Canada. I thought if I was going to die, I didn't want it to be in India. I'd be just another unclaimed body, dead on the side of the road, waiting to be picked up and thrown into a cart."

Her first impressions of Skylar as a rebellious girl who hadn't grown out of her juvenile ways were fading fast. "I never knew you had such a tough time. How awful for you!"

"Well, I managed to get myself to the Mumbai airport and tried not to look too sick to travel. If they'd looked more closely at the whites of my eyes—which were yellow—they might have stopped me from getting on the plane. Anyway, I slept through most of the trip home to Vancouver. I had emailed my mom to tell her I was sick and what time I'd be at the airport.

"When I got to the arrivals lounge I could hardly stand up. I found a place to sit and wait. Hours went by. I lay sideways on lounge chair with my backpack under my head. Every once in a while I tried phoning again, but I kept getting Mom's answering machine. Finally it was late enough that my brother, Dan, would be home from work by then, so I called him.

"He was surprised I was still at the airport. I told him I'd been there for five hours already and did he know where Mom was. By this time I wasn't even sure she had got my email. But Dan assured me that she had. Imagine, she told him if I had got sick in those foreign countries it served me right for gallivanting around. Dan came and got me."

Tears welled up in Skylar's eyes. Marlie hugged her and said, "That was a tough time."

Skylar sniffed and wiped at her nose with her sleeve. "Yeah, I'm okay. I've proven that I don't need her. My brother is good—I mean, he saved me, took me to the hospital—but our mother did so much damage over the years that none of us will ever be really close."

They trudged along the beach a little farther and talked about lighter things, and about how they both had tough times and were going to make it just fine.

The Baileys were still way up ahead of them when they decided to call it a day. Their packs were getting too heavy for comfort and neither of them wanted to give up any of the treasures they'd picked up. Skylar put two fingers into her mouth and got their attention with a powerful whistle. When the Baileys turned to look, the women waved that they were going home. They waved back, and Marlie and Skylar turned to go home.

"I've always wanted to be able to do that," Marlie said.

Skylar frowned. "Do what?"

"Whistle like that." She put her fingers in her mouth and blew what sounded like a raspberry—nothing more than a splutter of air.

Skylar chuckled. "You need a brother to teach you things like that."

They picked their way through the sand and tidal pools to go back to Skylar's van. As they neared the road that led from the beach to the grassy edge of the woods where the van was parked, she stopped abruptly, grabbed Skylar's arm, and pointed. "Holy smoke! Look at those dogs. They're huge."

Six mangy dogs the size of German shepherds were sitting in the sunshine along the grassy ledge between the beach and the forest. The women were on the beach, about 200 meters from the van, still with time to retreat. Marlie hesitated behind Skylar who had taken a few tentative steps forward. She'd heard about what packs of dogs had done on other reserves and was about to say, "I think we should turn around and maybe come back later."

Just then the lead dog spotted them and sat up tall, ears pricked up. The other five did the same.

Adrenaline surged through Marlie preparing her legs for flight back to the water's edge, but Skylar bent down and picked up a long piece of driftwood. She raised it in the air and ran towards the dogs. Marlie hardly recognized the roar that came from Skylar's throat. Ferocious and aggressive, Skylar ran forward waving her stick menacingly. Seeing this, Marlie would have been ashamed to follow her instinct to run away, so she grabbed a stick too. She raised both arms in the air to make herself look bigger. She caught up to Skylar, yelling and running towards the pack.

The dogs fell into line and trotted off at a leisurely pace along the treeline to let the women go by on their way to the van. The pack did not look the slightest bit intimidated and retreated only a short distance. A

frightening thought crossed Marlie's mind that maybe
Skylar might have misplaced her key, but after patting
down a few pockets she found it. The keys rattled as
her shaking hands finally poked the right key into the
lock and opened the door. Once inside, their legs shook
uncontrollably and they laughed with relief.

"Oh my God, Skylar! You were so brave!" she
shrieked.

Skylar laughed. "You too! You too! Look at us," she
said, as she bumped fists with her. "Women rock!"

CHAPTER 11
Brent

Leaving Masset Inlet, Brent passed the old village of Haida on his starboard side and kept the Huckleberry pointed north toward Alaska until he cleared the shallow entrance of the inlet. By the time the sounder showed that he had come to the drop-off into deeper water, the first rays of the sun were struggling to penetrate the light cloud cover.

He thought he'd throw out some coho gear and try a pass or two right out in front of the inlet. You never knew where there might be a school of fish until you dropped a line. Turning east toward Prince Rupert, he could tack along the north shore of Graham Island, the northernmost island of Haida Gwaii. He was hoping that maybe he wouldn't even have to go far to get a trip in. Why burn extra fuel? That was one of his biggest expenses. He wanted to get one more decent load of coho and he'd be happy.

It was late in the season. He didn't want to be out there when the storms started and in a few weeks only the desperate and the foolish would be taking their chances with the weather.

Just the same, he was glad to get out of town. All he kept thinking of was Marlie. Yes, she was a naïve city girl, but maybe, if he got to know her, he could turn her to his way of thinking. She was the best-looking chick he'd seen up here in years. And last night when she was walking home, and he nearly ran into her, he was going to stop to give her a ride, but then Clancy appeared out of the dark and pulled her close. Pissed him off to see him hold her like that. Goddamn, no-good Clancy. She didn't seem to mind him though. Looked like he was all over her and she wasn't exactly fighting him off. He'd gotten the hell out of there. He should just forget about her, but each time he put her out of his head, within minutes she crept back in.

He climbed into the cockpit and adjusted the monitor at the back of the boat so he could watch his depth while he put the gear out. He'd put most of his spring salmon gear away and had the bright pastel-coloured coho spoons lined up ready to be hooked onto the trolling wire. As the brass fathom markers on the wire passed by him, winding down off the gurdies and into the water, he snapped on a monofilament line with a spoon on every second marker. Flashers with hoochies went on the in-between markers. But the spoons were fun. Bright pink, bright pink with black dots, bright yellow, bright yellow with black dots—they all worked on cohos. They'd make funky earrings too, if a girl were brave enough to wear them. He imagined himself brushing back Marlie's cinnamon curls and tucking the pink and black dotted one behind her pretty ears. He'd have the spoons fitted with earring hooks and put them through her pierced earlobes. She'd be his fishing queen and bring him good luck. He snorted and shook his head to clear the image. He didn't even know if she had pierced ears.

Dammit! He lunged for the handle of the hydraulics control to stop the gurdies. The trolling wire had gone down way too far. He'd better watch what he was doing.

He was hung up on Marlie, but if he didn't pay more attention he'd get hung up on the bottom and lose a lot of expensive gear.

He should forget about Marlie. But she was headed for trouble, and he couldn't let her blunder into Clancy's clutches without at least warning her. He knew Clancy was just having fun with her and if she took him seriously, she was going to get hurt. If she knew what he knew about Clancy, she'd tell the asshole to get lost. But how could she know? Someone should tell her, but he had a pretty good idea how it would go over if he were the one to tell her. Lead balloons came to mind.

He pulled his mind away from Marlie—again—and forced himself to concentrate on fishing. He would be out here all week and he couldn't afford to be distracted every few minutes. Watch the tack. Keep an eye out for crab pots. The pots sat on the bottom but had a rope going to the surface held up by a float so the crabbers could find the pots and retrieve them after they'd soaked for a bit. Wouldn't want to get the stabilizers tangled in the line. One guy got hung up in a crab line and it nearly pulled his boat over as he kept motoring, unaware of having snagged it.

***

After five days Brent had a good load of coho aboard. He had room for more fish, but he was getting tired of it. It had been a long season, especially fishing without a deckhand, doing all the work himself. He ran the boat from the stern most of the time rather than sitting in the wheelhouse, so he could bring the six trolling lines up and down, clearing them of seaweed, jellyfish, and other unwanted debris that he might have hooked. With any luck he might have a coho or two on the lines. When the bite was over and it seemed all he did was burn fuel going back and forth on the tack, he used that time to gut and clean the fish, dropping them into the chilled hold until he could ice them properly. Sometimes that meant he had to head out towards deeper water where there was almost no chance of meeting a boat, and he could hop down into the hold to ice the fish and lay them out on their backs, side by side, their cheeks and bellies filled with ice. He put a layer of ice chips over the fish and started a second layer of fish. In between doing the layers of fish he frequently popped his head out through the hatch cover to look around, checking for other boats or logs and kelp mats. He didn't like being down below deck for too long, but without a deckhand, he had no choice. He had to get those fish on ice.

He'd been lucky and caught all the spring salmon his quota allowed; even leased more quota from a guy whose engine packed it in. Brent's leasing of it gave the unlucky fisherman at least some income. It allowed Brent to catch more spring salmon, but he would have to deduct the lease price from his earnings. Still, it was worth it. Now that springs were closed to fishing, Brent had a reasonable season in. He didn't need more money, but why not go for the coho and top up the kitty. Call it gravy. But, he was bone weary from the long hard days and the sleep deprivation. Anyway, with his accounting background, he could always do a few fishermen's tax returns for extra money if he needed it in the spring. He had several steady clients and that helped him with his startup costs each year; that way he didn't have to dip into his savings.

"Huckleberry ... The Serenity. Are you on here, Brent?" The VHF cut into his thoughts.

He picked up the mic. "What's up, Jim?"

"See you're still wandering back and forth up there. Had enough yet?"

"Getting pretty tired of it. I was thinking of pulling the pin," he told him.

"Heading in to sell?"

"Yeah, but I meant pulling the pin for the season. Enough is enough. Besides, I think the coho are heading up the Tlell. More fun to do some river fly fishing."

"Sounds like a great plan. We're making this our last tack and heading over to Rupert. We'll sell most of the fish and bring a few home for ourselves. We saw the ducks and geese heading south. We should too."

"Why don't you come in to Masset and sell there? You could get cleaned up and we could have a last get-together at my place. Stay overnight so we can have a few drinks. Then you can get your laundry done and get the boat cleaned up for the trip home. What do you say?"

"I like the sound of that. Let me check with Andrea and I'll get back to you. Oh wait. She's already nodding 'yes.'"

"All right then. Say tomorrow, Saturday? I'm pulling my gear after this last tack and I'll see you in town." And maybe he could get Marlie to come out and join the party.

CHAPTER 12
Marlie

The kids were settling in, arriving at school with smiles on their faces. Marlie tried to make learning fun. She'd had them make special books—a few pages of lined paper cut to notebook size and covered front and back with coloured paper. This was to be a spelling practice book and the only one in which they were allowed to use a pen. Already the pen was an incentive to work on the notebooks.

She used an overhead projector and the class watched the screen while they practiced their spelling. She drew a line for each letter, like playing hangman, and the kids guessed the word she was looking for from clues that she gave either verbally or with a drawing on the projector. Every once in a while a funny-looking character crept into the lesson.

The kids pointed and laughed. "Ms. Mitchell! Look!"

"What? Where? What's wrong?" Marlie asked.

"The little cartoon man! There! He's peeking in at the edge of the screen."

While Marlie pretended to be oblivious to his presence, every child's attention was focused on the screen. They couldn't see her drawing on the plastic sheet on the projector. It was a great way to keep their attention as they learned to spell words they didn't know they could spell. When the children put away their special spelling notebooks, they all beamed with happiness, even those who once had little confidence in their academic abilities. Each day when it was spelling time, Marlie had no trouble getting the class to pay full attention to the lesson.

They liked learning about animals, and so did Marlie. She wondered if she could find an expert to come and talk to them. She thought about asking Brent to come in to give a talk about salmon. That is, if she ever saw him again.

She'd been so immersed in her work at school she was almost surprised when Friday night rolled around so quickly. She stopped at the liquor store to buy a bottle of wine, dashed home to her trailer, grabbed a quick sandwich for supper, and got her volleyball gear together. She wore stretchy pants, and, remembering Mike's party, put her jeans in the drawstring bag to change into after volleyball was over. She put her runners with them in the bag and threw a hoodie in the back seat of the car.

She hadn't counted on how hard it would be to find new friends, especially in such a small community. One of the hardest things for her was to approach people she didn't know well. She was terrible at making small talk, thought it was insincere and a waste of time. At least going to play volleyball beat sitting around in the trailer alone on a Friday night. Clancy had mentioned wanting a ride to the party. It wasn't exactly a date. Just someone to go with. He wasn't Brent, but she wouldn't feel like such a loner walking into Mike's place when they all knew each other and she hardly knew anyone.

She would rather have been with Brent. He was handsome even in his grubby fishing clothes, and she knew he was a kind person or he wouldn't have stopped to help her when she had the blowout. He'd said something about going for coffee with her but except for the time he nearly ran her over on the causeway, she hadn't seen him around at all. She guessed he was just being polite when he said that coffee bit.

By 7:00 p.m. she was back at school in the gym. Some of the men were setting up the posts for the volleyball net. She looked around at the players. Same crowd as last time plus a few extras. She scanned the gym looking for Clancy, but didn't see him. A cluster of women stood around in the far corner, all looking down at someone sitting on a bench. Voices got louder and the women seemed to close ranks, standing together, hovering over the seated person. "You need to visit your son more often," one said loudly. "And take some responsibility. I need more money!"

A man got up from the bench, shoved the towheaded toddler at her. "You shouldn't have come here. I don't have any money right now. When I sell the next piece, I'll pay you." He put his face close to hers, but still the words he hissed reached Marlie on the other side of the gym. "Now get the fuck outta here."

Marlie gasped and her jaw was gaping when she saw Clancy handing the child over. She spun around and helped the fellows finish tightening the net, hoping he hadn't seen that she saw.

Ryan smirked at her from the other side of the net as he tightened the bottom rope. "Tsk! Tsk! Tsk! Clancy's gonna get himself in trouble if he keeps that up."

"Keeps what up?" she mumbled.

"The guy can't keep it in his pants. He's got a trail of kids from here to Sandspit." Ryan pulled on his earlobe and fiddled with the diamond stud in it. "Oops! You didn't know?"

She felt rooted to the floor. "A trail?" She shook her head, dazed.

"Well, two or three, anyway. Sorry. I thought you knew. You let him walk you home last week. I thought you must have known him from around town." Ryan's face reddened. "Not my business, but if you don't know him well, all I can say is be careful."

Ryan tied off the knot with a flourish and ducked under the net to go join a small group who were bumping a volleyball in a circle.

"Heads up, Marlie!" someone shouted, but the ball hit her on the back before she could look around.

"You okay?" Clancy ran up and put his hand on her shoulder. "Didn't mean to hit you. Wanna bump the ball around and warm up?"

"Ah ... sure." It would have been rude to say no, but what else could she say? Has your baby gone home? Is that your wife? How many children do you have? How old are they? Probably all close to the same age. Oh God, how could she let herself get mixed up with him? No, wait! She wasn't mixed up with him. Not yet.

Clancy brushed the unruly blond shock of hair out of his eyes and smiled at her. One cheek had a dimple and his teeth were straight and white. "I've missed you all week," he said.

Her harsh judgment of him, made only moments earlier, eased somewhat. Maybe she'd gotten it all wrong and he was an innocent victim of those women's venom. He had seemed pleasant enough whenever he'd talked to her. "Well, here I am," she said. "I brought my car this time."

"Great! We can go over to Mike's after we're done here."

He must have thought she was throwing herself at him. "I meant, I have my car so you don't have to walk me home."

His brow wrinkled. "Oh yeah. Sure. Whatever. I'll see you at Mike's afterward though." He pushed his hair back again. "Let's play."

"Play?" She stood there, puzzled, and then he flipped her the ball. "Oh."

***

Masset was a small town of about 850 people. The apartment block where Mike lived was only about a ten-minute walk from the school, Clancy told her.

"But if you give me a ride over, I can show you where it is," he said. The lot behind the building was already full, so she parked on the street.

"Don't the neighbours mind if Mike has a party?" she asked.

Clancy's brow wrinkled. "Why would they?"

She reached behind the driver's seat and picked up her brown bag of wine and her purse. "Well, the noise, of course."

"Naw! Nobody cares about that kind of thing here. Everybody has a party sometime. As long as they don't go on too late, nobody complains. Too bad for them if they do."

"What do you mean?"

"Well, what do they expect will happen if they complain? The police don't come for noise complaints. There's not enough cops to go around as it is." He shrugged. "I don't know why they bother to have any police here at all. Nothing happens here and if it did, they'd be useless at dealing with it."

"What do you mean? Aren't they trained to respond if there's a problem?"

"Oh, I suppose ... but they're lazy." He snorted. "All the better for everyone. Less hassle."

Marlie frowned at Clancy's revelation and his nonchalant attitude. "What do you mean 'less hassle'? For whom?"

Clancy shrugged. "Who cares? For anybody. People can sort out their own problems. There's always shit going on around town and it all gets straightened out. We don't need police to do it for us."

"That may work out for men, but what about women and old people? They might need help."

"The men can look after things." Clancy walked ahead of her towards the apartment lobby. "Don't worry about it. It's just a small town."

Marlie was shocked at Clancy's attitude. Men can look after things. Did he really think women wanted men to look after everything for them?

What if it were a man who was causing a problem for a woman—maybe robbing her—and she needed the police? Why should women settle for having the men look after the problem for them? She hoped she was wrong to be concerned. If Clancy was right about police not responding, she would have to make a point of taking care of herself.

The door to Mike's second-floor apartment was wide open and people were laughing as they milled around in the musty hallway and inside the door. "Just throw your coats on the bed," Mike called to the group.

Marlie put her wine on the counter. "Hi, Marlie," Josie said as she pulled at the elastic band of her ponytail and released volumes of her wheat-coloured hair letting the waves cascade over her shoulder. "Glad you came along." She took a big plate of chips and dip out of a bag and set it on the coffee table. Most of the guys stood around holding cans of beer to their chest. Clancy had brought nothing, but he headed for the fridge, helped himself to a beer and then parked himself in a chair in front of the chips on the coffee table. Sheila smiled brightly as she wiggled over to make room for him on the couch. She patted the space beside her.

"How's it going, Clancy?" She put her hand on his shoulder and let it slide slowly down his upper arm as she reached for a chip, dipped it, and fed it to Clancy.

Marlie hadn't moved from the counter when Ryan came over to stand beside her. "Want me to open that for you?" He held the bottle at an angle and read the label. "That's a nice wine. Too good for this crowd." He pulled the cork out and poured a glass for each of them. They clinked glasses. "Looks like your boy is enjoying Sheila's attention."

She glanced over towards the couch. "He's not my boy. He just came over with me to show me where Mike lived." Clancy grinned as he looked adoringly at Sheila. "But he is having a good time, isn't he?"

Ryan nodded wryly. "And Sheila has her hooks into him."

Ryan took Marlie by the arm and pulled her farther away from the crowd in the living room. "She and Clancy used to be an item, but she told me they had a fight over something a couple of weeks ago...."

Marlie looked at Ryan over the rim of her glass as she sipped her wine. "Why would she tell you that? Are you guys close?"

"We teach together at the high school, but yeah, you might say we were close. We used to live together, before Clancy."

A small cough and a gasp escaped Marlie before she composed herself. She held her wineglass away as it threatened to spill onto her shirt. "Don't you care that she's flirting with him like that?"

"She knows what he's like, and she's all grown up. It's up to her if that's the kind of guy she wants to mess with. I have no interest in her love life anymore. We're just friends who happened to live together for a while." He shrugged. "Welcome to the Charlottes. People change partners a lot here. We call it the Queen Charlotte Shuffle."

"But don't you care? I mean you obviously cared about her at one time." She waved her free hand in front of her, erasing the airspace. "Oh, never mind. It's not my business. I shouldn't be so nosy." She knew she was babbling, but she was shocked.

"Not at all. That's not being nosy. But I can understand how you'd be surprised at all the switcheroos people do up here. Small gene pool to sample from I suppose. People all know each other just a little too well. So we trade around and there's no hard feelings."

"Really? You can turn it on and off like that?"

Ryan shrugged and looked at the floor.

"Not me," Marlie continued. "Maybe I'm too possessive, but if a guy and I are an item, I don't want him making googly eyes at someone else any more than he would want me to be looking to hook up with some other guy." She waited for Ryan to say something, but he seemed lost in thought as his gaze rested on Sheila across the room. "I don't think you're quite done with Sheila yet."

At the sound of her name, Ryan came out of his "Sheila daydream" and mumbled, "Maybe not. We'll see."

Clancy's arm was around Sheila's shoulders. He rubbed her upper arm as if to comfort her. He put his head down close to hers and talked in a low voice. Across the room, Marlie couldn't hear what he was saying but his body language said a lot. He still had feelings for Sheila, too.

She wasn't so enthralled by Clancy that she cared whether he went back to Sheila or not. She hardly knew him. His chauvinistic attitude about men taking care of things still niggled at the back of her mind. Sure, he had a certain attraction; that "little boy" look, and that shock of hair that kept falling over his deep blue eyes. Beyond that, though, he was just a diversion for her.

She thanked Ryan for the wine and the chat and wandered into the kitchen where Skylar and Josie were having a heated conversation.

"Those days are gone, Skylar. You're fooling yourself if you think these kids smoking pot have the same ideals that pot smokers had in the Woodstock days of peace and love." Josie hesitated. "Not that any of us were around back then.

"What do you mean, it's not the same?" Skylar asked. "A little pot never hurt anyone. I think it's kind of cool. Makes people more mellow."

Josie turned to include Marlie in their conversation. "The drug scene has gotten way out of control up here. Kids aren't just smoking a bit of pot. They're popping prescription pills, mixing it with alcohol, and some are doing coke and heroin. And instead of peace and love, it's smash and grab. It's a real mess."

"Is it really that bad?" Marlie asked.

Josie shrugged. "Well, if it isn't drugs, it's alcohol. I've been up here for quite a few years now, and the problems are only getting worse. I don't mean to sound like I'm judging, but I feel sorry for them. The drugs and alcohol problems are literally killing them."

"For example...," Skylar said.

"Okay," Josie said, "I play basketball on the local town team, and one of my biggest fans was this Haida fellow, Archie James. He was just a friend, but I really liked him. He'd holler my name and cheer me on from the bleachers when we were having a game." Josie looked into her glass of wine and swirled it around. She swallowed a lump in her throat and her voice got quiet. "One morning last winter he was lying on the sidewalk in front of the Co-op, dead of exposure. I guess he passed out drunk and no one found him in time."

"That's awful," Marlie said quietly.

"And have you noticed all the plywood nailed over the business windows around town? Smash and grab prevention. The kids have expensive habits to finance."

Skylar added, "I guess you can also add the fetal alcohol problem. The mom drinks while she's pregnant. Then those babies grow up having fetal alcohol babies of their own. It's a vicious circle and I don't know how it's ever going to stop."

"That's all so sad. Can't anything be done?" Marlie asked.

The girls shrugged and sighed. "I don't know what the answer is," Josie said half to herself.

Just then Clancy tapped Marlie on the shoulder. "Can I get you to give me a ride home?"

"Sure," she said. "I'm ready to go. It's been a long week." She gave the girls a crooked smile. "Thanks for the chat. See you next week, ladies."

Skylar grabbed Marlie's arm and pulled her aside. "You sure you know what you're doing here?"

Marlie frowned. "What do you mean?"

"Just be careful."

She picked up her jacket from the pile of coats on the bed, and raised a hand to the group in the living room. "Night, everybody," she called. That was a strange thing for Skylar to say.

"Sorry I didn't get to spend much time with you," Clancy said, as he followed her out into the hall. "Sheila needed to talk, and anyway I could see you were busy with Ryan."

"No matter. They're nice people, this group. They seem to know each other well."

Clancy shrugged. "Small town. After a while, everybody knows everything about everybody else."

Just now she wasn't sure if what she'd been learning about Clancy was such a good thing. To be fair, Ryan did have an agenda, so maybe he wasn't unbiased.

CHAPTER 13
Clancy

Clancy had been hoping Sheila would show up at Mike's place for the party. Her house was almost next door to the apartments where Mike lived. She hadn't been to volleyball yet but he went to the volleyball nights each Friday, hoping that she'd start coming out again like she did last year when he first met her.

Marlie was a hottie; Sheila was a woman. A very sexy woman. She wasn't a pushover either, and he liked a challenge. It heightened the pleasure of the conquest when a woman played hard to get. He could probably have insisted that Sheila have sex with him last year when they met, but she was a big girl and he wasn't sure if she might be more than he could handle. She worked out and had arms on her like a wrestler. Beautiful arms, but strong. He wanted those arms wrapped around him again.

She belonged to the Haida royalty. Her face had a hint of Polynesian features, and her eyes were like dark chocolate. She had cut her long hair to shoulder length and styled it in a modern way, not hanging down and straggly like some of the native women he'd seen in the pub. Sheila stood out in a crowd. She wore good quality clothes and with her beautiful face and long lean body she could have been a model. Clancy was smitten by everything about her.

He had moved in with her last September but by June they had broken up. Somehow she got wind of one of his dalliances. The Haida network was thorough. Not much got past them.

"Where were you?" she asked him one morning. She raised her chin and looked down her nose at him, daring him to lie.

"At the pub," he said, looking at the floor. Her gaze was powerful and he couldn't bring himself to meet it when he lied.

"Bullshit!" Sheila spat the words. "You were with that girl off the sailboat. My Aunt Florence saw you driving with her in Declan's car. Her cousin Hilda saw you in the Masset Grocery loading up on junk food. She was coming after you to say hi but then she saw the girl in the car."

"So what? I gave her a ride to the store. That's all."

"No, it was not all. Hilda wondered why you were with a girl, so she followed you and you went to Declan's place with her."

They had the biggest row that day and Clancy had to be extra nice to Sheila for days before she forgave him, but the next week, when he got tired of playing nice, it all backfired on him.

It was some small argument and a bit of pushing and shoving, but that's all it took to put Sheila over the edge. She threw him and his backpack out the door, and turned the key.

Luckily Declan came through for him and let him sleep at his place. He was hardly ever there anyway. His dreary shack often smelled of kitchen garbage and dirty dishes, but it was a place to sleep. The crude house was off the main road, close to town but hidden by thick growths of alder. A good, private place for Clancy to bring girls he picked up.

He liked having sex without any responsibility attached, but there were times when he also wanted someone he could have a conversation with over breakfast. If he played his cards right he could have both lifestyles at the same time. Sheila was a steady, no nonsense kind of girl, so tonight when she told him she missed him, he had to remind himself to play it cool. He told her he'd think about it and they could talk later. Since getting back together was what Sheila wanted, keeping her guessing was the best way to make it happen.

Besides he still had Marlie on a string. Didn't want to waste that lead. He'd try to get her to smoke a doobie with him, relax her, and then Bingo! She'd be his. His motto about girls was: Leave no tern unstoned. This little bird would sing for him first and after that he'd see about pulling Sheila out of his back pocket. No reason he couldn't have both.

CHAPTER 14

Marlie

"A re you sure there's a house down here? It looks like
nothing but bush." Marlie had followed Clancy's
directions with increasing misgivings. It was a clear,
but moonless night, pitch black without streetlights.
The road narrowed until the alders were so grown in
that they brushed against the sides of her car. "Yup! I'm
sure. Almost there. Right around this bend here."

The car headlights lit up a small shack with cedar
shake walls. A bare light bulb over the door revealed a
set of saggy wooden steps.

"Come on in. Let's smoke a doobie and have a glass
of wine," he said.

No way. Smoking dope was a quick way to get fired
and she needed this job. "I don't think I'd better...."

Clancy got out. "You want to see my carvings, don't
you?" As the door opened and the interior car light came
on, disappointment showed on his face.

She did want to see his artwork. She'd heard he
was good, but images of Sheila stroking his knees and
thighs kept popping into her head. "I do, but...."

"Great. Come on in." He pulled at her hand. "I'll show
you my latest work-in-progress. It'll be fun."

"It'll be fun?" Looking at artwork was going to be
fun? She liked art, but "fun"?

Clancy was bouncing on the balls of his feet. Hyper! "Yeah, it's interactive art."

She had no idea what he meant by that, but it was awkward to keep refusing when he wanted to show her his artwork. She would just have a quick look to be polite and then she'd go home.

"Let me just turn the car around before I come in. With so many bushes and trees, I want to make sure I'm facing the right way while you're out here to help guide me." She maneuvered the car around as Clancy waved his arms and shouted at her through the driver's side window to stop, turn the wheel to the right, to the left, back up, go forward. As soon as the car was turned, she had misgivings again. "Clancy, I think I should get going home."

He yanked the door open again. "Nonsense. Come on and see my art. You might as well, now that you're here." He took her arm and gently, but firmly, pulled her out of the car. "C'mon, Marlie? I really want you to see it. I want to know what you think."

"Okay, okay. Just for a minute, but then I should go."

Inside the musty cabin, the acrid smell of the cold woodstove and a hint of a full garbage can filled the room. The place was one big room. Off to one side the door to the bathroom stood open.

"Did you build this place?"

"No, that would be Declan."

"Who's Declan?"

"This is Declan's shack. He's letting me crash here until I find something else. He's out tonight. Spends Friday nights at The Bunker. He'll be there until closing time."

She gathered that Clancy had no home of his own. But who was she to criticize? She didn't have a home either, except for the stupid trailer.

Clancy opened a beer for himself. He held one up for Marlie, but she shook her head.

"You were going to show me your carvings," she said.

"Oh yeah." Clancy took a swig and set the beer down on a wooden crate that served as coffee table. "But first, I need a little kiss." He pulled her close and kissed her with that horrible beer breath.

She pushed him away, but he kept an iron grip on her upper arms.

"Clancy!" She hit at his shoulders and twisted away. "That's not funny."

He grabbed her wrist tightly. "No, not funny," he said, "but it's fun." He laughed and yanked her closer and tried to kiss her again, groping at her breasts with one hand. "Told you we'd have fun."

Now she was scared. She was all alone in the bush with a guy she hardly knew. What ever had possessed her to come here alone with him? She must have been crazy. She didn't know Clancy. She'd only met him two weeks earlier and the comments from people who knew him had nothing good to say about him. Why hadn't she listened? She was only trying to be polite, coming in to see his artwork. Suckered! She couldn't believe she was so stupid.

Clancy grabbed the back of her hair. "I love your hair, Marlie. There's so much of it." He pulled it back so hard that her knees buckled and she fell backwards onto the couch, just as he must have planned it. She scratched his face to make him let go, but he threw his bloodied head back and laughed like an insane man, taunting her with a sound like a cat yowling. "Bit of a wildcat, eh?"

When she bit his arm he jumped back, shocked, and then slapped the side of her head with the back of his hand. Her head roared inside like blood rushing around in her skull, and her ears were ringing. Clancy reached up and grabbed a coil of rope that hung on a nail by the door.

"I've been trying to be nice to you, Marlie, but you aren't playing along. I'll have to tie you up." He grabbed her wrist as she tried to push past him to the door, and twisted an arm behind her back. The pain was excruciating, and her other arm flailed uselessly as she tried to reach for him. He dragged her across the room and shoved her under the table, mashing her face into the floor. She thought her shoulder would break when he put his knee on it. With three quick wraps around her wrist he tied it to one leg of the table. He caught the other wrist and tied it to a second table leg. She kicked at him like a wild horse. That was probably a mistake. He just stepped back and grinned.

"Sorry I don't have a four-poster bed, Marlie, but this will be even more fun. Do you like to improvise?" He looked around the room, studied the table, and nodded. "Are you enjoying this like I am, my dear?"

"Untie me," she yelled, "and then you can go to hell. You sonofabitch. Untie me!" She kicked at the air around him. He managed to stay just out of reach, laughing as if this were all a big joke.

He put a wrap around a third table leg and tied one of her ankles to the table. She yanked at the ropes around her wrist, but the knots were tight. She was helpless as he grabbed her free foot and pulled her jeans off that leg before tying the ankle to the last table leg. Then he pulled the second pant leg the rest of the way down to her ankle.

"Don't do this, Clancy," she sobbed. "What's wrong with you? Stop!"

"One could say you are literally 'under the table.'" He giggled at his joke. Then he smiled and pulled at the loose skin around his Adam's apple, studying her for a moment. "I like the way you're bucking, my dear. You'll see this can be really fun. Don't be upset. We're just playing a bondage game."

"I don't WANT to play a bondage game," she shrieked hysterically.

Clancy's hand connected with her face. "I didn't want to have to do that but you're not playing the game. Now, come on, Marlie, be nice or I'll have to hurt you."

He stood over her behind her head and slowly pulled down the zipper of his cargo pants. He unfastened her blouse, popping some of the buttons off. Then he left her lying there. She thought he was finished with the game but then he dropped to the floor and crawled under the table and up between her legs.

She screamed. Clancy clamped a hand over her mouth. "Nobody's going to hear you out here in the bush, but if you keep screaming, I'll have to gag you. Do you want me to gag you?"

She shook her head wildly. "No!" she cried out, muffled by his hand.

"I'm going to take my hand away then. So play nice or I'll get out the duct tape." His erection was huge and her eyes reflected her surprise. He grinned, satisfied. "Too bad your hands are tied or I'd let you feel it. On second thought, I don't really trust you anymore, so you'll have to do without the pleasure."

"You pig!" she yelled.

He crawled back out from under the table. "That's it! You're getting the duct tape." He yanked open a drawer by the sink and brought out a wide roll of duct tape.

"No, don't do that," she pleaded. "I won't say anymore. Please, don't—m-mph."

"That's better now," he crooned. "Now where were we?" He brushed his unruly shock of hair out of his face, an action she now despised, and crawled back under the table. His fingers tickled the inside of her legs on their way up to her panties. "We'll have to get rid of those."

One forceful rip tore them right off her. All she could do was whimper behind the duct tape and gasp for breath through her nose.

Clancy was anything but gentle as he satisfied his urges. She lay still and shut her mind to what he was doing and thought how ironic it was that she'd started taking the pill again in hopes that something would come of her and Brent. It didn't look like that was going to happen but at least she wouldn't be another mother of Clancy's trail of illegitimate children.

When he had spent himself, Clancy rolled off her and untied the ropes. "There you go. Wasn't that a fun game?"

She pulled off the duct tape the second her hands were free, and yanked her jeans up. Sobbing, she ran for the door, grabbing her bag with her keys on the way out.

Clancy followed her out to the car. "Marlie! Don't get any ideas of telling anyone about our little game, will you now? You don't want to get hurt. I mean really hurt. And anyway, what would the school children think if they heard what you'd been doing?"

She slapped the button down with her elbow to lock the door as she stepped on the gas and spun the tires until they got a grip and lurched her out of there.

CHAPTER 15
Brent

The Huckleberry was tied to the dock. She was a sturdy and reliable 40-foot troller. Wood, so that meant constant work to keep it maintained, to stop the rot from setting in, as it always wanted to do in the damp climate of Haida Gwaii. Brent had dreamed of trading it in for a fiberglass hull, but then there would still be the engine to get to know and maintain. He knew the Huckleberry from stem to stern; every change in pitch and every rattle or groan told him how the engine and the boat in general were running. It would also be a huge financial leap to trade up to a bigger, more modern boat and he didn't need that kind of stress. He was doing okay. He was comfortable. His house was paid for, thanks to his dad, who had given him a good deal. It was an almost perfect situation, but he was tired of the constant work involved in maintaining the boat year round.

He'd delivered his last coho trip to the fish plant in Masset. Everything was clean and tidy. If he'd been unsure about whether he was going to do another trip, he would have left the gear out in the cockpit ready for next time, but he felt like an old man in a young man's body. Fishing was hard work and he'd had enough for this season. He packed the gear away in a big tote. Later he would cut off the monofilament line and sort the spoons, hoochies, and snaps. Some guys let their lures and hooks sit out in the weather and rust over the winter, but his father had taught him to take care of the boat and its equipment.

So he was finished for the summer. No point in wasting time fishing when the price wasn't there. And anyway, he had put in a good season on springs. He wasn't rich, but he wasn't hurting. He could afford to quit until next year.

His dad would be proud of him when he told him how his season went. He got Brent started in fishing when he was about fourteen. A skinny lad, Brent was probably not much use to his dad as a deckhand, but he tried to make up for it by working hard to please him. The old man put up with a lot of screw-ups—fish Brent lost by knocking them off the lure with his gaff, expensive gear he lost by not hooking the snaps on properly or trying to go too fast and missing the trolling cable completely, cutlery he accidentally threw over the side when he dumped the dishwater from the plastic tub. His father cursed for a few minutes, but he always came around quickly, and showed him what he'd done wrong. Soon he was slapping him on the shoulder and laughing again.

Brent's mother died of breast cancer four years ago. His dad had practically given him the house as he intended to live in Victoria while Brent's mother went through cancer treatments. After her death, Brent's dad never wanted to come back to the Charlottes.

Brent's dad had been good friends with Jim's, and he took Jim under his wing when his dad died of a heart attack on the boat about eleven years ago. Jim had brought his dad's boat home to Vancouver Island with the help of a friend from Lund and they all thought that was the end of his fishing career. The next year, Jim had sold his dad's boat, bought the Serenity, and was back fishing again. Brent's father helped him get on his feet, fishing near him and making sure he didn't go out in bad weather. Jim and Brent got to be good friends in the process.

Now that the nightmare with Andrea's abusive husband was over, Jim and Andrea could fish together. They had gone in to Masset already and would sell their load in the morning. Brent was looking forward to having them over to his place Saturday night for supper and one last visit before going home to Vancouver Island.

He picked up his truck from Lennie's place. Lennie used to fish in his younger days but was too old to do it anymore. He lived just a block up from the wharf and let Brent park there while he was out in the boat. Saved him hitching a ride out to his place way out of town to get the truck when he came home between trips. He always made sure to bring Lennie some fish as a thank you.

It was getting late by the time Brent finished up at the wharf, cleaning the boat and shoveling the old ice out of the hold, but he figured Marlie would still be up. After all, it was Friday night. No school in the morning.

On his way over to the trailer court, he went over a hundred different opening lines for inviting Marlie to come for supper tomorrow. He was surprised at how nervous he was. He never had trouble approaching women. Not that he had a lot of time for female company lately, but until now, if he met a pretty girl, she was usually throwing herself at him before he had to think about what to say to get her interested. He'd grown up confident and self-assured. Even after his failed marriage to Nicole, he never lacked for girlfriends. He found it harder to find excuses to let them down easily when he got bored with them. And he always did get bored. He'd slept with some gorgeous girls, but any he'd met so far had very little inside their pretty heads. It wasn't as if he was an intellectual, but he liked to think he was pretty smart. He liked knowing what was going on in the world and how it was going to affect the market. If there was a coup happening someplace on the other side of the world, his shares in the stock market would probably go down, so it mattered. He worked damn hard for his money. He didn't want to lose it all overnight. Sure he cared about what was going on in the world for other reasons besides money, but the stock market always reacted to the headlines and he had learned that they could cause his portfolio to go up or down. Seldom did he find a like-minded girl – one who cared about the world and also realized the far-reaching effects of news stories on everyday finances.

Nicole was the exception. He was a student at the UBC Sauder School of Business for three years and it was during his last year that he met Nicole who was also taking the accounting courses. She was pretty and smart, too. She was eager to marry Brent and moved to the Charlottes with him at the end of his last year. She got work right away in Masset, as an assistant to a guy who did taxes for a lot of the fishermen. The accountant got her hooked on drugs and Brent found out about their affair and her addiction too late. They had talked it through and Nicole was sorry about the affair, but she couldn't shake her heroin addiction. The problem was too big for both of them and it spelled the end of their relationship before it had a chance to work.

He had no illusions about Marlie being an intellectual. In his limited experience, most teachers weren't. For sure, his hadn't been anyway. To be fair, he hadn't had much chance to talk to her at length. Except for her naïve city ideas, she seemed to be fairly level-headed, but he didn't get his hopes up. Still, he wondered if he might have been too quick to judge her that first day he met her.

Something special about her got his attention when she'd come down to the dock last week. She seemed to be a bit lost and alone, out of her depth in the fishing community, but making a valiant effort to be independent. He sensed that she was quietly gutsy. She had no one holding her hand when she came to see if she could buy a fish for a dinner she would probably eat all by herself. Maybe she wasn't just a flake like he first thought.

He needed to see her again. After Nicole, he'd had a flurry of one-night stands but he was tired of that lifestyle. He had sworn off women. Life was so much easier without all those theatrics, all that stress. So how was it that Marlie stirred something in him that wouldn't leave him alone? She had a way of popping back into his head no matter how much he pushed her out. She had a great figure—kind of lean and athletic, his preference—and she wasn't a loudmouth—also his preference. Those were the obvious reasons for the attraction, but there was something else about her that he couldn't quite put his finger on. Her eyes said she'd been hurt. She was wary, and yet needy at the same time. It puzzled him how both those components could be part of one person.

Brent pulled into the trailer court and plowed through the potholes to Marlie's door. The trailer was dark. No lights. He checked his watch. 10:30. Too early for bed, but maybe she wasn't home. It seemed to him it was a Friday last time he saw her, too. With Clancy, that jerk.

It hadn't occurred to him that she might be out. Shit! If she was with Clancy again, he'd have to set her straight. She was too good for him and she probably had no idea what a sleazebag Clancy was. How could she, being so new here?

Her car wasn't there, but there was a small chance it might be parked somewhere nearby. He knocked on her door, just in case she was in there with the lights off. No answer. He'd have to try her in the morning, but it would be short notice for a dinner invitation, and maybe she wouldn't want to come. Damn. He didn't like striking out.

Brent drove along the roundabout driveway, cursing the School District for not fixing those bloody potholes. He was about to leave the trailer court when Marlie's Corolla lurched in and pulled up by her trailer. She was alone. *Whew! No big date with Clancy then.*

He did a quick U-turn, parked behind her car, and turned off the truck. She didn't get out. Just sat there slumped forward over the wheel. He got out and stood by her car door. She reached for the door handle and jumped when she saw him standing there. Marlie's head spun away from him, and her hands went to her face, wiping at her eyes. He could see her shoulders heaving.

Brent frowned. What the hell? "Marlie?" He tapped on her window. "You okay?"

She nodded and reached for her bag. He opened her car door. She hesitated and then got out and quickly hopped up the steps into her joey shack.

He followed right behind her. "What's wrong, Marlie? Can I help?"

She flipped the keychain around in her hand looking for the trailer key. Her hand trembled as she pushed the key at the door, missing the lock. The bundle of keys fell and disappeared into the crack between the joey-shack porch and the trailer.

"Oh no-o-o-o!" she wailed, and sat down on the steps with her head in her hands.

"I've got a flashlight in the truck. I'll find your keys."

Brent shone the light under the trailer. The grass was high under the porch steps but in the beam from the flashlight he caught the glint of metal. "I see them. I'll have to crawl under there to get them though."

"I'm so sorry," Marlie whispered.

Brent snaked under the porch on his belly and reached the keys. He brushed at spider webs in his hair, not his favourite thing. He studied the keys in the light of the flashlight and picked one out of the bundle. "I'll get it." He opened the trailer door.

As Marlie turned on the light, Brent had a better look. Her hair was a mess. Her shirt was askew and some buttons were missing. He reached for her hand and as she jerked it away, he noticed her wrist was bright red. So was one side of her face. "What the hell happened to you?" He reached and held her by the shoulders. She winced and he let go immediately. "Something happened," he said.

"I can't tell you." She twisted away and sat down on the couch sobbing into her hands.

He sank down beside her, put his arm gently around her shoulder, and pulled her close. Talking into the top of her head, he said, "Sh-sh-sh! It's okay. It's okay."

She quieted down after a few minutes. He handed her a tissue from the box on the coffee table. She blew her nose and frowned at him in a puzzled way, "Why are you here?"

"I came to invite you to dinner."

She burst out laughing and immediately began crying again.

"Hey! I'm not that bad a cook," he said, stroking her hair. "Look. Why don't you go have a nice hot bath and I'll make a pot of tea for when you come out? You'll feel better and then you can tell me what happened." He felt her tense up. "Or not. If you don't want to, we can just talk about other things. But you look like you need cheering up."

She nodded. "Bath and a cup of tea sounds good. Okay ... if you're sure you don't mind."

CHAPTER 16
Marlie

When Marlie woke Saturday morning, the events
of the previous evening came rushing back. She
squeezed her eyes shut, rolled over, and sobbed into
her pillow. She woke again an hour later, drained and
confused, not wanting to face the day. Every part of her
body ached. When she finally dragged herself out of
bed, she downed a couple of Advils hoping to dull the
pain. She winced as she passed a wet facecloth over
her cheeks, and gasped when she saw her face in the
bathroom mirror. A raised welt ran down from her eye
to her jaw just in front of her ear. The bruising that
was bright red the night before now took on a purple
tinge. She showered and tried to fix herself up to
look presentable. With shaking hands she dabbed on
makeup and managed to hide the worst of it.

She wasn't worried about getting pregnant, but she
prayed that Clancy didn't have an STD. In a small place
like Masset it, would be embarrassing to have to ask
to be tested for a venereal disease. The doctor would
want to know why she was concerned and, if it was
positive, whom she'd been sleeping with so they could
know for their records, and stop an outbreak. *Christ,
what a mess.*

She couldn't risk anyone finding out what happened.
She'd never live it down. Jean and Tilly, the bitches,

would be the first to call the newspaper, a small-town gossip rag, and of course they'd be telling everyone who would spare them a few minutes of their time. She was sure if the kids in her class heard the story, they'd stare at her crotch and wonder how you did a rape. Then again, some of them probably knew all about that from abuse at home. Heather most likely did. *Oh God, the poor girl.* No child should have to go through that. Bad enough that it happened to adults.

And Brent? Tears welled up just thinking about how kind he was to her last night. He poured her a cup of herbal tea and offered her cookies he'd found in the cupboard. He didn't pressure her, but by the questions he had asked, Marlie knew he suspected what happened. She wanted him to hold her and tell her everything would be all right. Wanted him to protect her from the fallout of last night's horror. But if she told him, two things could happen. He might toss her aside as someone he had misjudged and who turned out to be a tramp, or he might get so angry that he'd go confront Clancy. That would be awful. She didn't want Brent to get hurt, and she knew that in most fights, the good guys finished last.

The best thing to do was to try to get over it and pretend it didn't happen. She wasn't so damaged that she now believed all men were evil, but she had learned that she couldn't go on being so trusting. And yet Brent was different. She trusted him. She sighed. Did that mean she was hopeless?

She really didn't want to go anywhere, but what was the point of sitting around feeling sorry for herself? If she spent time with anyone, she wanted it to be Brent. He said he'd pick her up at 2:00 and they'd pick up Jim and Andrea from the wharf.

She put on her good jeans and a bright top, wanting something that looked happy. Her hair was easy to deal with. She brushed it, twisted it into a knot and stuck a big clip in it. Worst case, a few curls would pop out of the clip, but at times like this, having curly hair made life easier.

She had to make a quick trip into town to get a bottle of wine at the liquor store. She didn't like to go empty-handed.

Marlie dreaded the thought of running into Clancy. A shudder ran down her body. She wasn't sure what she'd say or do. She knew what she would like to do, but that wasn't legal. One thing was sure, much as she loved playing, she wouldn't be going to volleyball next Friday. Maybe never again. The winter ahead looked bleak.

***

Brent showed up in his truck and Marlie was about to jump in when she remembered that they were picking up Jim and Andrea. "Maybe I should bring my car," she said. "There's not going to be room for all of us in the truck."

"Sure there will," Brent said. "They don't mind sitting close together. Don't worry. We'll fit."

Marlie kept her head down as she got into Brent's truck. She had covered her bruises as much as possible, but was afraid they still showed. She felt as if last night's rape shouted out from every body part, and the world could see what she'd gone through. Nowhere to hide. The experience was so much in the forefront of her mind that she was sure Brent could see into her head.

"How are you feeling today?" he asked. "Better?"

Marlie nodded. "I took a couple of Advils and that helped a lot."

Jim pulled Andrea close and they barely took up more than one space on the seat. Marlie was pressed up against Brent who had his arm on the back of the seat to make more room for her. That arm soon slid down onto her shoulder and he gave her a light squeeze and a smile that took away a lot of her insecurity and pain. She knew that men like Clancy were not the norm. Bad luck for her that she had walked into his trap. Sitting close to Brent, she felt only warmth and caring. She wanted to lean into him and have his protection forever.

Brent drove along the road that ran eastward parallel to the beach and away from town. Huge spruces, hemlocks, and a few cedars grew on either side of the road, but the forest stretched farther inland on the right side of the road. It was like a mythical forest. Marlie expected gnomes to peek out from behind the trees and go leaping along the mossy forest floor. Way past all the other houses, Brent turned down a long driveway that went on for about a quarter of a mile.

They tumbled out of the crowded cab of the truck and stood around in awe of the natural beauty of the place.

Brent picked up some firewood from under a tarp and headed for the brake drum fire pit in the clearing by the river. "Andrea, you've been out here a few times now. Do you think you could take Marlie on a tour of the property? Jim and I will make a fire while you two do the tour."

"Sure thing," Andrea said. "C'mon, Marlie."

They headed down to the river—the Chown, Andrea called it.

"The property's ten acres but we're not going to explore all of it," she said. "Not today anyway."

Marlie turned to look away from the river. Giant hemlocks with beards of Spanish moss on the branches rose above clumps of huckleberry and salal bushes. A soft wind waved the Spanish moss gently like laundry in a breeze. "What a beautiful piece of land. Brent is so lucky to have a place like this. He must make a lot of money fishing."

"Well, he works hard at fishing and he's careful with his money but he bought the property from his father. His dad and Jim's dad used to fish together a long time ago, until Jim's dad died—heart attack on the boat— and Brent's dad was kind of lost without him.

"Brent fished with his dad on the Huckleberry and they looked out for Jim till he got used to fishing without his dad."

"And now they're both on their own. Well, sort of. Jim's got you. How did you meet him?"

"At the wharf in Lund." Andrea shivered.

"Cold?"

"No, just remembering my first husband." Andrea hesitated. "I met both Jim and Robert at Lund. With bad timing and worse luck, I married the wrong one. Robert enjoyed ... being in charge. The bastard." She stopped walking along the riverbank. They stood, looking out at the water. After a moment, Andrea shook herself as if shedding bad thoughts. "So, Marlie ... what happened to you?"

Marlie gasped involuntarily. "What do you mean?"

Andrea pointed at her face. "I recognize myself when I look at you, covering your bruises with makeup. Men might not notice it, but I've been through a lot of abuse and it looks to me like someone mistreated you."

Marlie shrank down into a crouch and covered her face with her hands. "I was hoping it wouldn't show."

Andrea crouched down beside her and put an arm around her. "Who did this? You can tell me. I promise I'll understand. I've been there."

"You can't tell Brent. Don't even tell Jim. Promise me, if I tell you, you won't tell them?"

She nodded. As Marlie told her the basics, Andrea's hands curled up. Marlie snorted a sad laugh and pointed to her clenched fists. "That's how I feel too. I want to punch him in the face, over and over and over."

"Is this the first time something like this has happened to you?" Andrea asked.

"Yes. I came close to getting hit when my live-in partner started drinking too much, but we split up before it got to that point."

"That was smart," Andrea said. "I wish I could have left."

"Why couldn't you?"

"Because he had taken me to his cabin on the coast. Not a soul around. No roads—only boat access. He controlled the radio on the boat and that was the only communication possibility."

Marlie clenched her back teeth. "That sounds bad. What did you do? I mean, how did you get away?"

"I escaped out the back window when he set fire to the cabin with me in it. It was rugged country and I nearly died."

"Oh my God. What a bastard!" And she thought she'd had a rough time. She reached for Andrea's hand and patted it. "Well, I'm glad you made it." Marlie stood and slapped the sand from her hands. "Jim seems to be really good for you."

"Yeah, he is. Speaking of whom ... I guess we should be getting back."

"Do we go back along the river or is there a path?"

"The path to Brent's house is just up ahead. We might as well go back that way. It's easier than walking along the riverbank."

As they turned onto the path, Andrea stopped abruptly and Marlie walked into her. "Oops! What— oh...." A huge black bear stood in the path about fifty feet away. "Oh shit," she whispered. Her knees felt like Jell-o. The bear lifted his head slightly to sniff the air. He stayed in the path, squinting his eyes in their direction.

Andrea didn't turn to look at her but spoke quietly. "Back up very slowly, Marlie, and keep looking at the ground."

She did as Andrea said and backed up, except she didn't do it slowly. The adrenaline was sending buzzing flutters to her stomach and the back of her knees. She wanted to get out of there, and fast. She couldn't keep looking down though. She had to know where the danger might be coming from. Marlie kept her head down but turned her eyes upward.

The bear sauntered into the bushes beside the path. His hips were massive and his muscles rippled under the shaggy coat.

Marlie checked behind her to make sure she was still on the path as she walked backwards. When she got the nerve to look forward again, the bear was gone and she turned around to walk faster. Andrea was right behind her. Marlie grabbed her hand and said, "Let's go!" Out of sight of the bear, there was no reason not to run and they were back at the clearing in seconds.

The boys whirled around at the sound of their running footsteps. "Back so soon? Did you show Marlie the house and garden?" Brent asked.

Between gasps for air, they giggled with relief. "No, we didn't get that far."

"There was a bear!" they blurted out together.

The bear was the topic of conversation for the next hour or so with Brent leaving the campfire only long enough to check on his dinner and to bring some more beer and wine. "I didn't know we had so many bear stories," Jim said. "I guess spending so much time up here we're bound to run into bears from time to time. More than most people do anyway."

The stories kept coming, about so many things. Mostly the three old friends told funny deckhand stories. It was the most fun Marlie had had in ages. For a short time, she forgot all about Clancy.

Brent let the fire die down and suggested that they move the party into the house. It was getting a bit chilly and the mosquitoes were becoming a nuisance.

Marlie was glad for the warmth of the house. Brent had a small fire going in the woodstove in the family room—just enough to keep the chill off—and the oven warmed the kitchen.

"Mmm ... something smells so good!" she said. "What is it?"

"Secret," Brent said, and she saw him glance over at Jim and smirk. "You girls keep out of the kitchen. Jim and I are in charge tonight."

"Oh that suits me," Andrea said. "C'mon, Marlie, let's have a glass of wine by the fire. We wouldn't want to interfere with their cooking." Andrea leaned over and whispered, "And maybe get put to work. This is our chance to relax and be waited on."

When everything was ready, Brent called them into the kitchen to load up their plates and bring them to the table. He had cut the roast into thin slices. Mashed potatoes, carrots, green beans, and gravy all in their cooking pots were ready for them to dish up.

They sat at a heavy wooden table that had been beautifully finished. "What an amazing table this is," Marlie said. "Did you make it, Brent?"

He shook his head. "I helped a bit, but mostly it was my dad. He was good at working with wood." He pointed at the counter and the coffee table.

"Just beautiful." She stroked the wood grain lovingly.

"My dad would be pleased that you appreciate his work."

Brent had some world music playing on a CD player–something Oriental that made her feel as if she were in Thailand. The kitchen was a warm and happy place with good friends chatting and laughing. She was the outsider, but they pulled her right into the conversations as if she had been their friend for years. She swallowed hard. It felt so good to be accepted and included as if they genuinely wanted her to be there. She had been missing that kind of friendship.

James's friends were so shallow by comparison. They all seemed to want something. Takers, they were. She had the feeling that Brent and his friends were the opposite—givers.

Brent poured more wine for everyone. Then he raised his glass and said, "Here's to good friends."

They all clinked glasses and sipped their wine, smiling at each other. Brent's eyes locked on Marlie's and she thought her heart fluttered some extra beats. She blinked back welling tears. This was someone she knew she would dream about.

As their plates were nearly empty, Brent said, "Would you like some more, Marlie? There's lots of meat. Lots of everything."

"I wouldn't mind another slice of meat and a bit of gravy to finish off those mashed potatoes."

Brent got up and reached for her plate. She laid her hand on his forearm. "Just a little bit, okay?"

"Sure thing." He had a huge smile on his face.

Jim and Brent watched surreptitiously as she ate the meat Brent had added to her plate. She loved meat and vegetables. Mashed potatoes, not so much. "This is really good," she said between mouthfuls. "You're a good cook, Brent."

"Glad you like venison after all," he said.

Marlie stopped chewing. She clamped her hand over her mouth. "You mean it's not beef?" All three of them shook their heads at her. "It's really tasty." She leaned back from the table and sighed. It was time to let go of her prejudices. "I guess I have to not think about how pretty deer look. I'm sure cows can look pretty too."

"That's right," Andrea chimed in. "If we're going to eat meat, we have to deal with the fact that the animal has to be killed. It's not something anyone likes to think about, but man has been hunting and fishing for thousands of years. Nothing unnatural about it."

"That first day when I saw the deer in the back of Brent's truck, I was stressed about my flat tire and my stuff not fitting back in the car and everything being new, and I'd been traveling all day. I wasn't prepared for the sight of a dead deer." She paused. "I may have over-reacted."

Brent's eyebrows went up and he grinned.

"And my parents had little to do with nature," she continued. "No camping. Certainly no fishing or hunting.

All meat came out of the store properly shrink wrapped. We lived in Victoria so we were city people. I guess I was a bit naïve when I first arrived here."

Andrea reached over and put her hand over Marlie's. "You're not alone. I was from Ontario, near Ottawa. I had never seen anything get killed until I was stuck with Robert in the cabin and we had to eat deer and fish or starve. It was awful being there, but learning to survive off the land was good. The only good thing." She hesitated and smiled at Jim. "Well, thankfully, that's all in the past now." She laughed nervously.

Andrea's voice betrayed her and told of the pain behind the comments but it made Marlie feel better to know she wasn't the only woman in the world who had been naïve about where their food came from. Andrea was a city girl once and had to learn about deer meat too.

"I think I'm a convert. I like venison."

Brent smiled. "So glad to hear that. We eat a lot of it here."

"But I still don't want to see them killed." She knew she was being a hypocrite but she couldn't stop herself from adding, "Just call me when the roast is ready."

CHAPTER 17

Clancy

Clancy was still tingling with excitement long after Marlie peeled out of the driveway. He went for a piss and did a double take as he passed by the bathroom mirror. He leaned in for a closer look and fingered his cheek gingerly.

"Why, the little bitch!" He splashed cold water on two long scratches. It smarted like a dozen hornet stings. He chuckled. "Feisty! Have to give her that much."

He lay down on his bunk, smiled, and sighed. He replayed the scene in slow motion, fondling his satisfied pecker. It came to life all over again. That Marlie was quite the wildcat. *Maybe it's the red in her hair, but man, did she have fire in her.* He wouldn't mind having a second go at her. Maybe he could get her alone somewhere.

When he reached the end of the replay and his penis lay limp in his hand, he pushed away the usual guilty thoughts that wormed their way into his head. He knew he shouldn't have done that to Marlie, but the lingering thrill was worth it. He had made up his mind to stop playing the bondage game at least with unwilling participants, but Marlie was such a turn-on. She shouldn't have smiled at him like that. She shouldn't have looked so sexy in those tight yoga pants at volleyball. She shouldn't have put her hair up like that, pinned with a leather barrette, all those tendrils swirling around, teasing her neck and cheeks. It was her own fault. She had no right to look that good and expect him to keep it in his pants. She totally ruined all his good intentions to stop forcing himself on women.

***

Saturday morning he got up early. Declan, fully clothed, was sprawled across his bunk, his greasy, black hair matted to his cheek. He lay on his back with his mouth wide open, rattling out the deep rumbling vibrations of a drunkard. Clancy threw his few belongings into a backpack and slipped out of the shack before Declan could wake up and pester him for rent money.

Half an hour later he was knocking on the door of Sheila's little green cottage in the backyard of a town councilman's property.

It took a while for Sheila to come to the door. She opened it a crack and squinted out under lids drooped over bloodshot eyes sunken into dark sockets. A crooked smile spread over her pale face.

"Rough night?" he asked.

"Hey, Clancy," she drawled.

"I came back ... like you asked me to." Clancy gave her his most angelic look and stepped inside while the door was still open and before she had time to change her mind. He dropped his pack in the entry and took her in his arms. Sheila hugged him tightly. Relief flooded over Clancy. He was stupid to have that fight with her. It had been over such a silly thing.

"Don't shove me like that," she had said.

She was in his way at the kitchen sink and he wanted a drink of water.

"Well, get out of the way then," he had told her, using the opportunity to show her who was boss.

"What the hell's got into you? You think just because your father pushed your mother around you can do that to me?"

"I just did, and you'd better get used to it. That's how things are done." But that small victory was short lived.

"Fuck you, Clancy. Get your stuff together and get out of here. I don't need this shit on top of your whoring around."

Apparently his father's way of doing things didn't work with all women. It had worked with Clancy's mother. As Clancy remembered it, when his father said, "Jump," his mother asked, "How high?"

His parents tolerated each other, but the warmth was gone. Even as a child, Clancy could tell. He was sure his dad had had lots of girlfriends on the side. But he admired his dad for being in charge and, though he loved his mom, he despised her for being weak.

He learned that this was how a man should do it; he had to be assertive and take what he wanted. It had worked for Clancy so far. Just not with Sheila. He'd have to take a different tack with her.

Now that he had Sheila back for regular sex and a place to stay, he'd be nicer to her. He could still get all the sweet pussy he wanted. Just had to be a bit sneakier about it.

"What happened to your face?" Sheila stepped back and frowned. "You didn't have those scratches when you left Mike's party last night."

"Oh, yeah, that...." He touched the scratches and sucked in air between his teeth. "That bitch, Marlie. I asked her to give me a ride to Declan's place. When we got there she wanted to come in and I told her I was just getting my stuff and moving back in with you."

Sheila nodded. "Yeah, and...."

He swallowed hard and hoped he'd sound convincing. "She grabbed my hand and said, 'But what about us?' I told her, 'There is no us,' and she got really pissed off and screeched that I'd led her on. For Christ's sake, I just asked her for a ride. Anyway, she scratched my face and yelled, 'You bastard!' It was all I could do not to hit her."

Sheila pulled him close for another hug. "What a stupid bitch that Marlie is. Well, come on. I'll make you a nice breakfast."

Clancy grinned and squeezed Sheila's hand. "That's my girl."

CHAPTER 18

Marlie

Marlie heard the rising wind. Brent told her gale warnings were forecast for the next couple of days, so Jim and Andrea were not in a hurry to get back to the boat that night. They wouldn't be crossing Hecate Strait to head for Prince Rupert until the weather calmed down. Brent had a spare room for them and they had already said good night.

Marlie felt a bit awkward about staying when Brent offered to sleep on the couch, giving her his bed. She really did want to stay, but....

She'd been dreading going home to the trailer, being there in the dark, alone. It had been almost a year since she and James split, so she was used to being alone, but what if Clancy showed up on her doorstep and tried to barge his way in? These trailers were damn flimsy. One good shoulder shove could pop the door open.

She didn't want to seem eager to jump into bed with Brent, and anyway, she wasn't ready for that, after what happened only last night. Any other time it would have been a dream, but she was too sore and beat up from Clancy—not to mention traumatized by the whole thing. Marlie wrapped her arms around herself. She couldn't deal with the thought of having sex with a man—any man. Still couldn't believe that nightmare was real.

"How about if I sleep on the couch?" she offered. "It looks way more comfortable than my bed in the trailer."

Brent smiled. "I just changed the sheets so my bed is clean. I'd feel bad if I let you sleep on the couch."

"Or you could just drive me home?" *Please say no.*

He was already shaking his head. *Thank God.*

"We all had too much wine. Staying will be easiest for everyone. If you don't mind, that is." He chewed on his lower lip. "Of course, I'll drive you home if you really want me to, but I thought we could have a cozy evening here ... if you'll stay." He put his hands on her arms and gently pulled her closer. "I'd like you to stay," he whispered. His kiss was gentle and barely brushed her lips.

Brent is not Clancy. I have to keep my head straight and not let this shit from last night get to me. "I didn't bring any overnight things...."

"I have spare toothbrushes," Brent said. "New ones!" He laughed. "And I'm sure Andrea won't mind lending you a hairbrush if you can't make do with my comb."

"Well ... okay. If it'll make things easier." She wasn't sure at all that she was doing the right thing, but again, somehow she trusted Brent. "Sure, I guess...."

Brent didn't even try to hide his grin. "The lovebirds have already gone to bed," he jerked his head in the direction of the spare room, "so how about a little Port wine for a nightcap?"

They sat on the worn leather couch in the living room with only the light of a candle on the coffee table. Marlie was thankful for the darkness so her bruises didn't show as much. She knew Brent had seen the redness on her face last night but the bruising was turning purple and she'd rather he didn't focus on that. He'd played it cool then and all of today too, pretending she looked normal. With his arm around her shoulders they slouched against the back of the sofa. He put his feet up on the heavy coffee table his dad had made and invited her to do the same. It was so comfortable and relaxing, she never wanted to move.

Their conversation went in every direction. He asked about her teaching and she had a few little stories to tell him—funny things the kids had said or done.

"When I was teaching grade one in Maple Ridge a couple of years ago, the kids and I were playing a game of listing all the things we could think of that started with a hard 'c' sound as in 'car.' They named a few things and then ran out of ideas, so I said, 'I know one we haven't said yet. I'll give you a clue. It's where we get milk from.' Little Paul threw his hand in the air and called out, 'I know! Safeway!'"

Brent chuckled. "Kids can be so cute, so innocent. I can see you love your job."

Marlie smiled. "Yeah. I do. But how about you? Do you like your job?"

Brent blew out a long puff of air and waggled his hand. "It's a real love/hate kind of thing."

She patted his arm. "Tell me one thing you love about it."

"Lots of things, really. Being out there on the water, sometimes I feel like it's just me and nature. Freedom, I guess. Yeah, it's pure freedom. You have to be out there all alone to appreciate the power of the wind, the waves, all the forces of nature. There's nobody to tell you what you should do. You have to make your own decisions and live—or die—with the consequences."

"You said 'love/hate.' What do you hate?"

"That's easy. I don't even have to think about that one. It's the sleep deprivation."

"Why can't you sleep?"

"Oh I could! But I wouldn't dare." Brent turned sideways to face Marlie on the couch and tucked one leg under him. "You're out there, sometimes all alone without a deckhand, and you run out to the fishing grounds before it gets light and don't come in to anchor behind some island until it's dark—and you know how long the days are in the summer up here. Then you try to sleep for a few hours before you have to get up and do it all over again."

"Can't you have a nap?"

"Would you have a nap if you were driving your car?"

"Of course not, but I thought—"

"I know, you thought it's just a big ocean with nothing in the way. If you were way out, where you weren't going to run into any other boats, you might put your head down on the steering wheel for a few minutes and set the watch alarm."

"Your watch has an alarm?"

Brent laughed. "No, the watch alarm is a gadget that's installed on the helm and you can set it—like an egg timer—for ten minutes or however long you want. You might set it to remind you to turn down the stove or shut off something, like a fuel valve if you're pumping from one tank to the other to even the load. When the time is up, a light flashes on and off and the alarm beeps, and to make sure you don't ignore it, you have to go over to the alarm and push a button to shut off the infernal racket."

"What if you sleep through the beeping?"

"Oh, they've thought of all that when they made these alarms. If you ignore the beeping or sleep through it, after about 30 seconds it blasts you with a blaring super-beep that you're guaranteed not to sleep through."

"Can you turn it off like the alarm clock at home? That's what I'd be afraid I'd do—hit snooze and go back to sleep."

Brent put one finger in the air. "Aha! But they've thought of that, too. If you seriously don't want to sleep through the alarm, or say you had a deckhand who is on watch while you have a nap and you're worried he might 'hit snooze,' there is a key in the alarm. If you take the key out of the alarm box, the alarm can't be turned off permanently until you put the key back in."

"Wow! Lots of safeguards then," she said. "There's so much I don't know about fish boats. I thought you just get in the boat, start the engine, go out someplace and put the gear in the water, go have a beer and wait for the fish to bite."

"Yeah, a lot of people do think that." Brent hesitated. "You could come out in the boat with me sometime, maybe on a Saturday if the weather's okay," he suggested. "Then you can get an idea of what it's all about. If you want to, that is."

Marlie did a silent handclap without her palms touching. "Yeah, that would be fun." *Wow! I'd love to go for a ride in the fish boat. With Brent!*

By the time they had exhausted those two subjects, Marlie had a lot more respect for how hard fishermen work, and she thought Brent's view of teachers was a little less cynical. They both loved their jobs and worked hard at them.

When they were yawning more than talking, Brent asked, "Do you feel like going to bed?" He raised his eyebrows and grinned. "We could both crawl into my bed and I'd keep you warm."

Marlie shrank down into the sofa and her stomach tightened. "Er ... ah ... I'd love to," she said, "but it's just a bit too soon for me." He was still snuggled next to her and she felt his shoulder sag. "Can I take a rain check on that?"

"Sure can. And what do you think about going for a boat ride with me next Saturday—just in the skiff—we'll leave the big boat for another time—weather permitting, of course?"

Yes, a boat ride, even in a small boat. Fun! "That sounds great. Where to?"

"Exploring the inlet. I think you'll be surprised at all the things you'll see."

CHAPTER 19
Marlie

Marlie pulled open the heavy double door and stepped out of the wind and into the school lobby. A few kids had begun to show up and were milling around the back door on the playground side of the school. Some of them pressed their faces to the glass of the door and waved. "Hi, Ms Mitchell," their muffled voices called. She gave them a smile and raised her hand to wave.

In the staff room Jean and Tilly, joined at the hip, sat in their place on the sofa. She said her usual good morning, but didn't expect an answer. She didn't know why she bothered, but her mother had taught her to be polite. She put down her tote bag, went over to the counter and plugged the kettle in for a cup of tea.

"What happened to you?" Tilly asked, pointing to the side of her face.

Figures, the only time they speak to me is when I don't want them to.

She turned back to put the tea bag in her mug. "Slipped on the wet wood of the porch steps."

"Hmph! Sure you did." Tilly's sarcasm was heartless. Marlie turned just in time to catch her rolling her eyes at Jean. She didn't wait for the kettle to come to a complete boil before she filled her mug and got out of there, sloshing drops of tea on the floor as she hurried, head down, to her classroom. Bitches! She hated herself for being such a coward and an easy target for those bullies.

The kids were kinder. When they came in, most of them remained unaware of the bruises. Long sleeves covered her reddish-blue wrists, and makeup covered her purple-streaked face. Heather must have noticed, but she was too shy to say anything. She kept sneaking glances at Marlie when she thought she wasn't looking. Her brow was wrinkled and she had a pained look on her face. Marlie thought Heather must have some experience of her own to be so quick to relate to hers. Poor dear. At lunchtime she sneaked her half a sandwich as she always did and Heather pointed to Marlie's face. "It's okay, Heather. I just fell down on the slippery steps." Marlie patted her shoulder. "Thanks for caring. I'm okay though, so don't worry." It broke her heart to see that frail child nod and bow her head. She wasn't buying it. She knew how things could get out of hand.

***

After school on Tuesday, Marlie had to make a quick stop at the Co-op for a few groceries. It was the day before freight day when the fresh groceries would arrive, but her fridge was depressingly empty. She'd have to keep today's shopping down to basics and go back for more in a day or two. Meanwhile, she needed to get some cheese for sandwiches and think about what to have for supper. Maybe an omelette if they weren't out of eggs. She parked on the main street across from the Co-op and dashed in. No cart needed today. A basket would do for the few things on her list. Eggs, bread, half and half for her coffee, maybe some cheese.

On the bread shelf, all that was left was some stale-looking Wonder Bread. No way she could eat that crap. She might have to resort to making a quick batch of bannock. She'd have to come up with something for Heather's lunch. Maybe she could throw together some muffins when she got home. She headed for the dairy section to find eggs and bumped into a man coming around the end of the aisle. "Oops! Excuse me—Clancy!"

"Well, well, look who's here? If it isn't Miss Easy," he drawled.

Marlie glared at him and hissed, "You sonofabitch! Don't you dare call me that!" She dropped her basket and with both hands on his chest, gave him a shove backwards. "Bastard!"

She didn't know where she found the nerve to do that. Anger had surged up in her like an uncontrollable tidal wave. She wanted to do much more than simply give him a shove, but managed to rein in her rage. At that second, she understood how otherwise normal people could kill in a crime of passion.

"Hey! Hey! Cool it!" he said when he regained his balance. "We don't want to attract a lot of attention, do we?"

"Don't we?" she said in a louder voice.

Clancy's head swiveled as he checked for any witnesses. "Crazy females!" he said, and made a beeline for the door.

"Yeah, you'd better run! You coward!" she called after him. The surge of emotion that threatened to explode into violence surprised her, but it was better than being a wimp and sniveling the rest of her life away. It frightened her though, to think she was capable of losing control as she had. If she'd had a knife in her hand.... She shuddered to think what she might have done. She stood still for a moment taking deep breaths, allowing her hands to stop shaking and the heat to fade from her face, before she could resume her shopping.

Over by the dairy section, three dozen eggs were left on the shelf. As she reached for one, she felt a tap on her shoulder and jumped. The shopping basket fell on the floor. She spun around. "Leave me alone!"

Brent took a step back. "Whoah! Marlie?"

She shrank together. "Oh, Brent. I'm sorry. I thought—"

Brent picked up the basket and slowly handed it to her. "You thought what?"

She shook her head wildly, "No, no, no. I-I'm sorry. I thought … you were someone else."

"Clancy?" Brent's blue eyes looked hard as steel. "I saw him rushing out the door...."

"Never mind," she said quickly. "So, are you out of groceries too? My cupboard is like Mother Hubbard's. Not the best day for shopping, day before freight day, but I—" She knew she was babbling but she had to fill in the space so Brent didn't ask more about Clancy.

"Just picking up some butter," Brent said. "Say, if your cupboard is bare, would you like to come for supper?"

"What? Now?" She waved her hands to erase the wrong impression she must have been giving. "Oh, no. I wasn't fishing for a dinner invitation."

"I know, but why not? I could throw together some stir fries. It would be quick and easy and guaranteed to be good." Brent cocked his head to the side. "What do you say? Yes?" And he was nodding for her.

She found herself nodding without realizing it. Maybe it was just what she needed.

She paid for her groceries and waited for Brent by the door. "I'll follow you in my car then?"

He nodded and grinned. "Yup! See you at my place."

Marlie put her groceries in the trunk of her car and pulled out into the road. At the corner, she saw Clancy standing under a tree. From there, he had a clear line of sight to the front door of the Co-op. Nothing cute about his unruly shock of blond hair now. His face was dark as a thundercloud. He unfolded his crossed arms, poked a finger at her, and shook it in warning. Marlie was shocked that he would be so boldly threatening. Not to be seen as easily intimidated, she squinted her eyes and glared back at him. As soon as she had driven past him, she started to shake. Two blocks down the road she pulled over. She dropped her head onto the steering wheel and groaned. She had thought she could start the healing process, but apparently she and Clancy were not finished yet. A tremor of concern burned at her stomach. In such a small community, they were bound to meet frequently. She had only been on the island for two months. So far she had a few acquaintances and fewer friends. It wasn't good to have made an enemy already.

CHAPTER 20
Marlie

Marlie was still shivering when she pulled into the driveway. When she had been here before, Brent had been driving. Now she was glad he had waited at the main road. It was already getting dark and she might easily have missed the turn-off. In the darkness it looked a bit eerie. The driveway was like a tunnel with the trees reaching for each other overhead. It reminded her of childhood games when they played London Bridge is Falling Down and they stood across from a partner and put their palms together to make an archway. It was a fairy tale driveway with the castle at the end.

Brent's castle was only a house. He and his father had built it, but it looked like Brent had put some creative finishing touches on it. Two electric porch lanterns lit up the entrance. Hanging from a driftwood banister, glass balls once used by the Japanese net fleet were tied up in old fish net to finish off the enclosure around the veranda. It was far more interesting than the usual railing of spindles. The front door made of heavy, oiled wood planks had the name Carlson carved and burned into the wood.

"You must be tired," Brent said as they entered. "Just let me put the stuff in the fridge and we'll have a little something. Wine?"

"Oh, that sounds perfect! It was a bit of a rough day today."

Brent handed Marlie the wine and they clinked glasses. "To a better day tomorrow," he said. "So tell me, what was so bad about it?"

"Well, to start with, first thing in the morning, I had supervision duty—basically it's just keeping the kids outside until 8:30. If we didn't, they'd start arriving at 8:00 if they thought they could come into the school."

Brent nodded. "I can see that. Probably a nicer place to be than home for a lot of these kids."

"I'm sure. Some of them would have such a better day if I could let them in and give them a cup of hot chocolate." She hesitated. "But they aren't all like that. One bunch of grade seven boys were pushing and shoving at the door. I told them to move back and most of them did, except for this one. He was one of the Haida toughies—at least, he thought he was tough. He just stuck his face up to mine and said, 'Bitch! I'll cut your eyes out with a razor blade.'"

Brent's eyes widened. "You're kidding!"

"I wish I was. But that's not the worst of it. Before I could say anything, he turned and ran, but something dropped on the cement landing by the door. It was one of those old-fashioned kind of razor blades."

"Oh my God! What a job you have. Did you report it?"

"I turned in the razor blade, but what was the point? That kind of thing goes on all the time and nothing is ever done about it. I asked Mr. Dupuis, the principal, if he was going to call the kid in to the office, but he just sighed and said, 'Nothing will change. There's no point. Most times, the parents' or guardians' attitude is "What's the big deal? So okay suspend him and we can go fishing for a few days."' You get the odd one who really cares, but many of them don't want to be called in to the school. To them, school is just one of those annoying things in life that you have to get through."

Brent took a sip of his wine. "That's depressing."

"They're not all like that, but quite a few are and those are always the ones you remember." Marlie relaxed into the back of the sofa. "This is nice though. Helps erase the bad part of the day."

Brent leaned forward and turned to face her. "Do you want to tell me why you snapped at me?"

Marlie took a deep breath and let it out. "I had a run-in with Clancy at the store just before I saw you. I thought he had come back."

"Aha! I knew it!" Brent set his glass down hard. "That lousy shit. He's the one that messed you up the other night, isn't he?"

"Please, Brent, just let it go."

Brent's face was a tight mask. "Okay. If you say so ... for now."

She got up and turned towards the kitchen. "Can I help you get some dinner together? Just tell me what to do."

"Sure, okay." He refilled their glasses. "Here's to you being here." His kiss on her cheek was soft and warm.

***

It was nearly ten o'clock when Marlie got home. Brent had wanted her to stay over but with school the next day she just couldn't do it. Besides, she had to get something together for her lunch in the morning with enough for Heather too.

The trailer was dark and uninviting. Downright gloomy. If she had stopped at home after school, she could have left a light on, but she'd gone straight from the Co-op to Brent's place. It was a wet night. The potholes in the driveway had filled with water. Maybe she could find something better for next year, or maybe even by Christmas. She'd have to start looking around.

Marlie opened the trunk and got out her few groceries. This time she was careful about the keys. Didn't want a repeat of dropping them. She got the trailer key ready in the light of the trunk. A fishy smell wafted over to her. Maybe Roger's garbage? As she took a step towards her porch, the smell got stronger. She wished she had some light. Mental note to self—buy a flashlight to have in the car at all times. She stepped onto the porch stairs and her foot slid away. Groceries flew into the darkness and Marlie landed on the sopping grass below the steps. The stench of fish was overpowering. She reached for the step to pull herself up and felt slime under her hand. *Oh God! What the hell?* The tread was slick with something wet and smelly. She tried again to get to her front door. Carefully she stepped up the three slippery stairs and put her key into the lock. At least then she could turn on the porch light and find her groceries.

The light from the bare bulb illuminated the stairs. Fish guts and blood covered the steps and some had splashed on the side of the trailer. Marlie got her dustpan and scooped away as much as she could, flinging the mostly liquid goo away towards the road where the rain would wash it away. She picked up the few eggs that weren't scrambled, and the handful of other groceries, locked her car, and carefully climbed back up the slippery steps. It was then that she saw the note stuck to the bottom shelf in the porch:

Have a good night. See you soon.

A shiver of goosebumps covered her body and a squeaky cry of fear escaped her. She had a strong urge to jump into the car and race back to Brent's house. Marlie looked at the Corolla and then the trailer door. *Choose!* She took a deep breath, put her shoulders back and shook off her fears. She stepped into the trailer and locked the door behind her.

CHAPTER 21
Marlie

Brent called Marlie on Friday night. "Oh, you are home. I thought you might be at volleyball."

"No, I'm not going anymore."

"Oh? I thought you loved playing volleyball."

"It just isn't what I need right now." Marlie changed the subject quickly. "So how are you doing?"

"Good. Between boat maintenance and catching up on jobs around the house, I've had plenty to do ... so I'm ready for a break. Are we still on for tomorrow? The weather looks good."

"Sounds great. What time? What do I need to bring?"

"Well, let's see ... how about I pick you up at 8:00? It'll take a half hour to get to where we'll launch the skiff and then we'll have the whole day. Bring a snack if you want. I'll have some food in my pack. Bring a water bottle and a change of clothes in case we get wet. You never know, out in the boat it's always good to have extra clothes handy. You have gum boots?"

"Yup! I'll get it all together. Should be fun."

"See you at 8:00 then."

Marlie took her backpack out of the closet and started putting clothes in it. Then she thought about where she would put the backpack. If Brent's skiff was like any other aluminum boat she'd ever been in, the pack would be sopping wet in no time. Those boats all had small leaks. She would wear the pack but just in case she had to set it in the bottom of the boat, she got out a big plastic garbage bag and lined the inside of the pack with it. She threw in a change of clothes—sweat pants and sweat shirt. Not that she planned to do any sweating but they were comfortable and warm and easy to change into. Her toque and a windbreaker with a hood. She was all set. She'd wear an old pair of runners and bring along her gum boots for getting in and out of the skiff.

In a small shoulder bag she packed a couple of sandwiches and put in some cookies she'd made, two apples and two bananas and her water bottle. A whole day with Brent. She hardly slept that night.

***

Brent arrived just before 8:00. He looked so ruggedly handsome Marlie wanted to throw her arms around him in a big hug. As it turned out, he came right over and hugged her.

"All set?" he asked, as he picked up her pack.

It was a gorgeous day, a gentle breeze, not a cloud in the sky, a rare thing for the Charlottes, as she had already learned. Brent drove south. They met the occasional vehicle, but actually saw more deer than they did cars. For the most part they had the road to themselves.

Brent reached over and took her hand. "How was your week at school?"

The warmth in that touch tickled her insides, sending flutters to her stomach, and heat to her face. She felt like a teenager again. She just hoped she didn't revert to behaving like one. Brent messed with her head like no one ever had before.

"Not too bad," she said. "I have wonderful kids in my class. It's the part outside my own classroom that isn't so great. Some snotty grade seven kids. Hormones getting the better of them, I guess. They think they're all grown up but they still act like little kids in a big body."

"No more razor blades, I hope?"

She chuckled without humour. "No. Thank God for that! I still have two eyes."

Brent looked over at her. "Beautiful ones too."

She swallowed and turned to look out the side window to hide her face—she could tell from the heat she was blushing.

Brent put his hand back on the steering wheel. "It's just up ahead where we turn. Nadu Road, it's called."

They turned off the paved highway onto a gravel road that soon came to a dead end. Brent parked the truck off to the side and got out to untie the skiff. Marlie stood still, staring into the woods, listening. "You could get our packs out. I'll get the skiff down."

She spun around. "Yeah. Of course. I was just amazed at how quiet it is here."

"Yup! Nobody around. No houses, no cars. It's people who make the most noise. The animals are pretty quiet."

They slipped on their gum boots and tucked the runners into their packs. With the packs loaded into the skiff and, each taking one side, they dragged the boat down a path towards the water.

"Whoah! This last part is pretty steep," she said. A huge fallen tree blocked the well-worn path which dropped steeply under the log for the last ten feet to the beach.

"We'll slide the boat under the log, but first I'll go down to the beach. You stay up here and hang onto the skiff until I get there."

Marlie did as Brent said. She could tell he had done this before, probably many times.

"Okay, give it a little push," he called from below.

She thought everything would spill out of the skiff at that angle but just as things started to slide forward, Brent had hold of the bow and pulled it up, setting it down at the edge of the water. Then he went back to the truck to get the outboard motor. It was a bit of a grunt getting the heavy motor to the boat, but he had obviously done that before, too, judging by how he maneuvered it onto the fallen log, ducked under, and then picked it up from the top of the log and carried it the rest of the way to the skiff.

With the boat in the shallow water at the edge of the beach, Brent lifted the motor onto the board at the back of the skiff and fastened the screws to anchor the motor. He pushed the stern farther into the water and held onto the bow while she got in. Giving it one last shove, he stepped into the boat. Marlie picked up an oar and kept them steady in the water while he lowered the motor into the water and got it started.

Brent kept the motor on slow at first as they went out into the inlet, cranking up the handle to increase their speed as the water became deeper. "That's Kumdis Island on our left," he said, raising his voice above the roar of the outboard. "Lots of geese here this time of year."

She noticed that Brent had put a guncase in the bow, muzzle pointing forward. "You're not going to shoot any today are you? I'm not keen on going hunting."

"No, of course not. I always bring a gun though. You never know when you might need it." Brent shook his head. She could tell he didn't think much of her attitude. "I also bring along a survival kit and first aid kit. It's just part of going on any outing up here. If you get into trouble there's only one person who's going to save you."

"Who's that?"

"Yourself, of course. Very often there's no one else around, and you always have to be prepared."

"Is that why you always have a knife on your belt?" she asked.

"I'm a fisherman. You always have to have a knife handy when you're fishing and even out here, you never know if you might want to cut kindling or cut a rope ... or fight off a bear." He grinned.

She knew he was joking, but had to ask. "Are there bears around here?"

"Big ones. You don't often see them, but they're around. They just run away," he said, "... most of the time.

"Smell that?" Brent asked. "That's the marsh." He slowed the boat down and steered closer to the island.

A family of raccoons stared at them from the beach. Mother stopped her digging in the wet sand and looked up. Her five little ones sat on the log, one masked face next to the other.

"Aw ... that's so cute!" Marlie couldn't stop smiling. "Wish I'd brought my camera."

"You'll just have to remember this scene inside your head then."

As they putted on, a few geese lifted off from the marsh. Then a few more and a few more until a huge flock of about 50 birds came honking overhead. Their wingbeats whooshed and pulsed as the geese circled around and then settled back in their same place again.

"Wow! They were so close! That was fantastic." The air smelled of grasses and tidal flats. The scenes of undeveloped nature had Marlie regretting more and more that she had left her camera at home.

Brent sped up the motor and headed out into the inlet again. Shivering, Marlie zipped up her windbreaker against the breeze made by the boat's increased speed.

"Look at that!" She pointed forward. "There's a little island."

Brent steered towards it. It was much bigger than she first thought, all rocky and in the middle of the inlet. The water swished past on both sides of the island as the tide came in towards the head of the inlet. Up on the shore, Brent jumped out and pulled the boat out of the water. He took the line and wrapped it around a boulder and set the tiny folding anchor at the end of the line on the gravel. "Let's have a walk around and see what there is to see."

Marlie stepped out onto the coarse gravel and rocks. A glance at the skiff told her it wasn't going anywhere and she followed Brent to the farther end of the island. "See these bigger rocks here?" he said, pointing at a low wall. "Someone's been hunting here. Probably for geese or brant. Probably a long time ago."

"How can you tell?" she asked.

"They've made a blind. The hunters crouch down behind the rock wall and call the birds. When the birds fly over, they shoot them."

"Don't the birds fall in the water and float away?"

"Often they fall into the water, but that's what you have a dog for. You don't go waterfowl hunting without a dog—as a rule anyway—unless it's in a place where there's no chance of losing the birds. Well, some idiots hunt without dogs all the time, but it's irresponsible to do that. A waste of birds."

"Do you hunt birds?" she asked.

"Yes, but not this year. My old dog died last year and I haven't got a new one. His name was Juno. Chocolate lab. So now I only hunt with my friend Jeff and his dog." He looked off into the distance and she saw him wince and shake his head. "They don't live forever."

"No. I know it's sad when pets die." She remembered the pain of losing her cat. It had slept with her for ten years and when it died, Marlie was heartbroken. She couldn't bear the thought of getting another pet and going through that pain again. She sniffed and wiped her weepy nose on her sleeve when Brent wasn't looking.

They wandered around the small island turning over the odd rock, picking up a shell here or there.

"I'm just going back to grab a tissue. Be right back," she said.

Marlie was nearly there when she noticed the skiff was now afloat. She ran the last few steps towards it just as the tide pulled the skiff around so it was facing in the opposite direction.

"Brent!" she called. "The skiff is afloat. Maybe we should get going?"

She waded in to grab the side of the skiff, but the drop-off was sudden and one of her legs went way down, only finding bottom when she was thigh deep in the water. She launched herself from the leg that was still only knee deep and threw herself over the edge of the boat, scrambling to pull her legs in behind her. The tide caught the boat sideways now and it drifted free, pulling at the small anchor and dragging it along under the water.

Brent had rushed over. He groped in the water, making wide sweeps with his arms, wet up to the shoulders, presumably searching for the rope that held the anchor.

Marlie got an oar out from under the seat and stabbed it down into the gravel about three feet down. The island was much smaller than when they first landed there. All that was left of it was a small mound of rocks. She couldn't believe the tide could move that fast. She felt the boat moving against the tide and saw that Brent had found the line and, hand over hand, was pulling the skiff back until he could grab the bow. He pulled them up onto what rocks were still above the water line and climbed in. Marlie stowed the oars in the skiff as Brent sat on the bench seat by the motor.

"Pull up that anchor, will you?" Brent said. Seconds later they were drifting again but this time Brent was able to fire up the motor and take them out of there.

"That's not an island," she said.

"No, it's a bar. I knew that, but I should have remembered the tides are extra high just now and I didn't take into account how quickly the bar would disappear at this time of year."

"Does this bar have a name?"

Brent shrugged. "It just shows as a rockpile on the charts."

"Well, it sure gave me a fright."

"That's what we'll call it then, the Bar of Fright." Brent shook off a shudder. "Lucky you climbed into the skiff before it got away too far. I'm sure I would have got hold of the line, but having you in the skiff was insurance, just in case I hadn't found it. I would have had quite a swim in chilly water if we hadn't got hold of the boat. You okay?"

Marlie nodded. "What if we hadn't noticed it and the skiff was gone?"

"We would have had to try to swim for it, but the tide is so strong here and the crossing is so wide, we probably would have died." From his face she could see he was embarrassed and feeling foolish.

"Seriously?"

"Seriously."

"Oh my God," she whispered. "Oh my God." And she started to shiver.

Brent got them to the shore of a small island—a real one this time—with trees and grass. He pulled the skiff way up the shore and tied the line tightly to a solid log.

Marlie grabbed her pack and hiked up the bank to a grassy meadow where she pulled out her spare clothes. "Am I ever glad you suggested bringing along a change of clothes."

She pulled off her gum boots and wet jeans and socks. Her underwear was a bit damp but not too bad so she left it on. She didn't have any spare anyway. The sweat pants felt so good. Brent changed out of his wet pants too, and somehow neither of them had time to play shy. The main goal was to stop their teeth from chattering.

Brent pulled on a sweat shirt and his shoulders shook as he shrugged into it. "Marlie," he said, as he reached for her, "I'm really sorry about the skiff nearly getting away."

She put her hand on his cheek. "Oh, that's okay. It turned out all right."

Brent took her hand from his cheek and kissed her palm. "But I should have known better. I can't believe I allowed that to happen."

Marlie placed a finger across his lips. "Shh…. It's okay. Don't worry about it."

"I feel so stupid. A fisherman!" He shook his head. "Won't happen again. I promise."

As they warmed up in their dry clothes, Brent took out two black garbage bags and spread them on the ground as a moisture barrier. Then he took the shotgun out of its case. He unzipped the case completely and opened it up, laying it on the garbage bags to make a soft woolly bed for them to sit on. The sun felt soothing and calming. Marlie lay on her stomach and let it warm her back. "I could just fall asleep right here," she said.

Brent looked at the sky. "It's going to be good for a while yet. We could stay right here. I can make a lean-to and a fire for the night."

"We have food and water," she chimed in. "You want to?"

Brent took her in his arms and with a mischievous smirk, said, "I want to."

Waves of nerves washed over Marlie as she contemplated a night alone with Brent. She punched his arm lightly, hoping he didn't notice her trepidation. "That's not what I meant, but … we'll see." *I sure hope I'm not making another stupid mistake.*

CHAPTER 22

Marlie

Marlie was pleased with the mossy spot on the high bank of Cub Island overlooking Masset Inlet. It was soft and comfortable the way Brent had fixed it up with his plastic sheet and the sheep wool guncase opened up. They were alone. Not another soul around. The skies had stayed clear—one of those rare, warm autumn days. Adding to Marlie's comfort level was the fact that the skiff was tied securely on the beach way up out of reach of the pull of the tide.

While Brent found sturdy limbs for the lean-to frame and cut cedar branches for the roof, she gathered firewood. Luckily it had been fairly dry for the last few days so she found dry wood at the base of the bigger trees.

The afternoon sun warmed them as they lay on their sides on the bed of moss and sheepskin. They studied each other's faces. Brent's eyes had lashes that any girl would kill for, and his irises changed like the sea from blue to green and gray, depending on how the light caught them. Straight white teeth and a beautiful smile drew her in for kisses. When he spoke, Brent's voice was strong, yet mellow. She loved the sound of it.

Propped up on his elbow, Brent lay on his side. "You puzzle me, Marlie." A smile played on his lips.

"I puzzle you too," she said.

After a moment's silence they both wrinkled their brows and laughed.

"I mean—"

"I know." And they laughed again.

"But seriously, what did you mean?" she asked.

Brent let his fingers run down the length of her forearm, stopping at her hand to play with her fingers. "Well, the first day I met you, I was sure you were one of those fanatic left-wing greenies who protest against everything and anything even if they know nothing about it."

"Hmpf! And now?"

"I … I think I may have been too quick to judge."

Marlie opened her eyes wide in mock surprise. "So how does that puzzle you?"

"I thought you knew nothing about real life—only living by what TV tells you to think, a superficial lifestyle. Plastic ideas, you know?"

She nodded, and made a face as if she'd tasted something bad. What an awful impression he must have had of her.

"So I was surprised when you liked the venison I cooked and you didn't freak out when you found out what it was."

"Maybe I was a bit quick to judge that first day too—about you killing a deer. I've learned a few things since then."

"Good." Brent smiled and leaned over for another kiss. "And two more things surprised me."

"Oh, what's that?"

"That night you were messed up."

A frown crept over her face, but Brent continued as if he hadn't noticed. "You were obviously hurt and traumatized, but you were tough too, keeping it together, at least while I was there. Some women would have wailed and blubbered, or been hysterical."

She blew out her breath. "Yeah, that was a tough night."

"Want to tell me about it?"

Her stomach tightened and she shook her head. "What's the other thing?"

"What other thing?"

"That surprised you."

"Oh. Today. What you did with the skiff. That was quick thinking."

"What would you have done if I hadn't noticed it and the skiff had gotten away?" she asked.

"I would've had to swim like hell to catch it. But you saved us a lot of trouble." Brent was silent for a moment, then snorted. "Huh! We could've died."

"Really?"

"Oh yeah. I mean a few more minutes and the skiff might have been gone. That tide can really run and it's pretty deep around the bar. It might have been too far away to catch the skiff. And too far to swim to shore in that icy water. I feel stupid for letting that happen. A fisherman! I didn't think we'd be on the bar that long, and I didn't think it would be covered up so quickly. I haven't spent any time there before—just thought it would be something fun to do." He shook his head. "I'll be more careful from now on. That was a wake-up call. Anyway, I hadn't expected you to do what you did. I would have jumped into the water to retrieve you and the skiff if I hadn't found the painter line, but you were quick and I was lucky. Most women would have watched helplessly and called for someone else to do something. That was quick thinking on your part."

Brent's words were like a tonic for her insecurities. Made her feel good. "Well, everything turned out okay. It sure hasn't been dull today."

Brent put his arm around her and reached up under the back of her shirt. His hand felt warm as it wandered up to her shoulder blades and over to unhook her bra. Their lips and tongues explored each other's faces. Brent's hands on her breasts set off tingles in lower parts but she tightened up when he reached inside the waistband. He must have sensed her body going rigid.

"Marlie, I won't hurt you," he whispered. "I promise."

She scrunched her eyes shut and nodded. "Yes, I know, I know. But I just don't think I'm ready for this. Not yet anyway."

"Okay, Marlie." He gave her a peck on the nose. "We can wait."

Marlie bit her lip. He would probably be pissed off now and say she'd led him on. How could she get him all tuned up and then dash cold water on him? She knew she had to get over this and put Clancy out of her head. This was Brent who had been nothing but kind to her. And besides, he made her heart race like it hadn't done in years. But, still she couldn't do it.

She stroked his cheek, about to apologize, but Brent kissed her gently. It was as if he knew that gentle was what she needed. Nothing else would do.

He lay down beside her, took the barrette out of her hair and spread the fingers of both hands through her curls. "You are really something special, Marlie," he murmured. "One day, when you're ready, we'll take up where we left off today."

CHAPTER 23
Marlie

Skylar sipped her coffee as she pushed through the doors. As usual, she was late getting outside for recess supervision, but things were pretty quiet on the playground. The kids all seemed to be getting along. "Hey, Marlie. How come you haven't been coming to volleyball?"

Marlie took a bite of her apple and wiped the juice off her chin. "Just been busy. How are things?"

"Not many people turning up. Ryan wasn't there last week. Neither was Clancy, or you, of course."

"Clancy didn't show up either?"

"Nope." She glanced at Marlie sideways, watching her face. "Thought maybe you and he had sneaked off on a date."

"Hah! No way. I have no interest in Clancy."

"Well, he's back with Sheila, but still.... He gets around."

"Don't I know it."

"Sheila was there, at volleyball, by herself. Maybe she wants to keep him out of your clutches."

"She doesn't need to worry."

"Well, why don't you come out this week? There's not a hell of a lot else to do in this godforsaken place."

"Maybe I will...." *If Clancy isn't going anymore, why not?*

***

That Friday, Marlie went to the gym. It had that familiar smell of slightly sweaty running shoes and floor wax. She scanned the room from one end to the other. If she got so much as a glimpse of Clancy, she'd leave. She couldn't help glancing around nervously every few minutes to check as she joined a group that was bumping the ball around.

Sheila was there, but Marlie had no beef with her. Part Haida and very pretty, she had a classic beauty like the Polynesian girls except that her nose was not flat, but rather fine and straight. She was the girls' phys ed teacher at the high school. Sheila played volleyball as well as any of the men. She got great height in her jumps when she was set up for a spike. Her arm came down on the ball with swift forceful smashes when she was at the net. More than once, Marlie had to move fast to avoid one of her spikes and still make a—usually futile—effort to return the ball.

They had two extra players on each team, so there were always two of them sitting out after each rotation. Marlie was grateful for a chance to catch her breath and lick her wounds when her turn came to sit out. Josie, sat next to her.

"Wow!" she said. "Sheila's got it in for you!"

"What do you mean?" Marlie rubbed a bright red spot on her thigh. "I don't even really know her."

"You don't have to know her. You know Clancy."

She gave Josie a puzzled look. "Everybody knows Clancy."

"No, but you know Clancy," she gave Marlie a meaningful look, "and she doesn't like that."

Marlie was stunned by the conversation. "There's nothing going on, and anyway, I thought he was living with her?"

"Josie!" Mike called. "You're up."

What in the world had Clancy been telling Sheila? All she wanted was to be left alone. As for Sheila, she hadn't even been formally introduced. Marlie knew who she was, saw her at Mike's party. She'd said "hi" a couple of times. And if she knew Clancy, worse luck for her!

They lost that first game and while most of them were milling around digging their water bottles out of their packs, Ryan came up and nudged shoulders with her.

"You did great out there," he said. "I like how you set me up for spikes."

"Yeah, it worked out pretty well." She took a seat on the bench, nursing her water bottle.

"Whoah!" he said. "That's some bruise on your thigh."

A bright red spot had goosebumps on the abrasion, and a purple raised welt filled the middle of the palm-sized bruise.

"Didn't get out of the way fast enough. That Sheila is one tough cookie."

Ryan swore under his breath. "Damn her. She was targeting you on purpose."

"Aw! I don't think so." She placed her towel over her legs, hoping to change the subject.

"Don't kid yourself." Ryan shook his head. "I know Sheila. Don't forget, I used to live with her."

"I'm just not used to this calibre of playing yet. Back home I played volleyball too, but it was more like a community team."

"That's what this is supposed to be."

"I mean old retired guys. This community is different."

He took a swig of his water. "I'll say."

They got up as the players switched sides for the return match. Marlie caught Sheila's eye and gave her a tentative smile. Her eyes narrowed and her chin came up ever so slightly, but there was no smile. Marlie hustled over to her spot and shook off a shiver.

At the end of the game time, most of the players helped put the nets and poles away. As Marlie came out of the equipment room, Sheila was waiting for her. "We need to talk."

"Sure. Here?"

"Out by the front door," she said.

Marlie followed her and wondered what could be on her mind. Clancy, of course, but what about him? Outside the school, Sheila spun around and faced her. "You keep away from Clancy. You hear me?" Her finger poked into Marlie's chest and she took a step back. "He's mine. Get your own boyfriend."

"I want nothing to do with Clancy."

Sheila's black eyes narrowed into slits. "That's not how he tells it."

Marlie put her hands on her hips. "Oh, and how is that?"

"He says you came onto him after you dropped him off at Declan's place. You scratched his face because he told you he was coming back to me."

"What?!" she shrieked. "That lying bastard." She was so angry she was sure her face was turning red, but she didn't care. "If you want to know the truth, Sheila, Clancy suggested I come in to see his artwork and then he raped me."

Sheila's lower jaw dropped slightly. Then she shook her head. "Oh, bullshit! It's people like you that are giving him a bad reputation."

"Wrong! Clancy doesn't need me to give him a bad reputation." She spun away, but flung one last comment over her shoulder. "He's doing that all by himself."

CHAPTER 24
Clancy

While Sheila was teaching, Clancy had the house to himself. Easier to work without being disturbed. He dashed off a few quick paintings. It didn't take long to slap on a bit of acrylic paint and call it modern art. He could sell those along with the carvings. The coffee shops and a couple of the gift shops always took the paintings on consignment and they sold pretty quickly.

He scratched some lines into a piece of argillite that Declan had scored for him a while back. A small piece of the soft black rock with a traditional Haida design would sell fast. He could whip off a reasonable facsimile of authentic Haida art in half an hour and make fifty bucks selling it in the bar. Easy money, as long as he could get the rocks.

Officially, only the Haidas had access to it, but like anything, a bit of bartering, especially with drugs or a case of beer, was all it took to make a few pieces available. Being part Haida, Sheila was a big help in sanctioning his stash of argillite and ensuring he could keep on carving. The good thing about this business was it was all cash. No tax to pay. No bank account needed. Nobody to know how much or how little money he had.

He'd have to make a show of working to keep in Sheila's good books, and he didn't mind doing the artwork. It was when she wanted help with the housework that he got his back up. It was a balancing act. He'd work on his art while she was at school and then just before she was due to come home, he'd plug in the vacuum and pretend he'd been doing housework all day. Clancy had a good thing going here. He didn't need to pay rent. He bought a few groceries now and then, but he never let on if he had any money. He kept a smile on Sheila's face in other ways, too. And if it didn't work out with her, there was always Declan's place, or some chick wanting a man around for security. For now, Sheila was the best solution. He'd try not to rock the boat, and that meant he had to keep her unaware of most of his activities.

Marlie's fingernails had left two scars down his left cheek. Pissed him off. He went out of his way to make sure she paid for that. Several times he had sabotaged her trailer, dumping fish guts on the steps, spray-painting graffiti on the trailer walls. He had slashed her car tires. He had shadowed her when she did her errands in town, always making sure she saw him but not coming close enough that she could speak to him or complain that she was being followed. He knew what time she left for school and made sure he was somewhere along her route to make gestures at her as she drove by on her way to work. That had to be getting her rattled. Sometimes, if no one was around, he even threw rocks at her car as she drove past. He made sure she was aware of him and did his best to keep her afraid.

Last time he saw her in town she told him if he didn't stop harassing her she would report what happened to the police.

"Go ahead," he told her. "They'll just tell you it's your word against mine."

"I don't care if they believe me or not," she said, "but they'll watch you and hassle you. And maybe it won't be just my word against yours. I saved the scrapings of your skin under my nails and I used my cell phone to take dated photos of my bruises."

That unnerved him a bit. "You're bullshittin' me." He shook his finger in her face. "You just watch yourself, or you'll find out what I'm really capable of."

"I already have a pretty good idea. I'm going to make sure the whole town knows about it too, if you don't back off."

"Tread carefully, Marlie. It'll be your funeral if you push your luck."

***

A few nights later Clancy was at The Bunker flogging some argillite carvings when a couple of Haida princesses came in. He sent over drinks before they could order their own and in minutes he was sitting with them at their table.

Laurie was stunning and he couldn't take his eyes off her. Clear, tanned skin, a fine nose, eyes as dark as midnight, and lips that begged him to kiss them.

"I think I'm in love," he told her, reaching for her hand. Such a slender little hand. He got tingles just touching her golden brown skin.

Her friend, Christy, picked up her beer like he hoped she would, and said, "I'll sit with Joey over there. See you later."

Clancy settled into his chair to face Laurie and turned on the charm, smiling so his small white teeth and blond hair would intrigue her, he hoped. "I've seen you around town, but I've never seen you in here before."

She leaned forward and whispered, "I'm not really supposed to be in here. Christy sneaked her older sister's I. D. for me."

Such a young thing! "So how old are you?" *Not that it matters to me.*

"Seventeen—well, almost. Just got my drivers' licence and Christy and I took my mom's car for a spin. Christy wanted to come in here and see if we could get served."

"You do look all grown up." He let his eyes wander up and down her body and nodded his approval. If he didn't get her alone someplace soon, he was afraid he'd come in his pants.

She smiled, sat back in the chair, and made a show of studying her blue painted fingernails.

In the far corner of the room, Declan sat hunched over, practically sliding across the table on one elbow, deep in conversation with two of his dope distributors, so Clancy knew his house would be available. He reached over to tuck a strand of Laurie's long hair behind her ears. "You have such dainty ears. I have the perfect earrings for them. I carved them out of deer antlers. I'd like to know what you think. If they're the kind of thing a girl might like. I'll even give you a pair."

Her eyes lit up. "Yeah, okay. Let's see them."

"They're at my friend's house, but I'd sure like it if you would wear a pair and kind of advertise for me. Then I could maybe sell a bunch? What do you think? Could you do that for me?"

"Sure. And I get to keep a pair?" She was beautiful. When she smiled she had the cutest dimples in her cheeks. He adored dimples.

"I'd love for you to have them. For helping me out. But we'd have to go get them. You say you have a car?"

She glanced over at Christy. "I'll tell Christy I'm going to give you a ride and I'll come right back."

"Aw right!" He high-fived her. "Laurie, you are so cool!"

When Laurie bent over to talk to Christy at her table across the room, Clancy's hard on was pressing to escape. He couldn't wait to get his hands on either side of that cute little ass.

***

Damn Declan! His house was a pigsty. He probably hadn't taken the garbage out all week. But if Laurie noticed the stench, she didn't say anything. Clancy turned on the CD player with the music on low. The fridge was nearly empty but there were a couple of cans of beer. He opened one for Laurie and one for himself. Then he rifled under Declan's mattress and found his dope stash. He rolled a fat joint and sat close to Laurie on the couch.

"You've smoked dope before, right?"

"Of course!" Laurie looked around the room, wrinkling her nose. "What about the earrings?"

Clancy held his breath after toking and nodded with his lips pressed together. "Nnn-hnn." He blew out the smoke and coughed a little. "Yup. We'll get to those. Here, have another toke."

After a few more puffs, the sweet smell of marijuana masked the ripe odour of garbage and he felt more comfortable. The dope was having its effect. Laurie giggled at anything he said. Her tiny teeth sparkled white when she smiled and he couldn't believe his luck in getting her to come here. She was such a doll. They laughed about anything and everything, even the dirty dishes on the table, how neglected they must feel.

He kissed Laurie gently. "But you wouldn't know anything about being neglected, would you sweetheart?" The kiss became more urgent and Laurie leaned back to pull away. He pressed his advantage and pushed her down. "A man would be a fool to neglect you, Laurie."

"Wait a minute!" She struggled to get up, her midnight eyes growing wider with concern. "Get off me, dammit."

He lay on top of her, pinning her down while he unzipped his pants.

"Get OFF!" She clawed his hair and pulled.

"Ow! You little bitch." He poked his fist into her ribs. She gasped and cried out.

"Get off me," she yelled, sobbing. She pushed at his chest and swung her fists around. "You're hurting me. Stop it!"

Clancy used his weight and his chin in her neck to hold her down long enough for him to undo her jeans and yank them down. She was like a live wire kicking and screeching. In all that kicking, her knee came up between his legs and connected with his balls. Fuck, did that hurt! Jeezus, she was going to pay for that. Clancy belted her a good one. She howled. In seconds she had a huge red patch on her face. Served her right. "Don't ever do that again," he yelled into her face. "Bitch!"

"Get off me," she screamed. She twisted and tried to turn and pull away, so he thought, why not? Let her turn. He'd fuck her doggie style. He grabbed her ass and started to put it into her, but she turned, twisting like a snake, and sank her teeth into his forearm.

"Jeezus, you fucking bitch. I'll teach you. You want to bite? Here you go." He bit her in the shoulder and she screamed. "Now you know what it feels like." He smacked her on the side of the face for good measure. Then he grabbed her by the hair, pulled her head way back to shut her up, and fucked her hard.

Oh my God, did she feel delicious. The way she squirmed and writhed only added to his pleasure.

"Stop it!" she screamed. "Damn you. Stop!"

He had just finished so he backed out of her and shoved her down. "Okay, I'll stop. I'm done with you anyway. Christ, what a fuss. I thought this was what you wanted."

She rolled off the couch and jumped onto her feet in one movement. "You fucking shit."

He waggled his finger at her. "Now, now. Language!"

She yanked her pants up. "You goddammed bastard," she yelled between sobs.

Clancy waved his hands in dismissal. "Oh, just get the fuck out of here."

Her hands trembled as she fumbled to straighten out her clothes. She staggered out of the house smashing into furniture in her hurry to get away.

"Oh. Laurie! Wait. Can I get a ride back to town?"

"You can go fuck yourself! You pervert!"

CHAPTER 25
Marlie

The week after she and Brent stayed overnight on Cub Island, Marlie had a permanent smile on her face. Well ... almost permanent. Clancy was still continuing the harassment but she was not going to let it get to her. She was crazy about Brent and thought—hoped— he felt the same about her.

Knowing she had a good friend in Brent gave her the strength to rise above Clancy's antics. One day a dead rat lay on the porch step of the trailer. It startled her, but it was only a second's work to put a plastic bag over her hand, pick up the rat, and put it in the garbage.

She knew it was Clancy's work when she found the words "Miss Easy" spray painted on the side of the trailer a few nights ago. One of her car headlights was smashed that same night.

Another day she had a flat tire when she came outside after school. Fortunately she knew how to change a tire, and luckily she'd had the spare fixed when she first arrived. Now she'd have yet another tire to replace. But this one was beyond repair. It had been slashed.

She didn't even seriously consider making an insurance claim. She had a high deductible to save on her premium, so she would have to pay that out before the rest of the expense could be claimed. That was bad enough but on top of that, her future insurance premiums would be higher if she made a claim. Insurance companies were not in business to lose money. They had it all worked out. Marlie would bear the expense of replacing the slashed tire and even though the insurance didn't do her any good in this case, she would continue to pay her premiums. Besides, one of the women in the insurance office was a parent of one of her students. She didn't need more gossip flying around.

It pissed her off to have to be dealing with all these nuisances, but she was determined that Clancy would not wear her down. He always seemed to be somewhere close by and she was getting nervous about being alone in the trailer at night. When he was on her route to work nearly every morning and started throwing rocks at her car, she knew it was time to report the harassment to the RCMP. She didn't expect anything to be done about it, only to have it all be on record. At least the police wouldn't spread rumours like the women in the insurance office.

"He follows me," she told Constable Woodley. "Lots of times he's waiting for me somewhere along my way to work. Sometimes he gives me the finger. Sometimes he throws rocks at my car as I drive past. I nearly had an accident the other day when he threw a rock into my windshield."

Constable Woodley was taking notes in his little black book. He looked up.

Marlie handed him a list of incidents all dated, telling of the fish on the steps, the rat, the smashed headlight, the graffiti, and the slashed tire.

Constable Woodley took the list. His eyes grew rounder as he read the items. ""Any particular reason he might be doing this?"

"He raped me, but I can't prove it. I can't prove he was the one responsible for this vandalism either, but I know he threatened to make my life miserable if I had any thoughts of going to the police."

The constable rubbed his chin, "I see...."

"And me being an elementary school teacher," Marlie continued, "it wouldn't be in anyone's best interests to pursue it further."

"I understand," he said. "We'll have to make some inquiries to follow up on the rape, but as you said, you can't prove it and some time has gone by now. It's too bad you didn't come in right away. We might have been able to do more. Meanwhile, we'll give him a warning and keep an eye out to make sure he behaves. Be sure to let us know if he troubles you again."

Marlie felt better when she left the police station. The time would come when Clancy would go too far. He seemed to think he could do whatever he wanted and never be held accountable. Like he could rape and steal and harass with impunity. He acted disturbed, too. She had seen him walking down the street talking to himself. And his logic was so bizarre—to think that he could make a game of rape. She didn't know why she couldn't see it at first, how unstable he was. She had wanted to think she might be friends with Clancy. His blond Beach Boy look and those blue eyes had her going. She was embarrassed to think that she let hormones take over. She felt like a fool now, knowing the kind of person he really was. And how pathetic was she to need someone badly enough that she would let her guard down and not check him out first. If she had been in Maple Ridge or Victoria, she would have made sure of who his friends were before going out on a date with him. What had happened to her common sense?

Maybe it was because of the small community. Everyone was chummy with everyone else. They knew each other's business. People hugged the first time they met at a party and hugged each time ever after. It was a different way of life up here. No one paid attention to the speed limits. The RCMP was too busy to bother with radar speed traps. You could drive after drinking and not get fined, as long as you didn't pile up the vehicle. You could stop in the middle of the highway to look at a bear in a meadow off to the side. No cars would come along and if they did they'd just stop too. People hitched rides all the time and didn't worry about being picked up by an axe murderer. Everything was easy going. Is it any wonder she assumed that everyone was to be trusted? But she'd made a mistake trusting Clancy.

One day after school, Marlie went into the local bakery-coffee shop. She bought her bread and was invited to have a coffee with Cheryl, whom she knew from volleyball nights.

Talk came around to Clancy.

"I know you saw us that night we tried to gang up on Clancy."

"Well, I couldn't hear what you were saying to him, but I figured there was a problem you were trying to clear up," Marlie said.

"There's never anything else with Clancy. Always problems," Cheryl said. "That girl with the kid was my cousin, Nina. She made a stupid mistake and let Clancy have his way with her. He was kind of pushy, but my cousin was kind of drunk, and she got kind of pregnant."

Marlie nodded knowingly. "Clancy likes to get his way."

"Well, Clancy promised Nina he'd pay her support for the baby but she's hardly seen a dime. She has to chase after him for money and he always says he doesn't have any but yet he always has enough to go drink at The Bunker. So we thought we'd gang up on him on volleyball night." Cheryl shook her head slowly. "Waste of time. She'll never get anything out of him. And anyway, he's got at least three other kids that I know of, and I don't think those women were willing participants."

"What a bastard," Marlie said. She didn't tell Cheryl she'd had the same experience.

"You can't keep doing shit like this to other people and not get some on you. His time will come," Cheryl said.

She hadn't realized how much Clancy was despised by so many. He went through friends, mostly women, like toilet paper. He used them, soiled them, and discarded them.

Somehow Marlie wasn't afraid of him anymore. She'd seen the worst he could do. At least, she hoped she'd seen the worst. She carried a small can of bear spray in her bag now. When she ran into him in town they exchanged threats but she felt safe enough with other people around. To her, he was nothing more than a pathetic piece of shit and she wasn't going to let him turn her whole world upside down—except that she thought about him all the time, and not in a good way, so maybe he was turning her world upside down.

About a week after Clancy raped her, she had found the courage to go to the doctor in town. She told him she wanted to be tested for STDs and she wanted it kept quiet because of her job. He agreed and said he was obligated to keep her business private anyway. "But shouldn't we test your boyfriend?"

"I don't have a boyfriend. It was an unwanted encounter and I'd rather not go any farther than that." She was relieved to see him nodding "Okay."

"How long will it take?"

"I should have them all done in a week. I'll call you as soon as I have any results—either positive or negative."

When she got the call she'd been waiting for, she chewed her nails while she waited for the doctor to give her the news. She thought her heart would stop before he finally gave her the information she was so desperate for—she was all clear. She was so relieved, she poured herself a brandy to stop her hands from shaking.

Brent visited her a lot. Sometimes he came over to her trailer. Sometimes he brought her to his place in his truck and brought her home again so she wouldn't have to drive alone in the dark.

The Sunday of Thanksgiving weekend, Brent cooked a white-fronted goose for supper at his place. She'd never tasted anything so delicious. For a wild bird it had a surprisingly mild flavour. And tender! She could have cut it with a spoon. After dinner, they sat on the couch sipping a glass of port wine. Marlie asked him how he usually spent Thanksgiving.

"Up until three years ago, I spent it with my wife, Nicole."

Marlie bolted upright. "Your wife?!"

"We're not together. Haven't been for years. We just never had the same goals, but we didn't find that out until after we got married. She was always looking for a party, and the accountant she worked for encouraged her to enjoy herself by adding some cocaine as hors d'oeuvres. While I was away fishing, she was quite the party girl and got involved with more drugs. We argued over it a lot. I lost all the arguments before they started because I didn't know she was already hooked on heroin. After we split, she moved to Vancouver, got all depressed and dabbled in more drugs to make herself feel better. I can only imagine the things she's done to feed her habit."

Marlie reached over and took Brent's hand. "I'm so sorry. Heroin is a terrible thing."

Brent grimaced. "Don't I know it? Two years ago I went to see her in Vancouver because she was always asking me for money. I'd been paying her plenty and yet she never had any. I told her I would pay to get her cleaned up and I'd give her enough to get her started on a new life afterwards, and then she would be on her own."

"That was good of you to do that. I know those rehab places charge a huge amount of money. So is she okay now?"

"Hah! I might just as well have flushed that money down the toilet. She went right back on drugs and she still calls to ask for drug money or for me to take her back. I just can't do it anymore. She disgusts me."

"Sounds like you've had some terrible times."

"My sister, Pam, is kind of a go-between. She phones Nicole once in a while and passes on the news to me, but I've told her I don't want to know anymore."

"Sometimes it's good to put the past behind you and start over. I know it was the best thing for me."

"You were married too?"

"Not married, but living with a guy. You don't have the monopoly on foolish moves. He moved in with me in our fourth year university. James was all fun and parties. He had no interest in making use of his university years or finishing to get a degree. He went from one job to another and every couple of months he'd come home with yet another crazy scheme for getting rich quick. All it took was a few thousand dollars here and a few thousand there to put into some investment. Before each new enterprise fell through he'd already be looking for another. I finished year five and we moved to Maple Ridge where I started teaching. My pay wasn't huge but that's what kept us going."

Brent had a look of horror on his face.

"Yeah," she said, "it was bad. So he soon ran out of friends." She hesitated.

Brent motioned for her to go on. "It was awful. I'd have strangers knocking on our door looking for James and the money he owed them. He'd already taken every cent I made teaching and he'd been beaten up a few times."

Brent winced. "That's not a healthy situation for you to be in. Why did you stay so long?"

"He wasn't a bad person. He loved me. Always buying me things—with my credit card. Not that I needed to be bought, but I guess it helped with his guilt. And there was something boyish and gentle about him. He was fun to be around and he always said that this time his idea was going to be good. He could never stick to one thing though and make it work. Guess you might call him a dreamer.

"One day two thugs pushed their way into our apartment, gave me a black eye and threatened to hurt me worse if I didn't pay by the end of the week. They said James had gambling debts. I hadn't known that he'd started playing backroom poker to try to get more money. I knew then it was time to get out. Funny thing was, the coward deserted me before I could leave him."

"What did you do? Go back home to your parents?" Brent asked.

"No, my mom and her boyfriend lived in a small house in a posh part of Victoria. I hadn't had much to do with them since I left home after my fourth year at U Vic. My mom was never that happy to have me around. Her boyfriend sure was though. I couldn't wait to get out of there."

"Too bad. It would have been handy to live at home while you went to school."

"Yeah, and it was okay the first three years, but once my mom took up with Dean, I had to get out of there," she said. "Dean—Mom's boyfriend—had cornered me in the house a few times. Luckily, I could yell for my mom, but when she came, I had to make up something stupid so she wouldn't have hurt feelings. She knew though, and she resented me being there, taking Dean's attention away from her. Dad had moved to Regina to teach at a college there. He'd been sending me money to go to school and after I moved out he sent a bit extra for rent."

"That was good of him."

"Yeah, it was. It was never quite enough, but it was a lot better than nothing, which is what my mom and her boyfriend were offering.

"My mom was always really strict. It was her way or the highway. She should have been stricter about her own behavior. She didn't blink an eye when Dad left. Just had more time for her boyfriends. Then she took up with Dean. He was disgusting. He saw a place to live, a warm bed with all the comforts, free meals, and a young girl to play around with when the old lady wasn't looking.

"I had met James and liked him, so by the beginning of my fourth year when things were getting really bad with Dean, James and I moved in together." Marlie chewed on her thumbnail. "I bet a lot of women do that. Move in with the first available guy, just to get out from under their parents and feel looked after.

"I can see now that my mother had James pegged way before I did. 'He attracts the wrong kind of company,' she often said. 'We don't need that kind of trouble.' Hah! She would know. She had lots of experience in that."

"Seems to be a lot of guys like that around," Brent said.

"He wasn't a bad guy, but he just didn't have any goals. My mother was disappointed in my choice. Rightly so, as it turned out."

"Let me guess," Brent said. "You applied to teach in the Charlottes to get as far away from everyone as you could."

"That's exactly right. I wanted to start over."

Brent reached for his glass of wine and turned sideways on the couch to face her. "And what are you looking for now, Marlie? I mean, what would your perfect life be like?"

"Oh, nothing really earthshaking. I always wanted to teach because I liked my teachers. Some of them made a big impression on me, made me like school, and I thought I'd like to help kids the way they helped me. I like working with kids. It's a good feeling to see the moment they realize they've learned something new. They're so surprised sometimes and always pleased with themselves. You should see the look on their faces when they discover that they can figure out almost any word. That moment when the light comes on. It's just so wonderful to hear them exclaim, 'I can READ!'"

"That's really great. But what about you? What does Marlie want?"

She thought for a moment. "I want to meet someone who will make me happy. I'd like to do more things and share those experiences with someone I care about. Build a life together, maybe have kids. You know—the usual."

"Not so usual if you go by our bad relationships."

"I'd like to think we both had bad luck. But what about you? What do you want, Brent?"

Brent closed his eyes as if he were imagining. "A partner who is sexy and smart, capable and brave. Maybe someone who would jump into a skiff that's drifting away, and save me."

This time, when the kissing led to further exploration, she allowed it to go on. She put Clancy out of her head and reminded herself that Brent was here for her and would never hurt her. Brent pulled her by the hand and led her into his bedroom. He was gentle but insistent.

"Marlie," he whispered, "I've been wanting you for a long time."

"Me too," she said. "I know it's right now."

"You don't need to worry. I'd never hurt you."

They made love and her world seemed perfect. They lay on the bed catching their breath and letting the steam rise off their bodies. Then Brent propped himself up on one elbow and asked about that night again. "I can't tell you," she insisted.

"Why not?" Brent demanded more forcefully than before. "If we're going to be together, we can't start by keeping secrets from each other."

"What do you mean 'if we're going to be together'?"

"I thought ... well, I thought you liked me. I know I like you ... and we seem to get along well." He looked away. "Or maybe I misread the whole situation."

"No, no, you didn't, but ... oh dammit anyway." She sat up, letting her head drop into her hands. "It's just that, if I tell you what happened, you might not like me so much anymore."

Brent sat up straight and poked his finger in her chest. "Now you have to tell." He folded his arms and waited.

Marlie took a big breath and let out a long sigh. "Clancy raped me. He said if I told anyone he'd get me and he'd make sure I got fired."

Brent pounded his fist into his hand. "I knew it! That scumbag. He's going to pay for this."

"That's what I was afraid of," she said.

"Why are you so concerned for him?"

"Not him! YOU! I don't want you to get involved and get hurt."

"I'm not worried about Clancy."

"No, but he has a lot of druggie friends who would do anything for another hit of something."

"Don't you worry about it. I can take care of myself."

"Does it change how you feel about me? Do you despise me for getting into that situation?" She was almost afraid to ask it out loud. She held her breath and waited.

"Hey! Come here." Brent pulled her close. "You didn't ask to get raped. This is all on Clancy. But yes, it does change how I feel about you."

Her shoulders sagged. She knew it. She had blown her chance with Brent.

"I feel different because I need to take care of you."

She bristled. "I don't NEED you to take care of me!"

Brent flapped his hands in the air in front of her. "Okay, okay. Not NEED." He groaned. "Why is this so hard? I WANT to take care of you."

"Why?"

He took hold of both her upper arms and looked into her eyes. "Is it so hard to see that I really care about you?"

She swallowed hard. "I do too … care about you, I mean." That was an understatement. She was totally lost, in love with this beautiful man.

Brent hugged her and muttered, "Clancy is going to pay."

In spite of the warmth of Brent's hug, she groaned and shivered in fear for him.

CHAPTER 26
Clancy

After romping with Laurie, Clancy wandered home to Sheila's house. As he opened the door, one look at her scowling face told him the jig was up. His first thought was, *She knows about Laurie.*

Sheila leaped off the couch and crossed the room in two giant steps. "You lying sonofabitch," she yelled. Clancy caught her wrist just in time as she hauled off to smack him. "You raped Marlie!"

"Wha-a-at?!" *Oh whew!* He thought maybe Laurie had been here and he didn't have an excuse ready, but Marlie's story, he could handle.

"Don't play the innocent." She spat in his face. "She told me."

He played up his indignation. "Of course she's going to tell you that. She had to come up with some bullshit story. I told you she was pissed off that I was coming back to you."

"And what about tonight? Where were you?" Sheila's eyes were slits

"I was selling some carvings and scoring some dope for us." Half-truths had always worked really well for him. Easier to keep a straight face.

Hands on her hips, Sheila sneered. "I don't believe you."

He dug in his pocket, pulled out a bag of dope, and dangled it in front of her face. "Believe it! Come on. Let's get high and then we'll see what comes up." He waggled his eyebrows and she gave up the stern look.

It took some cajoling, but finally Sheila calmed down. Give her a little poke, tell her some lies about love and all that stuff women like to hear, and she's happy. When she drifted off to sleep, he lay back in bed, relieved that he'd weathered that storm. *Fuckin' Marlie. I'm gonna have to shut that big mouth of hers for good.*

CHAPTER 27
Brent

A thick blanket of low cloud covered the sky, but at least there was no wind. The water would be calm. November could be a brutal month for storms. Brent had been hoping all week it wouldn't be windy so they could take the Huckleberry down Masset Inlet. With Marlie working all week they were limited to weekends. Today it looked like they might be lucky. He had loaded the boat with all the necessities for an overnight trip. With any luck, Marlie would see a whole new world via the Huckleberry. He picked her up at 8:00 a.m. and brought her to the dock. They unloaded Marlie's pack and a few last minute things onto the boat. Brent started the engine and left the boat to warm up while he parked the truck at Lennie's. Meanwhile, Marlie got her things organized on the boat. When he came back they untied the lines and were on their way.

"I remembered to bring my camera this time," Marlie said.

"Great! I have a feeling you'll get lots of good pictures."

Brent asked Marlie to sit in the captain's seat and keep an eye out. "I'm going to put away a few things and put the kettle on."

"What about steering the boat?" she asked.

"No need. I've got it on autopilot. It'll steer itself. I've got the route marked on the plotter. The only thing is, the plotter can't let us know if there's a big log or a boat in our path, so you still need to watch."

He had made up his bunk a few days ago. There was a spare bunk in the fo'c'sle for a deckhand to use and he'd made that one up with fresh, clean bedding too, just in case Marlie wanted her own space. He had to have everything he needed on the boat for the whole summer of fishing anyway, so the only thing he'd had to do for this trip was to top up the food supplies and refill the fresh-water tank.

The wheelhouse was set up like a kitchen and bedroom combined. The bunk took up one side, and the other accommodated a diesel stove with a small oven, a sink with running water, and a small counter. Next to the bunk was a drop-down table. The only thing it didn't have was a fridge, so he brought along a cooler and ice.

Brent didn't know when she found the time to bake them, but Marlie had brought along a bag of blueberry muffins. He put water in the kettle and set it on the stove.

"In about twenty minutes we should have boiling water to make our coffee. Or tea, if you'd rather."

"Coffee's fine. I like both. We could have a muffin with it if you want—except they're still frozen."

"No problem. I'll just set a couple of them in the oven and they'll be thawed and warmed up in no time," he said. "How's it looking out there?" He'd been watching to make sure they were on the right track and that there were no unexpected obstacles ahead, but he wanted Marlie to build up her confidence and also to show her what was required to manage a boat. It was always good to have a second capable person aboard.

"Looks all clear," she said. "Hey! Isn't this near the Bar of Fright? But I don't see the bar. We're not going to run aground on it are we?" Her voice betrayed a touch of panic.

"No, we're fine." He showed her the spot on the navigation monitor where the bar was and where the boat was in relation to it. "The tide is covering the bar already so you can't see it. The sounder would show you if we were getting too shallow, but we don't want to get that close. Don't worry. I've plotted the course to give that bar a wide berth."

"Oh, there's our lean-to on Cub Island! It's still standing!" Marlie pointed and smiled. "That was fun."

"Nyah." He waggled his fingers in a so-so gesture. "It was okay, I guess."

That earned him a playful punch in the shoulder. He hugged Marlie. She smelled so good. "What's that perfume?" he asked.

"I don't wear perfume."

"Your hair smells like ... like flowers growing really far away. Not overpowering but just delicate."

"Must be my shampoo I guess."

He buried his face in her hair. "You know this boat is equipped with two beds?"

She answered with little mumbles between kisses. "You mean one for each of us to sleep in?"

"No, two beds for us to christen together."

"Mmm...." She chuckled. "We'll see...."

They crossed the wider part of the inlet where it opened up into a big bay. "That's Port Clements at the far end of the inlet."

"Not much there, is there? I took my car exploring last summer, after I first got here. Just two main streets, really."

"It's got a wharf, a store, a school, and a pub. That's about it, I guess."

"So why is it here?"

"Logging town mostly. At least it used to be. We're going past it to the areas near where they used to log."

About an hour and a half after they went by Port Clements, he turned the boat in to a bay and pulled up to a tiny dock. Marlie was almost speechless except for saying, "Wow!" over and over again.

"This is Shannon Bay. What do you think? We could make this our home base for tonight?"

"I don't think I've seen a more beautiful place. Yes, let's stay here tonight." She snapped photos of the bay and the dock. "Wow! It looks like a calendar photo."

Brent docked the boat and got the skiff down from where it was tied to an overhead boom. He lowered it into the water beside the Huckleberry and tied the lines to the big boat.

He took some meat out of the cooler and put it in the roasting pan. "I'm going to put this venison roast in the oven and it can cook while we're out. I'll throw in a couple of potatoes when we get back.

"Bring your camera and water bottle, and make sure you have your gum boots on. I've got the handheld VHF and a few Band-aids in a backpack."

"What do you need the VHF for?" Marlie asked.

"You never know. If we get stranded we'll have a way to call out. I keep the VHF in a Ziploc bag in case I end up in the water. It'll float with the air in the bag and stay dry. Just a safety thing I always do. I'm going to take us over to that island and we can get out and have a walk around."

"Is that why you're taking the shotgun?"

"It's just a precaution, but if there's any geese on the island, I might want to shoot one for dinner."

Marlie made a face, but quickly turned her head away. *Well, tough shit,* he thought. *I hunt to eat.* They rode out to the island without talking, not that they could say much over the noise of the outboard motor anyway.

Brent cut the motor as he pulled up on the island's beach. "Look, Marlie, I'm not going to slaughter wildlife just because I brought a shotgun, but if I see a goose, I'll get it for our dinner. You liked the venison ... you liked the white-fronted goose...."

"I know. I just don't like seeing things killed."

He put his hand out to stop her talking. "Listen!" He turned his ear towards the sound. Sure enough he could hear quiet gabbling and muted honking somewhere inland from the skiff. "Geese!" he whispered.

"Now Marlie," he said quietly, "I know you don't want to be part of any killing and I can respect that, but would you do something for me?"

"If I can...."

"Okay, I'll get out here. You stay in the skiff and row it around to the back of this island quietly as you can without clunking the oars too much. I'll stay here and if there's any geese in the grassy field in the middle of the island, they'll soon know you're there and with any luck they'll fly out right over my head."

"Okay," she said. "I guess I could do that."

"Here. Take my whistle and if you have any problem, just blow on it."

"Yup, okay."

"And keep your lifejacket on just in case." He gave her a kiss, and once she had the oars in place he pushed the skiff off. "Thanks for doing this."

***

Marlie didn't mind going for a row around the island. She would focus on the beauty of the place and not think about whether or not the geese flew in Brent's direction. Although it was early November, it was mild enough, as long as a person was dressed for the weather. Hard to believe that just a few weeks ago, they stayed overnight on Cub Island. The week following that outing it rained and blew and she realized how quickly the weather could change here. Today she was dressed for any kind of weather. She had a wool sweater on over her long-sleeved jersey and a waterproof windbreaker over that. A toque had become a standard necessity. Most people up here wore them every day once summer was over, and actually, even in the summer if they were on the beach or on a boat. The wind could cut through layers of clothes and freeze you even on a sunny day.

The water was without a ripple and clear enough to see down about eight feet or more. She rowed quietly away from where Brent stood on the beach. Some good-sized spruces grew in a tight group near the beach, but beyond them were tall marsh grasses. A few mounds and shrubs dotted the meadow and tidal rivulets snaked through the grass.

The deep greens of the spruces and the many hues of yellow grasses seemed to have been painted by a wildlife artist. The aroma of the marsh grass reminded her of the sweet smell of marijuana, delicious in the fresh salty air.

Marlie stopped rowing and rooted around in her backpack to get out her Nikon. She wanted to remember this beautiful spot. Too late to get a picture of Brent waiting for the geese. She had rowed around a turn and was coming up to the back end of the island. Looking straight ahead, she framed a scene on the mainland side of the narrow channel and zoomed in for more detail. A black blob in the side of the picture moved. She lowered the camera and tried to see what the camera had seen. It must be a stump. Plenty of those around. Big ones too. Wait a minute! Didn't she just see this stump move? She lifted the camera again and zoomed it. At that moment the blob raised his head and turned into a bear. It was huge and slow moving ... and moving in her direction. Her lungs tightened up and she struggled for the next breath. She told herself to relax and immediately felt better. She clicked a picture and looked frantically around for someone to tell her what to do. All was quiet except for a few seabirds and the muted conversation of the geese around the other side of the island. She didn't know if the bear was aware of her, but he continued nibbling as he headed for the beach. If she didn't do something, they would meet near the beach at the far end of the island. But Brent was hoping for a shot at the geese. That meant she had to get to the far end of the island fast and hope the bear lost interest. And yet, it would be so easy to turn the boat around, go back and say, "I can't do it." As soon as she had that thought, she dismissed it. Brent would be so disappointed in her. So would she.

Marlie's heart pounded harder as she snapped a couple more pictures and then laid the camera on top of the backpack. She picked up the oars and rowed faster. It was a race to the end of the island, but she hoped the bear didn't know it was a race. If he got to the beach at the same time as she did ... well ... she couldn't bear to think about it. She chuckled nervously at her own joke and thought this was how it happened that people died laughing.

She was counting on the bear not being interested in her. Pulling on the oars with all her strength, she made good headway. As she reached the end of the channel and started to turn the corner to go back to Brent on the far side of the island, the bear stopped, stood on his hind legs and sniffed the air. He was huge. Marlie wanted to snap that picture, but she was shaking so badly she didn't know if she could hold the camera still enough. In that split second, she thought, "I'll never have a chance like this again." She grabbed the camera and got a picture of the bear standing up looking like a sasquatch. Then she threw the camera down and rowed as if her life depended on it, and maybe it did. The bear continued to head for the beach but unlike her, it took its time. She became aware that she was making whimpering noises as she rowed. She hoped Brent couldn't hear her. He wasn't that far away now. There was no doubt that the geese heard her though. A cloud of them flapped into the air honking out distress calls and, rising up over the trees, headed for the open water. A shot rang out, and another one. Marlie turned to get one last look at the bear. His hind end was bounding through the high grasses into the woods beyond.

She pulled on the oars and moments later, beached the skiff around the corner where Brent stood. Proudly he held up a bird in each hand.

"White fronts," he called. "The best!"

She took his picture. "Want to see it?"

Instead of the picture of himself and the geese, she showed him the picture of the bear standing on his hind legs. "Whoah! Is this for real? Where? When? Here? Unbelievable!"

"I know," she said. "I knew you wouldn't believe it unless I got that picture."

***

As Brent had hoped, Marlie loved it at Shannon Bay.

"I can't believe how peaceful it is. We've got the dock to ourselves. Not a soul around," she said. "Is it always like this?"

"Without active logging nearby there's no reason for anyone to come out this way," Brent told her. "Just as well, since there's only enough room for a couple of boats here."

"It feels so remote, like we're the only two people on Earth."

"And yet it isn't that far from town," he added. "If we needed to be, we could be back in Port Clements in a couple of hours."

"I like it out here," Marlie said. "Away from the mad world."

Brent gutted the geese and hung them on the davits at the back of the boat. The pipe frame was handy for more than just holding some of the trolling wire rigging.

"Why are you hanging them by the legs?" Marlie asked.

"They taste better after they've been hung like that. There might be some pellet holes that need to bleed out and everything runs to the head and neck this way and doesn't taint the meat."

Marlie's face mirrored her distaste. "Oh," she said in a small voice.

Brent knew she would feel differently about it all once it was on the platter. "I'll cook one up for us in the next few days. You liked the one I cooked for Thanksgiving, remember?"

She nodded but still looked doubtful.

"And you liked the venison."

"Yeah ... I did ... but I don't like to see the animals lying there dead."

"You don't mind seeing them lying there dead in the meat department at the Co-op, and those have already been dismembered."

"Oh, stop it. I know you're right." She frowned. "I just have to get my head around the emotional part and think of the logic of it. Can't happen overnight."

"I know," he said. "It may take some time, but at least there's hope for you." He let out a big sigh. "You know, if you could see the fishermen out there during fishing season, you'd be surprised at how often you'd see a deer carcass hanging from the overhead boom."

"Really? I thought they'd be too busy fishing to go hunting."

"There are lots of days when the weather is too rough to go fishing, and you're anchored near a beach. You take the skiff and go ashore and lots of times there are deer on the beach. Somehow they don't expect danger to come from the water side. You shoot one and bring it back to the boat and you have fresh meat. The deckhands are always happy to have a roast of venison instead of the usual packaged stuff from the store."

"Isn't that a lot of meat to eat all at once? I mean what do you do with it all?"

"Well, for one thing, the deer up here are not as big as the ones on the mainland, so we're not talking huge amounts of meat. It's good for a few days, hung on the boom with a tarp wrapped around it. It's cool out on the water even in the summertime. And I have a little freezer on top of the wheelhouse to put the rest of the leftover meat in. I freeze it in ziplocs and it's good for a long time."

"Makes sense, I guess," Marlie said. "I've never had to think about that kind of thing. I always went to the store and all the dirty work was already done. I just bought my shrink-wrapped chicken or beef or pork. I didn't have to think about who killed the hen, the cow, or the pig, or how the animals felt about it."

"At least you can see how unfair it is to judge someone like me for hunting for my food."

"I think I'd probably starve out here if the grocery store shut down. I don't even know how to shoot a gun."

"Maybe we can change that and do a bit of target shooting with the rifle tomorrow. I brought both— shotgun for birds, and rifle for deer, either will do for scaring a bear. There's not a soul out here so it won't bother anyone if we shoot a couple of rounds. Would you like to do that?"

"I ... I ... I guess.... I still wouldn't want to shoot an animal."

"No, just a target. You can decide tomorrow if you want to or not. But now, let's open that bottle of wine and see if our supper is ready." And after that, who knew what might develop?

***

The next day they took one more trip to the nearby goose island and explored it together. Brent brought his rifle this time, mainly for safety. After seeing the size of that bear in Marlie's photo he didn't want to take any chances. He didn't plan to shoot a bear, but a warning shot would usually deter an emboldened bear. He'd brought the guns along in the fish boat; he might as well take them in the skiff. He would sure feel like a fool if they were mauled by an angry bear and he had both a rifle and a shotgun in the fish boat where he couldn't use them.

Marlie took pictures until her battery was depleted, and then she switched to another. When it came to her camera, she was well prepared. Her photos were exceptional. Somehow she found beauty in the simplest things that most people would miss seeing. Brent asked her when she'd had time to take all those photos he'd seen on her blog. She said she had gone on a tour of Graham Island in July. She had parked the car and walked in to meadows, or on the beaches, and snapped photos of the creeks and marsh grasses, the rocks and seaweed, the sea anemones clinging to the rocks just below the low tide level, anything she felt city people would find different from their urban lives. She had a great eye for composition and could add a few touches with her Photoshop program to fix up the few that weren't perfect. She always managed to produce exceptional photos.

At last she shut the camera off and let it dangle from the strap around her neck. "I think that's probably enough."

"What will you do with all those pictures? More blog posts?" Brent asked.

She laughed. "I'll probably delete two-thirds of them, but the rest, I hope, will be useful at school sometime. I can use them for all sorts of things: nature lessons, story starters for creative writing, art ideas."

"How will you set that up?"

"I'll connect the laptop to the big TV screen." She chuckled again. "Anything on TV will hold their attention.

"But that reminds me," she continued. "Would you consider coming to the school one day and doing a little talk about salmon?"

Brent stopped walking. "Er ... I don't know. Not sure how to do that kind of thing...."

"It's part of our science curriculum—we've talked about the life cycle of the salmon, but we haven't mentioned how important it is to have a fishing industry. Maybe you could talk about being a fisherman.

"I'd help get you set up, and decide what to talk about. We could have some pictures—or maybe you have some frozen fish you could bring? Some examples of the real thing?"

"Well ... maybe ...."

"And then you can let them ask questions and that will make it easy. They would LOVE it!"

"I guess I could make a stab at it."

They were about to get back into the skiff and Brent was putting the rifle into its case when he remembered their conversation from the day before. "Would you like to shoot the rifle at a target?"

"Could I?"

"Of course." He looked around. "See that log washed up on the beach way down there? It's got a piece of branch sticking up. We'll set you up here on this rock and you can rest the rifle on it to aim." He got the rifle loaded, went over some basic safety rules, and laid his jacket on the rock so the rifle wouldn't get scratched.

Marlie got in position and he coached her through the process. "When you get the little branch in the crosshairs, breathe out and don't pull the trigger. Just gently squeeze it."

"Okay, I think I've got it."

"Make sure you press the butt of the rifle into your shoulder. It's got quite a kick and you don't want it jumping back to hit you in the shoulder. Now breathe out slowly and squeeze."

Marlie squinted one eye closed and peered through the scope until she had the crosshairs on the stick. Then she squeezed the trigger. "Holy smoke! That's sure loud! Did I hit it?" She laid the rifle on the rock.

"Well, the branch is gone. I'd say you hit it. Good shot."

She grinned. "Wow! I hit it! I hit it! That was really something. But it sure does have a kick, doesn't it?"

She was smiling and shaking her head in disbelief all the way back to the Huckleberry. "That was fun. I wouldn't mind doing some target shooting again someday. Not killing anything. Just shooting at a target."

"Whoa, there's hope for the girl yet."

Marlie stuck her nose in the air in mock pride. "Hey! Just because I'm a city girl, doesn't mean I can't learn a few things."

Once they had the skiff hoisted back up on the boom of the Huckleberry and the boat was warmed up, Brent asked Marlie to untie the lines and they pulled out of Shannon Bay to head home.

As they passed Port Clements and turned north on their way up the inlet, Marlie gave him a hug. "This has been a really fun trip. Thanks for taking me out in the boat."

Brent pulled her toque off and ran his hands through her hair. He touched her cheek and was about to kiss her. "What the—" He held his hand palm up. "Where the hell did that come from?"

"What?" Marlie ran to the mirror in the corner of the wheelhouse and pushed her hair back. "Oh, shit!"

"Here let me look." Brent dampened a paper towel and dabbed at her forehead. "Looks like you've got a cut here, probably from the rifle scope when it recoiled."

"Guess I didn't hold it tight enough." Marlie's face was pale. "Is it bad? Do you have a Band-aid?"

"Yeah, we'll put a Band-aid on it, but when we get back you have to go straight to the clinic. That's going to need a couple of stitches." He shook his head. She had a gash about an inch long that had opened up and bled quite a bit, but her hair and the toque must have absorbed a lot of the blood. "Didn't you feel anything?"

She shrugged. "I thought I got a little bump, but in all the excitement of hitting the target, I didn't think anything more about it."

"We'll have to say you fell and hit your head on a sharp rock. You're not supposed to be shooting a gun without a licence."

"Out here? Who cares?"

"Believe me, there'll be some officious jerk who will make a federal case out of it. So you tripped and fell on a rock, okay?"

"Sure. No problem. Not their business anyway."

Brent pulled her close. She was such an enigma. She hated killing, but she didn't mind shooting the gun. She gave herself a deep cut on the brow and yet shrugged it off as nothing. And then there was that incident with Clancy. She was a lot tougher than he had first given her credit for. "Marlie, you're something else."

CHAPTER 28

Marlie

Marlie smiled when she arrived at school in the morning and she was still smiling when she walked out the door at 4:30. She thought maybe her happiness with Brent rubbed off on the kids as they behaved extra well. Whatever the reason, they were fun to work with. Heather seemed happier—maybe because she was getting more to eat, now that Marlie brought her something every day—and even Donnie, who was usually apathetic, perked up and joined in their project about animals of the islands.

Marlie discovered that the Haida kids, especially, had a lot to contribute to their talks about the habits of the deer, raccoons, and eagles. They worked together in small groups to produce booklets about these animals, writing reports and drawing pictures of them. Time seemed to fly by.

On Tuesday, about a week following the Shannon Bay trip, Brent came to the school after recess carrying a cooler and a huge canvas bag. He had the attention of the class from the second he walked through the door.

"Have any of you ever been out in a fishboat?" he asked. Several hands went up. "That's great. I'd like to hear all about it in a little while. But first, what do you think is in this big bag?"

The kids had fun guessing.

"A salmon?"

"A crab pot?"

"Ropes?"

"Your lunch? That one was followed by laughter.

Brent smiled and accepted all the suggestions as valid, without giving any hints whether they were right or wrong. It helped build the curiosity and the anticipation. At last he pulled out one item, a pair of rubberized bib overalls. He let everyone feel them and asked what was different about those pants.

"They're rubber on the outside," Darren said.

"They're a bit stinky," Samantha said, giggling and holding her nose. That got everyone laughing again.

"Why do you think they have rubber on the outside?" Brent asked.

"So the fish guts can wash off better?" Donnie suggested.

"It's like a raincoat, only pants," Daryl said.

"That's right," Brent said. "They're waterproof. You're always getting wet in a fish boat. Either it's raining or you're washing down the checkers where the fish are brought in, or you're in the hold putting ice on the fish. They keep you dry."

Brent put on the overalls over his jeans while the kids looked at each other giggling with embarrassment. He reached into the bag again, pulled out a rubberized jacket, and put it on. "What's missing?" he asked.

"Boots," said Donnie.

Brent fished out a pair of gum boots and slipped them on. "Anything else?"

"A toque," said one.

"A rain hat," said another.

"You're both right," he told them. "If it's just windy and cold out on the water, I can wear my toque, but if it starts to rain, and I still have to be outside to pull in the fish and gut them and clean them, I want to have ...," and he reached into the bag again, "this!" He held up a rubberized hat with a wide brim that would shed the water down his back.

"There's one more thing that's missing," he said. He took some more guesses and then opened up the cooler.

He took out a medium-sized fish and talked about the four kinds of salmon and how to tell the difference. A few of the kids held their noses and made noises about the smell of the fish, but when Brent put the fish back in the cooler and brought out a platter of cook-smoked salmon, the squeamish kids stopped their complaining.

Marlie handed out napkins and a bun to each of the kids as they sat in a circle on the mat. Then Brent followed around the circle with a platter of enough smoked salmon for each kid to have a good-sized piece.

The class was thrilled with the presentation. They dismissed for lunch right afterwards.

Brent got out of his slicker outfit and they sat at Marlie's desk sharing buns and some smoked salmon.

"Thank you so much for this, Brent," she told him.

He smiled, looking very pleased with himself. "It was more fun than I expected. Wish I'd had teachers like you when I was in school."

CHAPTER 29
Brent

Ever since Marlie told him about what Clancy had done to her, Brent discreetly followed Clancy around and asked a few questions about him. He heard very little that was good. The artist was a great one for not returning things he borrowed. A few of the fishermen even said they were sure they'd seen him hanging around the floats just before they had lost electronic equipment. Jack, on the Solitude, said Clancy had sold him a laptop for a bargain price, and later he learned that Harry had his boat broken into, a laptop was missing, and it turned out to be the one Clancy had sold. When he was questioned about it, Clancy said he had found it on the beach.

Brent spent a few nights in the pub. He didn't normally go there. The Bunker was a dark windowless brick building. It catered to a rough crowd and he didn't relish getting into a fight over nothing. Still, he needed to find out more about Clancy's habits.

It didn't take long to learn that he and Declan dealt a lot of dope, mostly marijuana, but some coke as well, and that Clancy had moved back in with Sheila. He spent most nights at The Bunker selling his carvings and dope, and hitting on young women.

Brent had an overwhelming urge to deal with him right away, just kick the shit out of him, but he reminded himself to be patient and not make any stupid mistakes by rushing in while he was still enraged. Luckily he'd had things to do to get the boat ready for the weekend trip to Shannon Bay, but once he got back he took up where he left off and followed Clancy to his usual hangout.

About a week after the Shannon Bay trip, on the Tuesday after Remembrance Day, he did the presentation at Marlie's school. That evening he put on his worn out stained jeans and his dark blue checkered work shirt with a tear in the elbow and found a quiet table at The Bunker. He studied the patrons and noted Clancy falling all over some girl on the far side of the hall. He picked out one of Clancy's many pot customers and had a beer with him.

"Listen, here's ten bucks if you'll pass Clancy this note and say you don't know who gave it to you."

The guy grabbed the tenner and pushed himself up out of the chair. "No sweat. Easy money."

Brent watched from the door as the note was delivered, saw Clancy's head pop up to see who the note was from, but Brent was quick and slipped out into the darkness.

"Come out to the parking lot. I want to make a big buy," the note said.

Clancy staggered out the door and stared into the darkness, his body swaying. From the bushes at the far edge of the parking lot, Brent called softly, "Psst! Clancy! Over here."

As Clancy threaded his way around the potholes of the parking lot to the edge of the bushes, Brent encouraged him. "That's it. Over here."

When he got close enough, Brent stepped out from the cover of the shrubs and punched him in the nose. That blow contained a good measure of rage for what

Clancy had done to Marlie. Brent was so charged up with adrenaline, he didn't notice until later that Clancy's teeth had cut into his knuckles. He wanted to kick him after he fell, but much as he hated him for raping Marlie, it seemed cowardly to hit a man when he was down. Clancy rolled over and groaned.

"That was for Marlie," Brent said. "Stay away from her or next time I'll beat the shit out of you." It had all been too easy, and the guy deserved a hell of a lot more punishment than one good punch. It didn't give Brent the satisfaction he'd hoped for. It was more like beating up a helpless dog. Still someone had to make him pay for what he'd done to Marlie. From what he'd learned, there were several other women who needed avenging, but that wasn't his job. He got out of there before Clancy could figure out who had hit him. When he got home he couldn't wait to shower off Clancy's blood.

The phone rang as he came out of the shower. He grabbed a towel and picked up on the fourth ring.

"Brent? Oh thank God. I've been calling all evening."

"Pam?" There was only one reason his sister would be calling. "What's up?"

"It's Nicole." Pam sounded tensed up just as she always did when she called to talk about his ex-wife.

"I figured that. I told her I wasn't paying for her habit any more. I paid for rehab, I paid to get her set up in a new place—"

"Brent—"

"I paid for her groceries, her Hydro bills—"

"Brent—"

"I'm not doing it anymore." He wanted it all to end.

"Brent! You don't have to."

"That's right. I don't. So what's the problem?"

"She's dead."

"What?" He sank onto the couch, stunned.

"She OD'ed."

"She—on purpose?"

"No, I don't think so. There's been some bad shit on the streets. This fentanyl is killing off addicts left and right. I thought it was somebody's idea of a prank, at first, but now it's in the news every day. Another addict overdosed."

"Whoah...." He'd forgotten to breathe. "That stupid girl." He shook his head to try to fling away the words he couldn't believe. "Holy shit. Now what?"

"You need to come down here right away. You're not officially divorced—"

"What do you mean, not officially divorced?"

"She never signed the papers or sent them in."

"That lying bitch!"

"Yeah, well, the only lying she's doing now is in the morgue."

"Shit, I can't believe this."

"Believe it. So, you have to come make arrangements and sign some papers. You know, like for her funeral, and for her apartment, the furniture, and her paperwork...."

"Fuck! This is not what I need right now."

"Brent! Can you stop thinking about yourself for a minute?"

"Okay, okay! I'll be on the plane tomorrow. Can you pick me up?"

"Sure. What time?"

"I don't know exactly. I'll have to see if there's room on tomorrow's flight. I'll call you tomorrow morning and let you know."

"Yeah, okay. I'm sorry, Brent. She was a nice girl before the drugs."

She hadn't been a nice girl for a long time. It pissed him off that he had to deal with this shit, but maybe he could salvage the trip and make good use of his time down there. He had other business he needed to attend to. But dead!? Nicole? Dead?

CHAPTER 30
Clancy

Clancy woke up shivering. He figured he must have been passed out for an hour or more because the parking lot was nearly empty. He crawled to the edge of the bushes and rolled over onto his back. His face hurt when he vomited the last of the beer left in his stomach. He clutched a skinny alder trunk at the edge of the gravel lot and dragged himself upright, his head pounding. His clothes were soaking wet and he shook uncontrollably in the rain. Luckily it wasn't far to Sheila's place. He staggered up to her door and let himself in as quietly as he could, trying to still one hand with the other as it shook, rattling the keys in the lock. Once inside, he headed straight for the bathroom. He dropped his sopping clothes on the floor, and stood in the warm shower until he stopped shaking. He had made sure to lock the bathroom door. He wasn't shy about being naked, but he didn't want Sheila walking in on him. Wouldn't do for her to see the bloody nose. He looked in the mirror afterwards and examined his face. Not too bad. Nose and lips were a bit swollen, but no black eye—not yet anyway. He flashed a smile to see how he'd look when Sheila saw him. Fuck! One of his front teeth was knocked out and another one broken off. Goddammit!

Sheila was pounding on the door. "Clancy?"

Oh shit! What am I going to tell her? I know. I'll blame it on Declan. He opened the door. She stood there in her T-shirt and bikini undies looking so sexy.

He took care only to smile with his mouth closed. He hugged her so she couldn't see his face.

"What happened to you?" she asked.

"Nothing. Why?"

"Your shirt. It's all bloody." She pushed past him and picked up the shirt from the bathroom floor.

Clancy opened his mouth to explain and she clapped a hand over her mouth. "And what happened to your face? Your teeth! Were you in a fight?"

He looked at the floor to hide his mouth. "It was some thug that Declan sent after me. He said Declan wanted the rent money I still owed, and he wanted it now. I didn't have it so he punched me."

"Oh, Clancy!" She hugged him again. "Jeezus! What is the matter with that Declan? I thought he was your friend." Sheila sighed and took his hand. "Oh, poor you! Does it hurt? Come on to bed. I'll have you feeling better in no time."

CHAPTER 31
Marlie

Marlie hadn't seen Brent for a few days. After the salmon presentation, he'd said he had some business to take care of in the next few days, but he'd call her Friday night. She waited around home for a call that never came.

Dammit! She was not going to spend her weekend by the phone. Saturday morning, she got out the second-hand bike she'd bought through an ad in the Queen Charlotte Islands Observer. The owner was moving back to the mainland. The bike was too bulky and complicated to pack—and the air freight too expensive—to take on the plane. It was a 10-speed in good condition and the guy practically gave it away for $20.

She packed a cheese and lettuce sandwich and a bottle of water in the carrier bags and set out on the road towards the Chown River. She didn't know why she headed out on the road to Brent's house when she knew he must be busy, but he was like a magnet to her. She promised herself she wouldn't go down his driveway. She'd stay on the main road to the end, turn around and come back again. That would be a good workout—several miles each way.

She had biked past the Circle—what the townspeople called the Department of National Defense's giant listening device; a giant circular stockade with a steel net around it. Beyond it, a few private driveways met the main road. Skylar had told her that the whole stretch out to Tow Hill used to be pretty much uninhabited. Now, more and more people were building houses on either side of the road that followed the beach across the north end of Graham Island, but there were still vast areas of untouched forest, especially on the south side of the road.

Long beards of mint-coloured moss hanging from the many broken and dead limbs, gave the trees an eerie look. Marlie filled her lungs and savoured the tannic aroma of the spruces and cedars. The spongey forest floor undulated with hills of soft moss. She and Andrea had walked across some of that thick moss at Brent's place. She stood straddling her bike at the side of the road and admired the fairy tale forest. A car was coming. What a rude sound, after the stillness of the woods. She twisted around to look behind her.

Oh no! Clancy!

She jumped back onto her bike and pedaled fast. Clancy crept along behind her in the car. This was silly. She could never outdistance the car. She stopped and waved for him to pass. "Go on then," she yelled. "Go on by."

He stuck his head out the window. "No, I don't think so. I'd rather follow and watch your ass." His eyelids drooped heavily like he'd been smoking dope or drinking. Probably both. Something was different about him. She did a double take. He had a shiner! And his teeth had a big gap. Huh! Guess he'd been in a fight. Not surprising. Maybe the next woman he tried to rape got a good lick in.

She pedaled on, her mind whirling, considering her options. She decided on a quick U-turn. It would be harder for Clancy to do the same with the car. Maybe he would just keep going. If not, at least she'd make some headway while he was turning. Maybe she could make it back to one of those driveways she'd passed about a mile back.

She spun the bike around and rode like crazy in the opposite direction. A glance over her shoulder told her that Clancy was again in pursuit. Moments later he had caught up to her.

"Leave me alone!" she shrieked as he pulled up beside her, keeping pace with her frantic pedaling.

He cruised alongside of her bike, an elbow on the window sill. "I would do that, Marlie, but you've been making trouble for me. I heard you told Sheila I raped you."

"You did!" she puffed out between breaths.

"Nonsense. It was a game, and you wanted to play it."

"Bullshit!" She pumped harder. "I did not want it, and if you keep harassing me I'll tell the police you won't leave me alone." She didn't dare tell him she had already done that or he might take revenge on her right there.

She cursed herself for not bringing her bear spray along, but if she had been expecting Clancy out here she wouldn't have gone for the ride in the first place.

"I see that I'll have to teach you a lesson to shut you up." He gave the steering wheel a hard yank. The car swerved into the bike and knocked her into the ditch.

Marlie yelped as the bike tipped. She jumped to get clear of it, rolling into the edge of the woods on the other side of the ditch. Clancy was already opening the car door. She scrambled up and ran into that fairy tale forest not knowing or caring where she was heading as long as it was away from this perverted maniac.

Clancy was in pretty good shape, but he staggered as he came after her, stumbling on a fallen tree. The forest floor was full of blowdown from decades of storms, and the deep, soft moss that covered fallen logs made some areas hard to negotiate. Clancy's being stoned gave Marlie the advantage she needed. She soon outdistanced him so far that she couldn't see him anymore. But she couldn't see the road anymore either, and there were no houses here.

She leaned her back onto a cedar to catch her breath and listen. Nothing. The moss seemed to absorb all sound. Her plan was to stay hidden behind this giant tree trunk. When she was sure Clancy had given up, she would go back to the road. She hoped her bike would still be there.

For several minutes all she heard was the hammering of her heart and wheezing of her lungs. She prayed that Clancy wasn't sneaking across the moss quietly while she was hiding behind the tree. When her heart slowed down and her breathing became normal, she peeked out. No sign of him. She took a few steps back towards the road. Or so she thought.

Marlie frowned. She should have been seeing familiar tree groupings and open spaces that she had passed on her way into the forest. She turned to look in another direction. Maybe the road was not where she thought it was. She studied the terrain in each direction, turning and turning again. The sky should have given her a hint but it was overcast and any bit of brightness from the sun was obscured by the canopy of treetops. No place was brighter than another. She wondered how far she could walk if she went in the wrong direction. Probably for miles before she came to the highway or the beach. If she walked north she would come to the beach in about twenty minutes. If she walked east or west, within about ten miles she would either come to Masset or to the east coast of the island. But if she went south she might walk for days, parallel to the highway.

The trouble was, she had no idea which way was north. She pressed her hands to her temples. *Oh God, I'm lost! ... But wait!* She knew that the moss grows thicker on the north side of a tree trunk where it got the least amount of sun. She looked for the mossier side, checking several trees. Her heart sank. So much moss grew all around every trunk here, it was impossible to tell which side might be facing north.

Marlie made a random choice and started walking. *Try to go in a straight line,* she told herself. *And stop shaking. Get yourself together.* She'd heard often enough about people who were lost, going around in circles.

She must have been walking for about an hour. Nothing changed. Moss, trees, more moss. Maybe she should try a different direction? She heard a gurgling sound, like water going over rocks. The river! It had to be the Chown. If she followed the riverbank downstream she knew it would eventually lead her to the beach. The hopeful plan renewed her courage. She picked up the pace.

Last time she was at the Chown was with Andrea. A shiver came over her when she remembered that day. She prayed she wouldn't run into the bear they had seen there a few weeks ago.

Two hours later she was slogging along, going over or around fallen trees, the detours adding to the time it would take to get to the river mouth. At last it was easier walking and she came to a clearing beside the river. *Wait now! The clearing! This looks familiar. Brent's place! Where we sat by the fire. Yes, there's the brake drum ring. Oh my God! I know where I am!* A burst of energy coursed through her and she stumbled across the grass and along the path to the house.

"Brent!" she called as she ran. "Brent!" *Oh please be home!* "Bre-e-ent!" Now was the time he should come running out and take her in his arms. But the house was dark and quiet. Her running steps slowed to a slap, slap, slap of tired sneakers on the driveway and then to a full, disappointed stop. It would soon be dusk, and yet no lights were on. She banged on the door with her fists and shouted Brent's name again, even though she knew no one would come. She looked around for his truck. Not there. Her heart sank and she collapsed on his deck chair, sobbing.

She was so thirsty. If she could get into the house she'd have a drink of water. She knew where he kept a spare key under a piece of driftwood on the veranda. Marlie let herself in. "Brent? Are you home? Please be home. Brent?"

No answer. She rushed to the sink to pour herself a glass of water. Next she found his phone and wondered whom she could call. Skylar? Her fingers shook as she punched in Skylar's number, one of three she had memorized. Skylar picked up after the second ring.

"Skylar! Oh thank God!"

"Marlie? What's up?"

"I'm in a real jam." She tried to keep the quaver out of her voice. "Can you help me?"

"Sure if I can. What do you need?"

"If you could pick me up at Brent's place I'll explain later. Come out Tow Hill Road almost to the Chown

Bridge. I'll be at the top of Brent's driveway watching for you. And thank you so much. I owe you." She put the phone back in its cradle. *Where are you, Brent?*

She locked the door and put the key back under the driftwood. Then she hurried down the long driveway to Tow Hill Road. She just hoped Clancy had gone home and wasn't still driving the road looking for her. Many hours had gone by so it was unlikely she'd see him. Just the same, she hid behind the nearest tree while she waited.

At last the VW van came barreling down the road. "I could kiss you, Skylar," Marlie said as she climbed in. "Thank you for picking me up."

"I'll pass on the kiss, but it's sure nice to be appreciated. What the hell happened? Did you and Brent have a fight? Jesus! You look like the wild man of Borneo. You okay?"

"I am now. Oh God! What a day! I just went for a bike ride—"

"So where's your bike?"

"Somewhere along the side of the road, I hope, but a lot closer to town." She glanced over at Skylar and saw her frown.

"Wha-a-at? That doesn't make any sense."

"It should be coming up soon, just this side of the Circle." Marlie leaned forward to scan the side of the road. "Slow down along here, would you? It could be anywhere here in the ditch."

"You were a long way from your bike...."

"I had to make a run for it.... There it is!"

Skylar stopped the van and Marlie got out. "Running from...?" she asked.

The bike looked just the way she left it except for two flat tires. "Bastard!" she whispered under her breath as they loaded the bike into Skylar's van.

They got back in and Skylar was about to start up the van again when she turned to Marlie. "Explain."

She did owe Skylar an explanation. "Okay. I know it sounds crazy, but ... oh what the hell. I might as well tell you. Clancy raped me after Mike's party back in September."

Skylar's sharp intake of breath stopped her for a moment. "Yeah, that's right," she said, "and he's been harassing me ever since. I threatened to tell the police what happened and he got really aggressive. He's trying to shut me up and it looks like he'll stop at nothing to do it. Which is pointless because I already went to the police just a few days ago."

She told Skylar about Clancy chasing her through the woods and how she outran him but then got lost. Luckily she came to the river and followed it down to Brent's place.

"What did Brent say?"

"He wasn't home. I don't know where he is. I haven't seen him for days."

Skylar dropped her off at her trailer. Marlie invited her in but, not surprisingly, she had a party to go to. She gave her a hug and thanked her again. "And Skylar? Do you think we could keep this just between us? About Clancy, I mean."

"Oh, sure thing. You went for a bike ride, had a flat tire, and I picked you up. No sweat. Now go inside, lock your door, and have a good soak in the tub."

"Will do. Have a good time at the party. Thanks, Skylar. You're the best." And she had to admit, even though she seemed a bit rough around the edges, Skylar had a heart of gold, and, once again, Marlie had been too quick to judge.

CHAPTER 32
Declan

"D eclan!" Russ called. "C'mere. Wanna talk to you." Russ was a huge Haida. Six-foot-four, he must have weighed 300 lbs, none of it fat. He and six of his cousins were hanging around outside The Bunker when Declan came out after making a small dope deal. "Over here." Russ pointed to the side of the brick building. "More private."

Declan was shaking in his boots. Seven of them, one of him. One kept pounding his right fist into his left. The right had brass knuckles on. Declan's mind whirled. He hadn't done anything to piss off these Haida toughies, had he? They were local mafia. There wouldn't be much left of him if they had a burr up their ass.

"This friend of yours, Clancy, needs to be taught a lesson." Russ's chin rose, daring him to defend Clancy.

"Oh? What's he done?" It was all he could do not to stutter. Thank God it was Clancy and not him they were after. But still, why were they ganging up on him?

Russ bent down and stuck his face close to Declan's. "He raped my little sister. Beat her up." Russ's fists clenched and unclenched and his cheek muscles worked.

The blood drained out of Declan's head and his words came out in a desperate whisper. "Oh my God. That stupid little prick."

"You got that right. And you're gonna help us teach him a lesson."

Oh fuck! "What can I do?" he asked, hoping it was nothing too messy. *Goddamn Clancy! The stupid fuck has crossed the line now.*

"You get him to come down to the wharf and get on our boat. You'll come too. Make it all seem okay, like we're going for a boat ride—maybe to pick up some dope."

"I can get him down there, but I really don't want to be involved in anything. I don't want to be on the boat." A wave of nausea swept over Declan and he thought he would lose his stomach.

Russ moved closer, so close that Declan could hardly breathe. "Too late. You are involved. You're his friend, aren't you?"

"N-n-not really." Declan had his back to the wall of The Bunker, his fingers splayed against the bricks for support lest his knees gave out.

The cousins swarmed him. He knew when to stop arguing. "Okay, okay. I'll come. I'll tell him we're making a pickup."

Russ flashed him a sneering smile. "That's smart of you, Declan. See you tonight at six, and you'd better have Clancy with you. Come to the Dixon E near the end of the dock."

Russ backed away a step and he was able to breathe a little easier. Then he stepped closer again and Declan nearly choked on his own spit. Russ put his finger up to Declan's nose and growled, "Don't let me down, Declan."

Declan hustled over to his beat up old Ford. He looked over his shoulder. The parking lot was empty. He opened his truck door and stood behind it to piss away the last beer he'd had. Just in time too. Those

Haidas had every nerve in his body jangling with fear.
He shook off the drips and jumped in behind the wheel,
locking both doors before peeling out of the lot. *Jeezus!*
Oh Jeezus, Clancy. What the hell have you done?

CHAPTER 33

Clancy

On Saturday morning, Clancy had convinced Sheila to let him use her car. "I'm going to see Declan and clear things up. I'll pay him the rent I owe him and pick up the rest of my art stuff," he told her.

"Just as well to steer clear of him from now on," Sheila said. "Once you get your stuff you don't need to have anything more to do with him. Imagine having someone beat you up for the rent. Sending thugs after you is not what a friend would do."

"Yeah, yeah, I know," he told her. *Except I need him to move my carvings and he needs me to move his dope.* Not something he had to deal with right now though. He wasn't planning on going to Declan's place anyway. Just needed a legitimate excuse to borrow Sheila's car.

He parked across the street from the trailer court where he had a clear line of vision to watch Marlie's porch. She would have to come out eventually and he'd follow her around until he got her alone. His plan was to scare the shit out of her, maybe get a bit physical, so there was no way she'd go to the police. Apparently she had already told someone—besides Sheila—or the guy wouldn't have jumped him. Clancy would get her good today. Teach her it was best to keep her mouth shut.

He got bored sitting there watching her trailer, like a cop on a stakeout—minus the coffee and doughnuts.

He rolled himself a fat doobie and put the seat back so he could doze with one eye open. No movement in the trailer. Curtains were still drawn. He knew she was home though. Her blue Corolla was parked out front. He cracked a can of beer. After the third beer he saw her come out, maneuvering her bike down the steps of the joey shack. Perfect. Her on a bike. Him in a car. He slid down in the seat and pulled up his hood to hide his face. He turned as if he was just some guy sleeping off too many beers—which didn't seem like a bad idea, actually.

He let her get a good lead while he opened the door to have a discreet leak before he started the car. She turned to go down Tow Hill Road. He rubbed his hands together. She was making it too easy. A bike ride down that desolate road? No more fucking around. When he got through with her she'd be too scared to talk to anyone. He'd rough her up a little so she wouldn't forget what could happen if she pushed her luck.

Clancy stayed well behind her while she went a mile or so down the road, past the last of the houses. Then in the first lonely stretch, he sped up and started harassing her to get her scared. She surprised him by doing a sudden U-turn, but she was no match for old Clancy. He was quick on the turn too, and came right alongside again. He could see that she was getting rattled so he ratcheted the game up a notch and swerved at the bike. The first swipe knocked her and the bike into the ditch. He got out to grab her, but she was like a rabbit, jumping off the bike and into the woods.

He chased after her but the damned moss covered the crisscrossed fallen branches so he couldn't tell where the solid footing was. Nearly broke a leg falling through the moss into a hole. Dammit, she was already way ahead. No way he'd catch her now. Next moment she was out of sight. She got the message anyway. Just to make himself feel better, he let the air out of her bike tires. Served her right.

He drove back towards town. He didn't really want to go back to Sheila's yet, so he dropped in to see Declan.

"Hey, Clancy my man!" he crowed. "I've been looking for you."

"Oh yeah?"

"Got an important job for—what the hell happened to you?"

CHAPTER 34

Brent

Now that Brent was finally free of Nicole and her problems, he should have been thrilled, but it was sad to see the mess she had made of her life. Even after he had no love left for her, he had wanted to believe that all the money he'd spent on her would solve her problems. He'd paid for rehab, a new apartment, new furniture, and a car thinking that was going to ensure that she could start over clean and make something of her life. He had underestimated the strength the pull of the drug lifestyle had on someone like Nicole.

When Pam called to tell Brent of Nicole's troubles, at first he didn't want to believe it. Later it got so he didn't even want to hear about it anymore. It disgusted him and made him angry each time she called.

Pam apologized for phoning. "I know how upset you get when I call," she'd said, "but I thought you should know what's going on."

"Yeah, I know. You're right," he told her. "I shouldn't take it out on you. It's not your fault I made a bad choice. I don't know why you're taking her under your wing so much though. You're a better person than I am."

"She used to be nice when you first married her. We got along like sisters. But drugs can do some ugly things to people. It's not her fault."

"Yes, it is her fault. She made the choice to take them." He sounded hard-hearted, even to himself, but Nicole had put him through so much.

"Okay, okay, I know. After she made that one little mistake, she really didn't have much of a chance."

"She had lots of chances, and I paid for most of them one way or another." The hurt pride her infidelity caused him, the shattered dreams of a future together, family, kids .... Hah! What a fool he'd been. "No, I don't owe her anything."

Pam sighed into the phone.

"Let's not argue over her," he said. "She's driving a wedge between us and I don't want that."

Pam kept calling to let him know what was going on and those were the only times they talked. He cringed when Pam called. Invariably her calls brought more bad news.

Nicole had promised to stay clean and go to work—H&R Block agreed to hire her on a trial basis— but it wasn't long before she stopped showing up for work without calling in. She had reconnected with the same old crowd and the parties now happened at her place because it was posh compared to the empty construction sites, back alleys, and abandoned buildings they were used to. Her street friends crashed there and it quickly became a flophouse. Anyone was welcome; to sleep, turn tricks, do drugs....

The car was the first thing to go. She'd practically given it away to pay for new debts she had racked up buying drugs, mostly cocaine, and then heroin and whatever was handy. The furniture followed until there was just a coffee table left, and a mattress on the floor.

"I hate to tell you this," Pam had said, "but I'm sure Nicole's been turning tricks to pay for her habit. She keeps mentioning this Leroy fellow. He's pimping her out and pocketing most of the money, and, of course, keeping her hooked on heroin."

"If I get my hands on him I'll kill the little prick," Brent growled.

"Let's hope you never meet him. Brent, these guys are bad news. You don't want to have anything to do with them. They'd as soon stick you with a knife as look at you. Just stay away."

That was a couple of months ago and now she was saying, Nicole's dead, come deal with the fallout.

"The landlord threatened to evict her," Pam told him, "but she OD'ed before that happened."

***

The smell was overpowering. Old pizza boxes and Chinese food containers with mould growing inside them littered the floor and counter. Spilled pop attracted crawlers of various sorts. The damage to the apartment was horrendous. With holes punched in the walls and doorknobs missing, there was no question of getting a damage deposit back. Brent gathered up the few personal items Nicole had left, mostly clothes and toiletries, and stuffed them in a garbage bag. The few dishes and pots and pans went into a box. He set it all beside the dumpster at the back of the building.

"Nicole told me she hadn't filed the divorce papers," Pam had said. He didn't want to believe it. Nicole wanted to be free of him. They had talked about it after the last rehab stay. They both agreed it would be best to divorce and start fresh. Pam was right, though. He found the papers in a cardboard box. She hadn't signed them or sent them in. Maybe she hoped they'd get together again.

Fat chance! More likely she was too high to deal with any business. And now, he was widowed, not divorced. Ironically, it would probably make it easier to sort out the legalities.

Brent replaced the doorknobs and hired a drywaller to fix the holes in the walls. He hired cleaners to scour the apartment while he went out to buy paint and brushes and a tray. Then he repainted the whole apartment. He saved a fair bit by doing the work himself, but he still ended up paying plenty extra, beyond what the damage deposit covered.

While Brent was painting the walls, he had a visitor. Big and burly, decked out in an expensive yellow shirt and black leather jacket, the man barged into the hallway and yelled, "Nicole! Where are you, bitch? You'd better not be holding out on me."

"Leroy?" he asked.

Leroy stopped short. "Who are you?"

"I'm Nicole's husband."

Leroy spun around, his eyes flitting back and forth like a cornered animal searching for an escape, and beat it for the door. Brent had never seen anyone move so fast. By the time he got the apartment door open again and stuck his head out into the corridor, Leroy was nowhere in sight.

A few homeless people wandered in asking if Nicole or Leroy were there. Some of them were so young, it was heartbreaking to think they were heading down the road Nicole had taken. Their whole lives ahead of them, wasted.

Nicole's funeral costs were minimal. She was cremated, no fancy box, no service, nothing. Her parents wanted nothing to do with the arrangements and other than the one phone call he made from Pam's place, he didn't hear from them again. Probably afraid they might have to reach into their wallets.

Brent slept at Pam's apartment, but Michael, her jerk of a realtor husband, treated him like a bad smell. Nothing had changed in his attitude since the first time he met Brent five years ago.

"Fisherman, eh?" he had snorted. "Guess that's an easy life. Drink a lot of beer, wait for the fish to bite. Collect employment insurance all winter."

"It's not like that at all," Brent tried to explain. "And I did go to school. Got my chartered accountant certification."

"So what happened? Couldn't get a decent job?"

"Fuck off." He wanted to punch the pompous little ass, but Pam was already biting her nails and pacing the floor. "I'll see myself out," he said. "Call you later, Pam."

Funny thing was, he had more university education than Michael did. After high school he went to the UBC Sauder School of Business, fishing with his dad in the summers to pay for it. When he got his accountant certification, he still couldn't see himself sitting in an office all day. Fishing was a good life and he had the fall to do his hunting and fly fishing. Why would he want to live and work in the city looking at cement and pavement all day? Acounting was a good skill to have to fall back on if he wanted to quit fishing, but for now, he liked fishing better.

To give Michael some credit, he was probably afraid Brent would bring some of Nicole's friends home to them. Couldn't blame him, but if Michael had given him half a chance and gotten to know him, he'd understand that Brent would never let that happen.

Brent spent little time at Pam's and she was probably relieved. Neither of them liked conflict. Even though it wasn't Brent who initiated it, he was on their turf, so he kept his mouth shut. He spent the days working at Nicole's place, eating out most of the time. He slept at Pam's, arriving late and leaving early. He bought a towel and showered at Nicole's. He would even have slept at Nicole's but he'd had to get rid of the soiled mattress right away. Probably full of lice and bedbugs.

When the Nicole ordeal was over, he took his rented car onto the ferry to Vancouver Island to visit Jim and Andrea. He stayed a couple of nights there to unwind from the nightmare. Then he did a quick detour to Victoria to have a visit with his father, before flying back to the Charlottes.

CHAPTER 35
Declan

Declan stood in the drizzling rain. The low cloud hanging over the dock mirrored his feelings. He chewed on his thumbnail. Christ! What if Clancy didn't show? Russ and his boys might take Declan for a ride in his place. He watched the road anxiously. He felt like a shit doing this to Clancy, but actually the asshole had brought it onto himself. Why the hell couldn't he keep his dick in his pants? More than once he'd told Clancy he was asking for trouble. His warnings had fallen on deaf ears. He was having too much fun, Clancy had said. Well, shit, he was going to pay for it now.

Declan waited up at the wharf head rather than down on the float, in case Clancy didn't show. He could still make a fast getaway from there. Where to, he didn't know, but for now he felt safer being out of reach. You didn't mess with Russ. He was big and mean, and seemed to get off on being that way. He'd put more than a few guys in the hospital.

Jesus, how did he get mixed up in this anyway? Just because Clancy used his house to rape his girls.... Declan figured he'd done Marlie there too. He saw the messed up house later that night, and her bruised face when he spotted her in the Co-op the next day. Clancy never even tried to cover up what he was doing. He thought he could go on forever and never get caught.

Declan had seen him leave with girls he picked up in the bar and come back for a drink later, always by himself, always with a satisfied smirk on his face. And he'd seen the wreckage at his house afterwards. He supposed he should have warned him—again—to clean up his act, but Clancy wasn't listening to anybody. Declan still didn't know why none of the girls went to the cops about his rapes. Embarrassed, most likely. Clancy was getting bolder all the time. To hear him tell it, he could jump any girl he wanted. Declan was surprised Marlie didn't go to the police. She seemed to be more educated and gutsy than some of the other girls. Clancy was always going on about her; what a feisty lay she was and how she was threatening to go to the police. He said he was managing to keep her in line and could have her again any time, but from what he could see, Clancy was forever chasing her around trying to intimidate her to keep quiet.

Declan had seen him—and smelled him—the night he came home stinking of fish after Clancy told him he slopped the fish guts on her step. He asked Declan to give him a ride to the school the day he slashed Marlie's tire. He got the hell out of there and made Clancy walk home after that. No way he wanted that kind of police attention in his business.

Only quiet time was last year when Clancy was living at Sheila's before they broke up. He still picked up girls then, but he wasn't taking them to Declan's place. Probably did them in Sheila's car. He was such a shit. But Clancy moved a lot of drugs for him, so he turned a blind eye.

"Hey, Declan!" Clancy, hood pulled over his head, came up and high-fived him. *Acts like a bloody teenager.*

Declan made a show of looking at his watch. "Jeezus, Clancy, cutting it kind of close, aren't you? I said 6 o'clock." He turned to head down the ramp.

"What's the big deal?"

"A big deal," he hissed at him over his shoulder. "That's what the big deal is. Now come on. We're running late." He glanced at his outfit. The crotch of Clancy's cargo pants near his knees nearly hobbled him as he shuffled after Declan. "You'd never make a seaman."

"Don't intend to. I hate the sea. I came to the islands from Rupert on a fish boat. Sick the whole way. I'll probably get seasick again today. Just so you know, I'm only doing this for you."

They stopped beside the Dixon E. Russ stood by the wheelhouse door, arms folded across his huge chest. "'Bout time," he growled. They scrambled aboard and Russ flicked his head towards his cousin Felix who hopped over the cap railing onto the dock to untie the big seiner. The other cousin, Hector, glanced over at them, nodding knowingly with a big shit-eating grin on his face as he caught the huge lines Felix threw to him and coiled them up on deck. Russ went into the wheelhouse and moments later, the boat slipped away from the dock.

CHAPTER 36
Marlie

A week had gone by since Clancy had run Marlie off the road to Tow Hill in Sheila's car. When that same car pulled up to her trailer she quickly made sure her door was locked, but it was Sheila, not Clancy, who came up the steps and knocked on her door.

"Sheila! What brings you over here?" Marlie opened the door wide. Sheila stood there beautiful as ever, but her face was a tight mask.

"I'm looking for Clancy," she said.

"Here?!" Marlie's eyes popped open wider.

"I've looked everywhere except here and I...." She looked away and blew out a sigh. "I thought maybe he'd moved in with you."

Marlie stared at her and her mouth dropped open. "Wha-a-at?! You've got to be kidding. I told you, he raped me. Weren't you listening?"

Sheila shrugged. "Still...."

"I want nothing to do with Clancy. Absolutely nothing. Ever!"

Sheila put her hands on her hips. "I don't believe you. He said you were always after him."

Marlie rolled her eyes and shook her head. "And you fell for that? Oh my God! Either he really is delusional, or, more likely, he's stringing you a line. Listen! The last time I saw Clancy, he ran me and my bike off the road in your car." She pointed at the car. "Check the driver's door."

Sheila's stare was expressionless and then she looked over her shoulder at the car. "I did notice a scratch.... When was this?"

"Saturday morning, a week ago."

Sheila's head tipped to the side, and she gave Marlie that "oh, come on" look. "How ridiculous! That could have been caused by anything. What possible reason could he have for running you off the road?"

"Trying to scare me. He's afraid I'll go to the police."

Sheila's pretty face turned ugly when she sneered. "I think you're just making all this up."

Marlie threw her hands into the air. "How else would I know your car was scratched?"

Sheila let out a big sigh. Then she mumbled, "I don't know....Well, he's gone. I don't know what to do. It's not like him to disappear for that long. I haven't seen him since Saturday afternoon. He said he had some business to attend to and he'd be late—not to wait up for him. I'm afraid something's happened to him."

"I don't understand how you can care about someone like Clancy."

"What do you mean 'someone like Clancy'? Like what?" Sheila asked.

"Someone who goes around raping anyone he can lure into a place where he can get away with it. He's raped several women in town."

"Oh, bullshit! And you know this because...?"

"Because they've told me. Because friends and relatives of his victims have told me."

Sheila shook her head. "No. That's not true. They're lying. He's always been really sweet to me."

Marlie snorted. "Hah! That's not the Clancy I know."

"I know you don't like him and I know he had some faults, but—"

"Some faults!?" Marlie shrugged. "Maybe you should go to the police, but knowing Clancy, he's probably off raping somebody else."

Sheila sniffed and raised her head. "You don't have to be such a bitch about it."

"Look! I can't help you. Apparently you don't believe what Clancy is capable of. I'd be careful of him, if I were you."

"He wouldn't hurt me." She began to tear up. "I really love him, and I think something bad has happened to him."

Marlie sighed, exasperated.

Sheila spun around. "I'm sorry I bothered you."

She walked away with her head down, wiping at her nose with the back of her hand.

Maybe she shouldn't have been so mean to Sheila, but the mention of Clancy's name brought out the worst in Marlie. Most likely he'd left town in a hurry after pulling some other stupid stunt. Her fist clenched and unclenched. If that creep ever showed up again....

CHAPTER 37
Marlie

No calls from Brent for nearly two weeks. Dumped. Marlie didn't know what she'd done, but he wasn't calling or dropping by. It was pretty clear he didn't want to see her anymore. She had to get over it even though all the joy had gone out of her life. Listlessly, she pushed open the staffroom door at school. She tried to pull herself together and put on a brave face as she poured herself a cup of tea. Didn't want to provide the old biddies on the couch with fodder for gossip about her. She had nodded at them as she came in, but didn't expect a response.

Tilly glanced in Marlie's direction and halfway through her next sentence to Jean, her head whipped around. "Marlie, hang on a minute." She heaved her large body off the sofa to go pick up her purse. She dug around in it and came up with a dirty, crumpled Post-it note. "Here we are. This message is for you."

Marlie reached for the note and read, "Out of town for a few days. Brent."

She stared at the note. "When did you get this?" She couldn't see Tilly taking a message this early Monday morning. She must have arrived only shortly before Marlie did.

"Let's see ... was it Thursday? No, last Wednesday. Yes, that was the day the secretary wasn't feeling well and I sat in the office over the lunch hour."

"Wednesday!? And you're just giving me the message now?" Marlie's heart beat faster as anger threatened to explode in her head.

"Well, it's not as if it was anything important. Nothing you can do about it if Brent is out of town." She sniffed. "I don't see what the big deal is."

Adrenaline continued to surge through Marlie and she fought to keep control. She felt herself getting hot and her fist itched to connect with Tilly's flabby face. She took a deep breath and tried to calm herself, but her voice came out loud and angry. "It's not your place to judge if it's important or not. You should have given me this immediately."

Tilly stuck her nose in the air and snorted. "Will you look at that, Jean? I do her a favour, and this is the thanks I get." Her eyes swept over Marlie from top to bottom. "Ungrateful wretch." She spat the words.

Marlie's hands shook so much that her tea left a trail of splashes across the staff room floor. The slopped tea trail was getting to be a recurring event, but she was beyond caring.

CHAPTER 38
Marlie

It was a cold and miserable day. Except for the note Tilly gave her, she hadn't seen Brent or heard from him since the day he did the presentation in her class more than two weeks ago. She shouldn't have let herself fall for him. Maybe she'd rushed into this relationship, too desperate to find someone special. And yet, she'd thought he could be the one. He'd said things that led her to believe they had a future together. Stupid to fall for all that sweet talk.

She should have known she didn't have that kind of luck. Men were always leaving her. James left even before she could leave him. Her father left when she was in her teens. And then there was Clancy coming on to her all nice and friendly and she was totally fooled by that predator. She shuddered.

It was the third week of November. Days were getting shorter. She drove to school in the dark and didn't get outside all day. Lately, when she left the school around 4:30, it was already dark again. With no classroom windows to the outside, the lack of daylight was starting to get to her. Even the kids couldn't cheer her up.

She told herself to snap out of it. It wasn't fair to her class. Forget about the damn sun. Forget about Brent. Concentrate on her job. The Halloween hype was long over and the kids had settled back to work, now that the sugar was out of their systems. Remembrance Day had come and gone. Time to take down the poppies they had coloured and displayed on the bulletin boards along with stories about how to get along with people so the world wouldn't have wars all the time.

A new theme was needed. This would be a good time to do something weather related—animals getting ready for winter. She wondered how she would do that herself too, getting ready to survive the long, dark winter. She tried to focus on the kids and teaching. No distractions. At least she hadn't had to deal with Clancy anymore. Sheila was always alone when she saw her in the Co-op, and Clancy was nowhere to be seen. He must have left town, maybe even the islands, and that suited her fine.

After school she cleared off her desk. She put the two big stacks of exercise books in her tote bag to mark at home. Someone knocked on her classroom door. "Come on in," she called without looking up.

"Hey, Marlie."

Her head whipped up at the familiar voice. "Brent!" Her heart thumped. "Brent!" She repeated, and ran over to him. "I can't believe it's really you."

Brent grinned. Dammit, he was so handsome. His arms pulled her in for a hug and he kissed her ... a few times. "I've missed you so much," he said.

Marlie gulped back the emotion. "Me too." She pushed away from him and held him at arm's length. "You look different."

"Is that good or bad?" He had new jeans, a soft cream coloured shirt, a tan leather vest and a black windbreaker.

"Good. Really good. Um ... I mean, you look great," she said, looking down at the floor.

"I'm sorry I didn't call but it's been a nightmare and I figured you got my message and knew I'd call as soon as I got back."

His offhand way of waving off her two weeks of misery irked her, but he seemed sincere. And yet, it was all about him and what a nightmare he had been through. What about her nightmare? She took a step back. "Actually, I didn't get the message until several days later. Tilly really has it in for me. The old biddy took that message and held off giving it to me."

"What?! Why that bitch!" Brent looked around as if to see where she was.

"Don't bother," she said. "She goes home right after the bell. Never does any prep."

Brent turned back to Marlie. "I'm sorry. I didn't think. Just thinking about myself, I guess."

Yes, you were. She put her head to the side and shrugged. "Well, I didn't know what to think. Even after I got the message, another week went by and not a sign of life from you. I thought maybe you didn't want anything more to do with me." She went back to her desk and tidied the last few things. She picked up her tote bag and turned to leave. "I guess I shouldn't have assumed...."

Brent reached for her arm. "No wait. It's just that ... well, it wasn't easy to call long distance from someone else's phone. I did try your cell phone a couple of times when I couldn't get you at home, but it said the number was out of service."

"I had to cancel my cell phone. Couldn't afford it. But there was still my landline...."

"Well, anyway I kept thinking I'd be home in a day or two."

"So why did you leave in such a hurry? You couldn't say goodbye first?" Brent's eyes widened and she regretted her question. "Never mind. It's not my business."

"No, I want to tell you, but ... not here." He hesitated. "Could we go to your place?"

"Sure. I guess so. Why not?"

Brent gave her a tentative smile. "I'll follow you over. We have a lot to talk about."

Marlie slid back into her depression. *Yeah, probably how best to end this relationship.* A black cloud settled on her shoulders and threatened to swallow her up.

CHAPTER 39
Brent

Brent had been looking forward to seeing Marlie. He had big plans for them. Her reaction to his return had him baffled. She had seemed glad to see him, but within moments she lost her initial enthusiasm. It was as if the wheels were turning in her head, probably processing his long absence, and she was spinning farther away from him with every word they exchanged. He should have thought about her feelings when he left town so suddenly, but he was all caught up in the shock of Nicole's death. He thought leaving a message at school would take care of it and that he'd be back in a couple of days. He hadn't planned to be gone so long; hadn't realized how much crap he needed to deal with to tie up the loose ends left behind by Nicole's overdose.

Brent pulled up behind Marlie's Corolla at the trailer park and stood beside her car waiting for her to get out. As she reached for her huge tote bag, he tapped her on the shoulder. "Here, let me get that for you."

She fiddled with her keys to open the trailer. Brent followed her in and set the heavy bag on the floor. "Do you always have this much work to do?"

"No. Usually I have more." Sullen. Dejected. Definitely chilly. *What the hell happened for her to pull away like that?*

He shook his head slowly. "Wow! I had no idea."

"Most people don't. They think all we do is sit behind
our desk all day." Marlie turned on the thermostat
and the furnace kicked in. She had lost her smile as
she said, "It'll warm up in a minute. Tea?" Just going
through the motions to be polite, putting up an ice wall
between them.

"Sure. That'd be nice. Here, I can put the kettle on.
You get your jacket off and sit down."

She took off her jacket and tossed it over the back
of a chair. "I think there might be some biscuits in the
fridge freezer." She turned to go get them.

"I can do it. You sit." He found the biscuits and a
plate and put them in the microwave. Moments later he
was serving tea and biscuits at the coffee table in the
living room.

"So how come you're all dressed up today?" Marlie
asked.

"I just got off the plane."

"Now?"

"Yes, an hour ago. I came right over to the school.
Haven't been home yet."

"Oh...." Marlie took a sip of her tea. "So ... you had
something you wanted to talk about?"

Brent took a deep breath and tried to muster some
courage. "I had a call from my sister. She said I had
to come to Vancouver right away to deal with some
business...." Here comes the hard part. "I told you I was
married before ... well, it turns out I never got divorced,
so I had to take care of some business—"

"You don't have to tell me all this—"

He put his hand on Marlie's wrist. "Yes, I do. I want to.
You need to know." He took a gulp of tea and continued.
"You know Nicole was a drug addict—a junkie whore—
and it finally caught up to her. She OD'ed."

Marlie's hand jumped up to cover her mouth as she gasped. "Oh no. I'm sorry."

"Yeah, it was too bad. She was a good person ... once ... but she hadn't been the person I thought she was for a long time now. She was always looking for a party, and that was great at first, but when you're trying to build a life together, you have to be serious sometimes too. She could never plan and save and wait until the time was right for buying something she wanted. Everything she did was about instant gratification."

Marlie turned to sit sideways on the couch facing him. "And how do you feel now that she died." She shook her head. "No, that sounds stupid. I mean, of course you're sad, but do you miss her terribly? Are you devastated? Or are you sad, but resigned?"

Brent nodded. "I was shocked at first when Pam phoned, but then almost right away, I wasn't surprised anymore. I always knew it was just a matter of time before something like this happened. A couple of years ago I got her into a rehab program, but when she came out, she didn't really change her habits. She didn't want to. It was right back to the drugs and parties almost as soon as she walked out of the rehab door."

"Nicole should have been married to my ex."

"We might all have been happier. Anyway, we haven't lived together for three years and the only feelings I had left for her were responsibility. Love flew out the window a long time ago."

Marlie reached for his hand. "I'm sorry you had to go through that."

He put his arm around her shoulders and pulled her close. "If I have you, I'll be fine. I'm really sorry I didn't call. I thought that with my message you'd know

I would call as soon as I got home. That bitch! I'm going to find her and talk to her—"

"No! Don't do that. It's okay. I understand now that you tried, and as far as Tilly is concerned, I'll take care of her."

"I thought I should try phoning you when it was taking longer, but it was awkward staying with my sister. And anyway, each time, I thought I'd be home in another day or so, and then something else would come up. You wouldn't believe all the stuff there was to take care of to tie up the loose ends. Paperwork and clearing out her apartment. Repairs. What a mess that was." He shuddered.

"Don't worry about it anymore. You're home now."

"And I'm so happy to see you."

"So am I." She looked towards the kitchen, bit her lip, and asked, "Would you like to stay for supper? I have some frozen spaghetti sauce I could thaw."

"How about if you bring the spaghetti sauce to my place and I'll make a fire. I could cook it while you do your schoolwork and then...."

"Then what?"

"Why don't you stay the night? Bring your pyjamas ... or not. I can keep you warm."

"Won't take me a minute."

CHAPTER 41
Marlie

Marlie's class buzzed with activity. Everyone was busy working on making a booklet featuring their favourite animal. Small groups at a time were allowed to go to the library to do research while the rest worked at writing reports and illustrating their work, or making the book cover special with their own art ideas. Half an hour before home time, Marlie gave the signal to start tidying up and putting their projects away. The buzzer rang and she dismissed the class. Moments later a crowd of children were squished together by the door.

"Ms. Mitchell, the door's stuck," Davie yelled.

They parted to let her through and she tried the door. "Hmm.... It does seem to be stuck." She took a step back and threw her shoulder into the door, which then flew open. Jared, one of the notorious little fiends from the grade five class staggered as he lost his balance after leaning against the door. "Wait a minute," she said to him.

Jared giggled and turned to run, but Marlie's arm shot out to catch hold of his collar. He swung around, yelled "Fuck you!" and swung at her with fists, first a right and then a left. Luckily, her reach was longer than his.

At that point, she said, "Okay, looks like we have a detour to make on your way home. Let's go see Mr. Dupuis."

Jared pulled and pushed all the way to the office. Marlie struggled to hang onto him as she knew he would run if she didn't. Mr. Dupuis' door was open just a crack and as they got near it, Jared's flailing arms pushed it open.

It took her a second or two to grasp the situation, but she nudged Jared toward the hall and said, "You go home and don't you ever mess with my door again."

She didn't have to tell Jared twice to get the hell out of there, but then she had to extricate herself from the embarrassing circumstances. Mr. Dupuis had spun around to face the wall away from her as they came crashing through the door, and someone dropped from her knees down onto all fours, saying, "I can't see it here. Your pen must have rolled away someplace."

Marlie stood transfixed, as Mr. Dupuis, having yanked his fly up, turned his red face towards her. "Never mind the pen, Tilly. I have others. The janitor will find it later."

Tilly stood up, grabbed a tissue from Mr. Dupuis's desk and rushed out of the room swiping at her mouth.

Before Mr. Dupuis could call Marlie back, she followed Tilly out of the office, nearly stepping on her heels.

Marlie's father had always said, "Don't put off to tomorrow what you can do today." She thought she might as well seize the moment. Why give Tilly time to make up excuses and tell Marlie later that she didn't see what she saw?

She followed Tilly into her classroom and closed the door firmly behind her. "Now wait just a minute," Tilly said. "If you think—"

"Shut it, Tilly." Power can be a wonderful thing sometimes, and at that moment, Marlie felt like superwoman. "I think you've had your mouth open enough for one afternoon."

Tilly spluttered and searched for words, but only, "But, but, but," came out of her mouth. She reached for a tissue from her desk and mopped her brow.

"Going through a lot of tissues this afternoon, aren't you?"

"It's not what you think—"

"It's exactly what I think. You're not going to weasel out of this one."

"What do you want here?"

"I'll tell you exactly what I want. So sit down and listen carefully." Marlie waited until she sank into her desk chair. She put her hands on the desk and leaned forward to put her face closer to Tilly's. Enunciating every syllable, Marlie told her, "You have been mean and rude to me ever since I arrived here. It's time you apologized for that."

Tilly's chin quivered.

She drummed her fingers on Tilly's desk. "I'm waiting...."

"I-I-I'm s-sorry," she whimpered.

"And you'll be polite to me from now on."

Tilly swallowed a lump in her throat. "Yes."

"Apology accepted."

Tilly made a move to get up, but Marlie put her hand up to stop her. "Uh-uh-uh! We're not done yet."

Her eyes flicked back and forth searching out escape routes, but finding none, Tilly had no choice but to sink back down into her chair.

"You also owe me a huge apology for keeping that phone message from me."

This time Tilly didn't hesitate. "Yes, I'm sorry about that."

"And you're sorry for talking to Jean about me so rudely, right?"

"Yes, yes, I am."

Marlie plucked a tissue out of the Kleenex box and handed it to her. "Here, Tilly. You're sweating. Most unbecoming for a lady."

"Are we done now?" Tilly asked.

"Almost." She hesitated, put her finger to her cheek as if she were thinking. "There's one more thing. Actually two."

"Yes?"

"I have recess duty every Wednesday. From now until Christmas, you'll do my supervision duties for me."

Tilly's jaw dropped.

"Close your mouth, Tilly. That has been the whole cause of your problem."

"Why you sassy—"

Marlie waggled her finger at her. "Uh-uh-uh! Manners please. You promised to be polite to me from now on."

Tilly clamped her mouth shut and let a long sigh escape through her nose. "And what's the last thing?"

"You will tell Jean that from now on I expect her to be polite to me too."

"I can't do that. How can I make Jean do anything?"

"Well, if you can't figure out a way, then I suppose there could be rumours starting around the school district about why some teachers are getting preferential treatment and what they do to get it."

"You wouldn't dare!"

"Try me. So do I need to put these things in writing— about recess duty, and getting your sidekick under control—or will you remember?

"I'll manage."

"Good." Marlie turned to leave Tilly's classroom. At the door, she turned and smiled at her. "And Tilly, I'm so glad we're going to be on good terms from now on."

CHAPTER 40
Marlie

That evening, doing her schoolwork at Brent's house, staying over, and going to school from there, Marlie realized how comfortable and secure she felt in that scenario. The sex was great and she found being around Brent such a turn on. If only it could last forever. But what reason did she have to think that this was going to last? After Brent's return from Vancouver, sometimes days went by without a phone call and then, suddenly, Brent would call and he acted as if nothing had changed since the last time they were together, as if she would always be there whenever he felt like calling. It was always on his terms. For Brent, she was probably a convenient bed warmer, and company when he wanted someone to talk to. The rest of the time he could do just fine without her. Of course he could.

He'd been living on his own for at least three years. His house was well looked after and he seemed to have everything figured out. And Marlie saw the way women looked at him. Even watched one practically rub up on him when she asked directions to the grocery store that was down the block. He didn't seem to mind, grinning the whole time he gave her directions, pointing down the street to the Co-op and her leaning on his arm to see where he was pointing. Did she need that in her life? Sure he hadn't done anything wrong except enjoy that encounter, but did she want to be in competition for the rest of her life?

Marlie didn't like feeling so vulnerable. She had job security, so she would be financially secure, but emotionally, she had almost no defenses left. She loved Brent so much. How could she have let this happen? He had never said he loved her. Sure, he said nice things, but he had never said those three magic words, "I love you." If she let herself believe in him and he dumped her, she would be a wreck. She'd already had a taste of that while he'd been away.

She had also been through this with James and although their relationship hadn't been anywhere near as hot as Brent's and hers, she hadn't forgotten how lonely and insecure she had felt for months while she tried to put herself back together after they parted. She had dreaded having to tell her mother that she and James were history.

Her mother's gossipy friend Madge worked at the bank where Marlie had her account.

"I'm opening a new account and you can take my name off the joint account I have with James," Marlie told her. She moved all but one dollar from the joint account to her new one – not that there was much left to move.

"Oh?" Madge raised her eyebrows. "Trouble in Paradise? I see you've got some bruises."

"We're history. So there's no way James should be allowed to access my money anymore, right?"

"That's right," Madge said. "You take care now."

She wasn't surprised when her mother called her soon afterwards. "Think you're better than the rest of us? You should have listened to me. I told you that lout was no good. But no-o-o-o! Marlie knows everything better."

On and on she vented until Marlie finally said, "Okay, Mom. I get it. I'm going to hang up now. Bye."

It was not what she needed just then. Her last nickel went to James's leg-breaking debt collectors. It was a good thing her mom couldn't see the bruises on Marlie's arms, and the black eye they had given her. She moved to a tiny basement suite that was barely affordable. She had no groceries and no money to buy any with, and it was still three days till payday.

Marlie knew she had less than $10 in her account, but she thought she could use her debit card to buy some hamburger and make a Sloppy Joe's kind of meat and gravy with macaroni for supper. She could make it last for two more days and then she'd be okay with another paycheque coming into the bank. She went to a local grocery store and picked up the cheapest pack of hamburger she could find. $3.49 was a pretty good price for three suppers. She waited in line for what seemed like ages. She'd had a long day on her feet and a shabby, empty suite to go home to. She'd cleared out of their old apartment quickly for her own safety. The one-room basement suite had a portable two-burner electric hotplate, and she had a couple of pots and a frying pan. She'd brown that mince and add some water and thicken it. Then she'd pour it over boiled noodles. She was hungry enough to eat anything.

At last she got to the cashier, who rang the hamburger through. Marlie took out her debit card and the cashier said, "Sorry, we don't take debit for amounts under $4.00."

"Well, that's all I've got with me to pay with," she said.

"Sorry. You could buy something else to go with it."

She knew she didn't have that much money in the account, and she didn't want to have the card rejected if she bought something else. "Look, couldn't you make an exception this once. Add on the service charge or whatever you need to do."

"Sorry. Those are the manager's rules. Would you like me to call the manager?"

"Over $3.49?" Marlie gave her a look of disbelief and walked out of the store without the hamburger. She knew her face was red. She was humiliated, angry, tired, hungry, frustrated, and desperately unhappy. She had worked so hard all day and now she was slapped down again.

After a few sobs in the car, Marlie went home to her dreary basement and sat in the armchair with her legs curled up under her. She stared out the sliding glass door to the backyard and watched the rain streaming down. After a while she didn't know what was rain and what was tears. It seemed as if she had nothing to live for. No matter how hard she worked, she would never be able to climb out of this hole.

She lay in her bed that night and listened to the rats chewing in the walls. That was when she made up her mind to apply for jobs far away. She got a job interview soon afterwards and was hired to work in Masset the following September. Maybe a change of scene would turn things around for her.

Now, as she looked back on the misery of those days, she didn't want to go through that kind of depression again. She had to get some control back in her life. So when Brent called the next day, she put him off. She had a lot of work to do. She had no time for dinner. She was miserable all night, but better to cut the cord now than be hurt badly later.

The next day he called after school. "Thought we might go grab a cup of coffee."

"Oh, I can't, Brent. I have to get report cards done. I'll be at it all evening."

The day after that Marlie had a meeting and couldn't come over. The next day they had parent-teacher interviews and she would be at school late.

"Marlie, talk to me!" Brent said on his next call. "We were good, weren't we?"

"Yeah," she said, wishing her voice didn't sound so mousy.

"Well, what changed?"

"I don't want to talk about it." Her voice choked up. "I can't. I just can't," she sniffed.

"I wish you wouldn't do this.... Marlie? Marlie, talk to me, please."

She hung up. Brent stopped calling. One rainy day in late November, reality hit her. She had her wish. She had broken off their relationship. It was then that she started to slide down the tunnel faster than before. She worked long hours and went back to school to work in the evenings. She was never home. Not that she ever called that trailer home.

CHAPTER 42
Declan

Inside the spacious wheelhouse of the Dixon E., Russ sat at the helm guiding the boat out of the Masset Slough into the inlet.

Declan couldn't bring himself to meet Clancy's eyes.

"Big job tonight, eh?" Clancy said to Russ as he held onto the walls for stability.

Declan winced and turned his face away lest it betray him.

Russ grunted. "Yeah. Sumpin' like that."

"Wow! Look at all the electronics."

"Don't even think about it," Russ snarled. "We know all about your sticky fingers."

Clancy raised his hands and ducked his head. "Just admiring, that's all." He backed away from Russ and turned to Declan for help. "Good to know this boat has all the modern stuff on it. Radar, sounder, radios, the best. Good to have for traveling at night. Can't see a thing. Crap weather, and dark already. But hey, this is a huge boat, so it's pretty safe, right Declan?"

"Why don't you step out onto the deck? In case you get sick," he said. "You never did travel well, did you?" He felt sorry for Clancy, but he had his own skin to look after, so he tried his best to keep Clancy calm and out of Russ's way.

Out on the deck, Declan lowered his voice and said, "Look, Clancy, I don't like doing business with Russ and his cousins—"

"No kidding, eh? That Russ has got to be the scariest guy I ever met. What is it with him anyway? Bad mood?"

Declan waved off the suggestion. "Naw, he's always like that." He took a big breath. "But look here. Let's just get this trip over with and try to keep out of his way. The less said, the better."

"Suits me," Clancy said. "I'll be glad to get back on dry land. I hate boats. After this, I don't care what the job is. Promise me you won't make me go out on any more trips like this."

Declan was glad for the darkness, as he had trouble meeting Clancy's eyes. "No problem. I can guarantee that."

CHAPTER 43
Marlie

Marlie couldn't figure out why she hadn't seen Clancy anymore. He'd been so persistent in his harassment of her. She saw Cheryl in the coffee shop one day and asked her if she had seen Clancy. "No, I haven't, but if I did, it would be too soon."

At volleyball nights, she saw that Sheila had given up on him and Ryan had moved back in with her. It was the Queen Charlotte Shuffle all over again. She heard a rumour that Declan had suddenly left town. He had flown out the day after she last saw Clancy, leaving behind all his belongings in his shack. That was over three weeks ago and he hadn't returned. Neither of them had. No loss.

Tilly's good behavior made life easier at work. Even Jean had somehow been enlisted to be polite, if not friendly to her. Marlie launched herself into her schoolwork completely, spending long days working in her classroom. As the first days of December passed, the short hours of daylight became even shorter. She certainly had nothing to go home to.

She focused on making life at school as happy as she could. These kids should not have to pay for her unhappiness. They had troubles of their own. She played Christmas music softly in the background while they worked. Marlie walked up and down the rows of desks, helping the kids with their spelling as they wrote Christmas stories and illustrated them. When she stopped by Heather's desk, the girl kept on working and seemed to be unaware of her teacher standing there. As she coloured her Christmas drawing, Heather sang so softly that Marlie could barely hear her. "Rudolf the red-nosed reindeer...." She had never imagined that this shy little girl would find an outlet in Christmas music. It was the first time she had heard her sing. Heather's voice was surprisingly deep and mellow for such a skinny girl, but she was right on key and sang beautifully. Marlie blinked back tears. *There's so much more to these kids than I thought.*

Marlie cut out a big paper Christmas tree and pinned it to the wall. Each child made a decoration for it using ribbons, beads, buttons, glitter, and whatever else they wanted to glue onto it. On the back they were allowed to make a wish and then they pinned the decoration onto the tree.

Those last days before the holidays were a flurry of activity at school. They baked Christmas cookies one day. While the cookies were baking, they decorated a party hat of the kind that came out of the Christmas crackers. They put their hats on and had a party at the end of the day with the cookies and juice. Christmas carols played and the class sang along. The kids were happy.

Christmas break was coming soon and Marlie had no plans to go anywhere. It would be a dreary two weeks. During those last days of school, she pasted on a fake smile, but her nights were long hours of misery where she cried her heart out. She had cut Brent out of her life, but she couldn't get him out of her head.

CHAPTER 44

Brent

When Pam called to tell Brent about Nicole, he had left abruptly. He didn't think he'd be gone for two weeks, so when he got home, in the middle of November, there were things he had to take care of—like the rotting food in the fridge. He'd forgotten about that when he asked Marlie to come home with him and have supper. The first time the fridge door opened, he was reminded that he had fucked up. It reeked! He told Marlie to leave it and not open the fridge again. They threw together a spaghetti dinner with his pasta and her tomato sauce that she brought along. The next morning after Marlie left for school, he tackled the mess.

The milk had soured days ago. The big smelly lumps didn't want to go down the drain until he stirred them to break them up. The lettuce in the crisper was anything but crisp. He brought a garbage bag over and dumped in the slimy mess. Mouldy oranges and limp celery were next. Half a loaf of bread and a stale muffin ... what a waste. It wasn't how he normally functioned, but times were anything but normal.

He tied the garbage bag tightly and took it outside to put into the garbage can. A vehicle was coming down the driveway. *What the hell? A police cruiser?*

The local constable, Jack Woodley, got out. "Hi, Brent. How's it going?"

Oh, shit! They know about Clancy. "Good ....
Everything okay?" His knees were Jell-O.

"Mind if I talk to you?"

"Sure, what's up?" he asked. "Kind of a long way
from town, aren't you?"

Woodley smiled. "Nice to get away once in a while."
He looked around as if wondering where to sit.

Brent pointed to the door. "Would you like to come
in?"

"Actually, this will only take a minute. Maybe we
can stand under your porch roof out of the rain. We're
looking for Clancy Morgan." He watched Brent's face
closely.

"Out here?" Brent's brow wrinkled. "Why would he
be out here?" *Holy shit. Maybe he put in a complaint
when I punched him.* His stomach did a flip-flop. He
fought to keep a neutral face.

"No reason, but he's gone missing. Sheila George
put in a missing person report. Said she hadn't seen
him in about two weeks."

"Sheila? Why Sheila? I thought he was staying at
Declan's place."

"Funny thing is, Declan's gone too." Woodley looked
puzzled as if this was the first time he'd thought there
might be a connection. "But apparently Clancy was
living with Sheila ... again, and she can't figure out
where he is. Nobody's seen him."

*God! I hope he isn't dead in the parking lot behind The
Bunker.* "And you're out here asking me because...?"

"We're checking all possible leads. You're friendly
with Marlie Mitchell." Woodley took out his black
notebook and flipped it open. "Yeah, here it is. She's
reported several instances of mischief that she's sure
Clancy is responsible for—fish guts dumped on her

porch, slashed tire, smashed headlight, graffiti on the trailer, dead rat on the porch, and some confrontations in town."

Brent's fists clenched. *Should have killed the bastard when I had the chance.* "What?! Really? I wasn't aware of that. She didn't say anything to me. I knew she'd had a run in with him at the Co-op one day because I was there and saw him stomping out like a crazy man and she seemed upset, but I didn't know about the rest."

"So you wouldn't have maybe taken revenge on him?"

He laughed. "I'd have to get in line. I'm sure there are a lot of other people who would like to teach him a lesson."

"For what?" he asked.

"He's got quite a reputation for making babies on young girls who didn't want his attentions. He doesn't know the meaning of the word 'no.' That's what I've heard around town anyway." Brent hesitated, and added, "But you probably already know that."

"You're sure you haven't seen him?"

He shook his head. "Nope, and it'll be too soon when I do."

"He was last seen on the Saturday before last. Where might you have been that day?"

Whew! So I didn't kill him with that punch. That was the previous Tuesday night. He snorted. "Hah! Normally I probably wouldn't remember, but I just got back from Vancouver yesterday. I've been gone for a couple of weeks. My ex-wife died and I had to take care of some business."

"Oh, sorry to hear that," Jack said. "Well, I won't bother you any more about this. It's strange that he dropped out of sight."

"Maybe things got too hot for him and he left town," he suggested.

"No record of him flying out."

"There are boats. He might have hitched a ride. Or he might have taken the ferry."

"Yeah, he might." Jack climbed back into his cruiser. "Nobody except Sheila seems too concerned, but we have to follow up. Seems like pretty much a dead end. Well, thanks for your time."

A dead end would be exactly what that prick deserved, but he doubted they'd be so lucky.

***

So with Clancy out of the picture, everything should have been on track for Marlie and him. What he couldn't figure out was why Marlie pulled the plug on them. No explanation. Nothing. He wanted to marry her—just hadn't found the right time to ask her. It didn't seem like a good idea to ask right after Nicole died. He never got the chance later. She dumped him just when he thought things were going really well. He couldn't figure it out.

Those first few times when she put him off, he believed her when she said she was busy and that they'd get together later on, but finally she came out with it—sort of—that they were finished. But then why was she crying? And he thought he understood women!

Brent sat around thinking about Marlie many a night, but it was pretty clear she'd had enough of him.

On days when Jeff wasn't hired out for a job with his excavator, Brent went duck hunting with him to keep busy and try to get his mind off Marlie. The weeks went by slowly. He had a lot of good duck and goose shoots all through late November, but in the evenings when he sat in the house alone, plucking the birds, all he could think of was Marlie.

November slipped into December. Going duck hunting meant getting up early—way before daylight. On one of those outings with Jeff, they drove the 28 miles to Port Clements and out the logging road to the mouth of the Yakoun River. In the dark, they put his skiff in and motored across to the other side of the river mouth. It was pretty wide there, but the point of land on the far side provided some shelter from the worst of the wind. In the first hint of daylight, he navigated by the silhouettes of huge tree stumps that dotted the mouth of the river. They were like islands, these uprooted trees that had floated downriver until they got hung up in the shallow sandbars of the estuary.

They set up a string of decoys at Cope and Johnny Point, and hid behind blinds they'd made up from folding aluminum frames with burlap stretched over them. Two small folding stools with canvas seats added some comfort in the blind and they were all set. It had been a lot of equipment to pile into the skiff along with Jake, Jeff's Labrador retriever, but they figured it was worth it, as they could then make a day of it, and it was only a short trip across the river.

They got the decoys set in the water and the blinds up with only moments to spare. The ducks started coming in at first light. Jake was in his prime, instinctively knowing what to do. He stayed behind the blind until one of them fired a shot. Then he sat tall and marked the spot where the ducks fell and on Jeff's signal, he bounded into the water and swam out to retrieve the ducks. He brought the birds to Jeff and slipped back behind the cover of the blind without even being told, to wait for the next flight. The only thing Brent could fault that dog for was that he always came over to stand by him to shake the water off his coat.

By early afternoon they had nearly all the ducks they were allowed to shoot. "This has been a great day, Jeff."

"You should get yourself another dog," Jeff said. "You love duck hunting. You need a dog."

"I know. And I wouldn't go hunting without one. But that's why I have you, right?"

Jeff laughed. "I guess you're stuck with me then, until you find another hunting buddy with a dog."

"It's going to have to stay that way for now anyway. I can't justify having a dog when I'm away from home all summer. I wouldn't be able to look after it. I felt bad enough asking the neighbours to take care of Juno in the summertime when I was away fishing. Now that he's gone, I'll hold off getting another one until I figure out what I'm going to do."

"That's the problem with being a fisherman. You're away from home a lot. But it's not as bad as those fishermen who come up here from Vancouver Island. They don't get to go home all summer. At least you can spend a night or two at home between trips."

"Still not enough to have a dog."

"What you need is a wife."

"What? To look after the dog?" Brent laughed.

"To look after everything. The dog and you."

He sat quietly waiting for ducks and Jeff kept talking. "Say whatever happened to that teacher you were seeing? What was her name? She was a looker."

"Marlie." He nearly choked on her name. "We're history."

"What happened? If you don't mind me asking...."

Brent hesitated as he tried to explain what happened. Then he snorted. "Hah! I don't really know what happened. Everything was great. I even thought I'd ask her to marry me, and then she started putting me off when I called. She was always too busy, or she had a meeting, or she had report cards to write. Always something."

"Do you think she found someone else?"

"No, I don't think so. I mean, she could have anyone, but she sounded miserable. Last time I talked to her I could swear she was crying on the phone."

"Sounds like she's not through with you yet."

"Oh yeah. She is."

"How do you know?"

"I never got anywhere with her on the phone. Finally she wouldn't even pick up when I called."

"What are you going to do about it?"

He shrugged. "Nothing to do. She's moved on."

"If you care about her, go get her. To hell with the phone. You need to go charm her in person." Jeff looked at him and shook his head as if he couldn't understand why he hadn't pursued such a simple plan yet. "Look, we've got enough ducks for today. Let's pack it up. I think you have a place you need to be tonight."

Brent knew Jeff was right, but what if Marlie just shut the door in his face again? Could he stand one more rejection?

They threw the decoys and the blinds into the skiff and headed across the Yakoun. A couple of times the skiff hit bottom and Jeff stuck the oar in the sand to push them off. "We're getting out of here just in time. Tide's going out. This place will be one huge mudflat in another hour."

"I know," Brent said. "I've spent a few extra hours in the skiff out here, waiting for the tide to lift me off the mudflats." Wouldn't have been so bad killing time if Marlie had been with him. He replayed their stay on Cub Island after she had saved the skiff at the Bar of Fright. What was the use? She was done with him. He let out a long sigh.

And yet, he thought about what Jeff had said as they drove home. He hadn't pushed Marlie very hard. Maybe she needed to know how he felt. But he had waited so long now, it felt awkward to approach her. He didn't know if he could do it. If he was wrong, and she turned him down again, he'd be embarrassed. Anyway, by the time he got home it was already kind of late. Maybe tomorrow ... or not.... He mulled it over as he drifted off to sleep that night.

It was getting close to Christmas and he had absolutely no plans. He wouldn't have minded going someplace warm—Mexico maybe—but there wasn't much point, without Marlie. He'd be just as well off to sit by his fireplace for warmth and save himself the plane fare.

CHAPTER 45
Brent

The following Friday was the last day of school before Christmas break. Brent put on a shirt that he knew Marlie liked, and a pair of his newer jeans. He got himself spiffied up as much as he dared without looking like a city dandy. He brought a book to read while he parked across the road, waiting for her to come home after school.

The wind whipped the tree branches around sending smaller broken bits flying. It wouldn't surprise him if the power went out. Normal conditions for December in the Charlottes. He had made a quick stop at the wharf to check the boat. He put extra lines on the Huckleberry for security against the wind, and made sure the bladders were in place. Didn't want some other boat rubbing up against his, gouging the wood. Around four o'clock, the sky darkened and black clouds scudded across the sky dumping waterfalls of rain. He hoped the weather was not an indication of how his meeting with Marlie would go.

Marlie's Corolla splashed through the potholes. He had a clear line of sight from where he had parked the truck. She pulled up the hood of her jacket before getting out to open the back door to take out two huge bags most likely filled with schoolwork, as usual. What else were holidays for? Then she rushed to her trailer door hunched over to escape the worst lashes of rain.

Brent gave her a few minutes to get her boots and coat off and made a dash through the rain to her trailer. On her porch in the shelter of the joey shack, he took a deep breath and knocked. She opened the door and stood like a statue, half in shock. "Brent!" she said. "Er … would you like to come in?" Her face flushed pink and she turned away quickly. He hoped that meant she still had feelings for him.

"I came to wish you Merry Christmas … and to see how you are … and to find out why … why you won't see me or speak to me." There, he'd said it. Breaking the ice was hard work, and from the expressionless face looking back at him, he needed to keep chipping. "I'm sorry to drop in on you without phoning, but you wouldn't pick up if I did."

"Come sit down. I can m-make us a cup of t-tea." She sounded flustered, stammering the words.

He came in and sat on the couch before she could change her mind. "No, don't bother with the tea, Marlie. I just want to talk to you. Is that okay? Just talk?"

She lowered herself onto the couch on the side farthest away from him. "Okay, what would you like to talk about?"

"I need to know what happened. Why did you cut me loose? Is it something I said? Something I did?"

Marlie had a pained look on her face. She chewed her lip, and her fingers fidgeted and trembled around the hem of her top. Finally she pulled herself up and sat taller. "I didn't think it was going anywhere with us. You didn't seem to care. You didn't even bother to phone when you were in Vancouver and then you thought we could just pick up where we left off—wherever that was...."

Brent sighed. *The phone business again.* "I told you it was hard for me to phone—"

"What's so hard about picking up a phone and dialing my number?" she choked out as tears welled in her eyes.

"I left you a message to explain. I didn't know that bitch hadn't given it to you. I thought I'd be back in a couple of days and then when it all took a lot longer, it wasn't easy. My brother-in-law doesn't like to have me around. We're like the city mouse and the country mouse only not that friendly. We tolerate each other because of Pam being my sister. I slept there and that's about all. I arrived late in the evening each day and left early in the morning. I didn't feel welcome there and didn't want to use their phone to call long distance. I don't have a cell phone. I use a satellite phone on the boat and a landline at home. Anyway there was no privacy at Pam's place and no phone at Nicole's. I didn't realize what a disaster Nicole's apartment was and it took a lot longer to make repairs and clean it up. I had thought I'd be home in a couple of days."

"Oh," she said quietly. "I had no idea."

"I thought things had been going so well for us."

She shrugged her shoulders and slumped on the couch. "I didn't know what you thought, other than that the sex was good. But where was it going with us? I had no way of knowing how you felt. I still don't know."

Brent reached over to touch her arm, but she pulled it away. *This is not going well. Come on, Brent, or you're going to blow it.* "You've got to be kidding me. You have to know how I feel about you."

"Well, you said nice things, but that's what friends do. And this is the awkward thing about friends."

"What do you mean?" he asked.

"Friends can be friends forever, but how do we know when we're more than friends? It may never go beyond that. Okay, I suppose we already have gone beyond that, but only in a physical way. It seems convenient."

He stared at her. "You think we had sex because it was convenient?"

"No, not like that, but I mean ... what if someone else came along that was handy and sexy and convenient? Then you could have sex with her and say 'That's okay. Marlie won't mind. We're just friends.'"

"Marlie! You know I wouldn't do that."

"How do I know that?

"Because we're friends."

"I rest my case. So, okay, we can stay friends." She got up to put her books away and fussed with a few things. "Have a good night, Brent."

Then she turned and said, "Was there anything else?"

"Yes, there's a lot more." He swallowed. This was so hard and she was not making it any easier.

One of them had to go out on a limb and be the first to admit to having more feelings than just friends. That person would be vulnerable to being slapped down hard with rejection. He supposed it might as well be him. What did he have to lose?

"Marlie, you know I care about you?"

Head hanging, she nodded and whispered, "Yup. I care about you too."

"And that's all?" he asked.

She let out a big sigh. "Okay, I admit it. I had to shut you out because I have very bad luck with men.

James, my 'ex-partner,' was a shit. My father simply left. Clancy took advantage and hurt me—at least that hurt was only physical. If I let myself feel what I feel for you and it doesn't work out—and with my luck, there's a good chance it won't—I'd be hurt all over again, worse than ever before."

He reached out and held Marlie by the arms and looked into her face. "Marlie, look at me, please. I will never hurt you. I promise."

She closed her eyes. "I'm protecting myself, just in case."

"But what about me? What about how I feel?" he asked.

"How do you feel? I don't really know."

He reached up to grab his head in frustration. "How could you not know?"

"You never said," she choked out. "You say nice things but you never say how you really feel."

"Marlie, you're the most important person in my life." He was close to begging, but if he had to beg, he would. "Don't you love me a little bit?"

She spun away from him. "Hah! You're asking me that? What does it matter what I think or feel? You don't care. Not really."

"I care. I care a lot."

She stuck her face close to his. "How much?" she asked defiantly.

"More than you, apparently."

She shook her head hard. "No. No, no, no. Never more than me."

"And you know this because...."

"Because you've never said you love me. Not once!"

"I didn't think you wanted to hear anything so mundane. Everybody says that so easily and it ends up meaning nothing. You don't want to hear that."

Tears spilled over as she fought through the words. "It's not so easy to say, nobody says it to me, it does mean a lot, and yes I do want to hear that."

He took her in his arms. "Marlie, shhh...." After a moment, he pushed her away from him gently to hold her at arm's length. "Well, dammit, if you're going to make me say it out loud.... I do love you ... with all my heart—"

"Oh, Brent," she sobbed into his shoulder. "Me too." She held him tightly while he stroked the back of her head.

"Please say you're not going to make us go through this again?"

"I promise, I won't."

CHAPTER 46
Declan

Declan wished he were anywhere but on the Dixon E. He had a bad feeling about what was to come.

Near the mouth of the inlet, the waves of the open water slapped harder at the bow but it hardly affected the motion of the big seine boat. The deck was wide and that added a lot of stability. The stern of the boat was messy. It smelled like some old humpies were stuck in the scuppers somewhere. Nothing like the stench of rotten fish to unsettle a queasy stomach. Upturned buckets, a couple of gaffs, and a rusty fish knife lay in the back of the boat. You'd have to watch where you walked if you were working in the stern.

Tonight, no one was going to be working—at least not at fishing. Declan didn't know what the plan was, but he knew Clancy was in for trouble. He suspected they wanted to give him a good beating for what he did to Laurie. He hoped they'd remember that he wasn't in on it with Clancy, and that they didn't get too carried away.

"How far out is this drop?" Clancy asked.

"Out by the weather buoy in Dixon Entrance. There should be a package tied to the buoy and we have to hook into it and haul it aboard." Declan was surprised at how easily he came up with this bullshit. "Not too much farther now."

Half an hour later the sea was heavier and even a boat the size of the Dixon E. pounded into the waves. An icy wind had come up, slicing through clothing like a knife to the bone.

Clancy came back into the wheelhouse. "Sure is pissin' down out there."

Russ and his crew said nothing. Clancy gave Declan a nervous smile. "We must be almost there, eh?"

"About another two hours."

"Jeezus! That long?"

"Have a beer." Russ tossed a can of Lucky over to Clancy. Felix and Hector passed a joint back and forth. They cranked up the music and the wheelhouse walls vibrated with the pounding beat of George Thorogood's "Bad to the Bone."

Russ joined in, singing the refrain, "B-b-b-b-bad to the bone." His grin took on an evil leer, his face and teeth reddish from the glow of the radar screen.

When the song was over, Russ turned the volume down and stared at Clancy. "I heard you know my little sister."

"I do?" Clancy frowned. "What's her name?"

"Laurie...."

In the dim light reflected from the instrumentation in the wheelhouse, Declan saw the fear in Clancy's face. His eyes were huge.

"Oh yeah, heh-heh." He swallowed hard. "Laurie, right. She's real pretty."

"She didn't look too pretty when she came home the other night ... with that big bruise on her face ... and a cut lip ... and a black eye...." With each injury he listed Russ moved closer to Clancy who was cowering in the corner of the bench.

"Y-y-you can't think I had anything to do with that?" Clancy stammered.

Russ backed off and drawled, "Naw... I don't think that...."

Clancy's breath came out in a shaky nervous titter. He gasped as Russ lunged forward and bellowed in his face, "I KNOW it!"

Declan was almost pissing himself and he suspected Clancy already had. Russ turned to his cousins. "Felix, go find the rustiest gutting knife we got." He rubbed his hands together and grinned. "We're gonna teach this little fucker a lesson."

Declan had never seen anyone move as fast as Clancy did. He was out through the wheelhouse door before any of the crew could lay a hand on him. He shrieked as he tore out onto the deck. "No-o-o! I didn't do anything. I didn't do it. It wasn't me."

Felix went out onto the deck and groped around in the stern. He found the gutting knife that had been carelessly left lying around. He sneered at Clancy showing a mouthful of bad teeth, and giggled as he waved the knife in front of his face.

Clancy was blubbering now, still babbling hysterically, "It wasn't me. I didn't do anything. You gotta believe me."

Felix took a swipe at Clancy and sliced the sleeve of his hoodie.

"Felix!" Russ bellowed. "Bring me that knife."

Reluctantly, Felix handed the knife over. "Now," Russ said, as he tested the knife for sharpness, "this isn't very sharp, but we'll have to do the best we can. Hector, you and Felix grab a hold of that little fucker. Hold him tight. I'm gonna cut off his balls so he'll never get the urge to mess with a girl again."

Clancy screamed like a stuck pig and they hadn't even touched him yet. He made a dash for the stern of the boat, slipping on the deck, grabbing hold of rigging as the boat lurched in the waves. Hector reached for him and snagged the sliced sleeve, but Clancy was desperate and found strength Declan was sure he didn't know he had. The bottom of the sleeve tore off and Clancy kept moving towards the back of the boat. He clambered over ropes and buckets. Felix lunged but missed him. Clancy held onto the side of the drum frame and made his way towards the back of the heaving boat.

Russ roared with laughter. He doubled over gasping for breath between bursts of laughter. "Felix, Hector, leave him alone." He wheezed and laughed. "This is more fun than getting it over with. Let him worry about it for a while."

Clancy looked around frantically with nowhere left to go. "Declan! Help me! For Christ's sake, Declan! Help me!"

Russ and the cousins sobered up and whirled to face Declan. "Sorry, Clancy," he called out. "You got yourself into this. It's out of my hands." He was nearly shitting himself in case they turned on him next.

"Okay, that's it," Russ said. "Let's get this job done. Grab him boys."

Clancy stepped out onto the stern roller that the seine net slides over. "Don't come near me."

He'd gone as far back as he could go.

Poor guy didn't know that the roller wasn't meant for standing on. It was, after all, for rolling, and roll it did. Clancy disappeared into the inky blackness behind the boat. Declan would never get that shriek out of his head as long as he lived.

"He's fallen overboard!" he yelled. "Russ! He's gone overboard!"

Russ straightened up and looked out into the darkness. "I don't see anyone. Did you see anyone fall overboard, Felix? Hector?" He looked at Declan then and felt the edge of the rusty knife in his hands. "Did you see anyone fall overboard, Declan?"

He shook his head vigorously.

"Good. No one saw anyone go overboard, so it didn't happen." He fingered the knife one more time and stared at him. Then, blessedly, Russ turned away and said, "Now let's get the fuck outta here."

CHAPTER 47
Brent

Brent asked Marlie how she felt about a low-key Christmas wedding. Low key was all he could handle anyway. She loved the idea. So the next Tuesday when the weather calmed down, they caught a flight to Vancouver, rented a car and took the ferry to Vancouver Island. It was a 90-minute drive from Nanaimo up island to Comox. The pace was slower there, much more to his liking.

The GPS in the rental took them right to Jim and Andrea's door. Christmas lights on the deck and nearby shrubs blinked a cheery welcome.

Jim and Andrea rushed out to the car. They hugged liked long-lost friends who had found each other again, and perhaps that wasn't far from the truth.

"We have so much planned for you two," Andrea said. "Marlie, you and I are going clothes shopping tomorrow. The caterers and marriage commissioner are booked for Friday. Nothing for us to do except make ourselves pretty and enjoy being waited on."

Jim took Marlie's bags and Brent picked up the rest. "Come on in," Jim said. "It looks like it might rain again. We need to have a hot toddy to welcome our guests. And speaking of guests, Brent, your dad called. He'll be here for the wedding."

"That's great, Jim. I'll call him later."

While Jim and Andrea were in the kitchen, Brent opened up his overnight bag and took out the little velvet box he had tucked away.

"Marlie, this might not fit, but if it doesn't, we'll get it sized right tomorrow." She blushed and fanned herself, and grinned, flashing her beautiful teeth. Then she closed her eyes and held out her left hand. He couldn't believe how gorgeous she looked at this instant. So trusting. Her face showed no sign of worry. Only complete happiness and devotion. He slipped the engagement ring on her finger easily and swore he would do his best to make sure she stayed this happy.

Marlie gazed at her ring and whispered, "It fits perfectly. Oh Brent, it's beautiful."

"And so are you." He kissed her and held her close. At that moment he was happier than he'd ever been in his life.

Marlie looked at her ring again and slowly shook her head. "I can't believe it. When did you buy it? I've been with you the whole time since we left home."

"I've had it since I was in Vancouver a month ago. For a while I wondered if I'd have to send it back."

"No way!!" Marlie said. "But I'm sorry you had to wait so long to find out if you could use it."

Andrea and Jim came into the living room carrying hot toddies and hors d'oeuvres. "There's one more bit of news," Jim said. "We hope you don't mind, but Andrea and I thought this might be a good time to have a double wedding."

Whoops and cheers filled the room.

"Here's to us," Brent said. "Friends forever. Happiness to us all."

THE END